EIGHT HOURS

LUCILLE LABOSSIERE

◆ FriesenPress

One Printers Way
Altona, MB R0G 0B0
Canada

www.friesenpress.com

Copyright © 2022 by Lucille LaBossiere
First Edition — 2022

All rights reserved.

No part of this publication may be reproduced in any form, or by any means, electronic or mechanical, including photocopying, recording, or any information browsing, storage, or retrieval system, without permission in writing from FriesenPress.

ISBN
978-1-03-912703-6 (Hardcover)
978-1-03-912702-9 (Paperback)
978-1-03-912704-3 (eBook)

1. Fiction, Thrillers, Crime

Distributed to the trade by The Ingram Book Company

EIGHT HOURS

LUCILLE LABOSSIERE

TABLE OF CONTENTS

Acknowledgements	vii
Chapter One 10:00 – 11:00 p.m.	1
Chapter Two Five Hours Earlier - 5:00 – 10:00 p.m.	7
Chapter Three 12:00 – 12:15 a.m.	13
Chapter Four 12:15 – 12:30 a.m.	18
Chapter Five 12:15 – 12:50 a.m.	25
Chapter Six 12:30 – 1:15	31
Chapter Seven 1:10 – 1:58	39
Chapter Eight 1:15 – 2:25	48
Chapter Nine 2:10 – 2:40	56
Chapter Ten 2:30 – 2:45	63
Chapter Eleven 2:00 – 2:45	68
Chapter Twelve 2:00 – 2:45	76
Chapter Thirteen 2:00 – 2:45	82
Chapter Fourteen 2:45 – 3:00	89
Chapter Fifteen 2:50 – 3:30	95
Chapter Sixteen 3:00 – 3:30	102
Chapter Seventeen 3:10 – 3:45	109
Chapter Eighteen 3:10 – 3:45	114
Chapter Nineteen 3:30 – 3:50	121
Chapter Twenty 3:30 – 4:00	127
Chapter Twenty-One 4:00 – 4:20	134

Chapter Twenty-Two 4:20 – 4:45   142

Chapter Twenty-Three 4:40 – 5:20   149

Chapter Twenty-Four 5:10 – 5:50   156

Chapter Twenty - Five 5:55 – 6:30   164

Chapter Twenty-Six 6:05 – 7:00   169

Chapter Twenty-Seven 6:15 – 7:00   178

Chapter Twenty-Eight 6:20 – 7:00   187

Chapter Twenty-Nine 7:00 – 7:30   196

Chapter Thirty 7:20 – 7:40   206

Chapter Thirty-One 7:40 – 8:10   210

Chapter Thirty-Two 7:55 – 19:30   223

Chapter Thirty-Three Two days later   231

ACKNOWLEDGEMENTS

A special thank you to my sister Margaret Soderquist who read my first draft copy and encouraged me to continue working on this novel.

I would be remiss if I didn't acknowledge my husband Jim who kept me on track. His support throughout this entire novel helped me to get to the finish line.

In memory of my mother, Agnes Kocurek
who was taken at too young an age.

CHAPTER ONE

10:00 – 11:00 P.M.

Three bear traps were set up outside of the secluded cabin at strategic locations. This allowed the person inside to only worry about the fourth side, which was a gravel road that approached the building. Each wrought iron trap had two sets of springs that, when forced downward, were hooked into place. The J hook was then attached to a stable object, usually a tree, to prevent the animal from dragging the entire trap off into the unknown. The setter tool on both sides opens up the trap, making it ready for whoever or whatever was unfortunate enough to step into it. The last step was to camouflage the entire trap in branches and leaves. Being fall, there was no shortage of leaves to place around and on top of the trap. This hunting method was not only illegal, but also barbaric, and any animal that was trapped died a slow painful death. The man needed to remember the location of each trap, so he broke a few branches on nearby trees as markers and put them into his memory. These traps, however, were not set to catch any animals, just humans, specifically one Sergeant Bill Smithe of the Blue Ridge Police Department.

Charles Lockman was a vindictive man and retaliation was at the top of his list. He felt Bill had crossed the line when the cop put his brother in prison, and tonight was the time to make right what he thought was a wrong. Approaching what would be his hideout for the next ten hours, he was full of confidence. The cabin was an ideal location, well hidden in the bushes and quite secluded. No hikers or fishermen were around as the season was finished for the year. It was too early for cross country skiers as the snow hadn't yet started to fall. Hunting season was just beginning, which could present a small problem; hence the heavy padlock he put on the door. He only needed the place until 8 a.m. tomorrow morning. Not many people knew this cabin even existed. It was a secret haven, known only by the builder and a few other people. Whoever built it was skilled at his trade. The logs fit together so well that no draft came between them. It had been built some years earlier as the logs were well aged and blended in with the surrounding forest. The door, on the other hand, had a gap at the bottom allowing some cold air to enter the building, but the wood burning stove, once lit, would keep the cabin warm and cozy and compensate for the draughty door. The other three buildings located around the area, but several miles away from this cabin, were dilapidated and on borrowed time, so were not a good choice for a hideout.

With everything outside completed, the stranger returned to the cabin, removed the padlock, and went to work on the next part of his plan. He lit a single candle to partly light up the rustic interior of the cabin and then worked his way to a second table set in the far corner of the room. The inside was chilly, but the wood stove didn't have to be lit until he returned hours later with his two victims. The first one was an innocent child, the other a relative who was not aware of his overall plan. She would either go along with it or she would be eliminated, either way worked for him. He took a seat in the only chair in the room apart from the couch and picked up his satellite phone. He entered a specific number. The woman at the other end hesitated a moment, then answered, "Hello."

"You're in bed already? Get dressed. I'll be there in an hour. We do it tonight."

She recognized the voice at the other end, but was puzzled at his comment. "We do what tonight?"

"Just be ready by the time I get there." He hung up his phone and shoved it into the pouch of his black hoodie. Glancing around the cabin he had chosen to use for the next ten hours, he picked up a paper bag from the table beside his chair and shoved it into his pocket before snuffing out the single candle burning in the center of the room. The cabin was immediately thrown into total darkness. He left the building. On his way out, he latched the bolt and sealed it with the huge padlock. He couldn't take a chance that anyone else got inside tonight, as he needed it for himself. He had planned his brother's release from prison for several months and was sure he had dealt with all the fine details. He had the perfect plan. By tomorrow morning, his brother Tom would be free as a bird. Sergeant Bill Smithe had put him there and now he was going to have him released and the murder charges against him dropped. Charles also planned on killing Bill, which would give him and his brother instant satisfaction. If the cop didn't step into one of the traps Charles had set, shooting him was another means of elimination. No one messed with him and got away with it.

His borrowed vehicle was tucked neatly behind the cabin, so was not visible from the gravel road leading to the building. The drive into town gave Charles time to consider the order of events that had to happen before midnight. On the outskirts of town, he pulled over to the side of the road and took a piece of crumpled paper from his pants pocket. Charles turned on his flashlight and read the address scribbled on the paper: . That was his first stop. He grinned from ear to ear while driving toward the house. If he had planned this to take place during the day, too many people would see him, so night time worked to his advantage. Already knowing the night shift officers were limited, Charles knew that Bill would have to call in his dayshift crew to help with the rescue operation. As the night progressed, Charles was hoping his opponents would show signs of exhaustion and hopefully make stupid mistakes.

The streets were clear of people and although lights were burning inside homes, they didn't hinder his overall plan. The outfit he chose to wear was all black, making it easier for him to blend into his surroundings. The overcast sky would also help to hide his presence. Charles parked several blocks from his final destination and walked the last several hundred yards.

Seeing the number on the house told Charles that he had arrived. Carefully opening the picket fence gate, he hoped it was well oiled and wouldn't squeak. He slipped into the front yard. Leaving the gate open was a smart decision on his part, as this was also his way out. From the front yard, Charles looked inside the large picture window and saw a man sitting in an armchair, legs crossed, and his head buried in a newspaper. Slowly moving around the house while hugging the fence, he kept out of sight. The whole plan would fall apart if he was discovered. The first window he saw was black, no lights on, so he moved to the next one. The second window was the one that he was looking for. Peering in from a safe distance, Charles saw a young lady sitting in a rocking chair holding a small child. The woman appeared to be reading a story. The child kept grabbing at the book and giggling when the mother pulled it away. Once the story was finished, she laid the book on the side table, picked up a bottle full of milk, and started feeding the baby. The child was wearing a pink one-piece nightie so Charles now knew the gender of his intended victim. The woman continued to rock the child while her mouth moved, probably singing a lullaby. Charles remembered his mother reading and singing to his little sister years earlier. He didn't want to hamper his overall mission so he cleared his mind and continued watching.

The man from the living room stepped in front of the baby's window and closed it, securing the lock in place before shutting the curtains.

Charles turned and quietly left, working his way back to his vehicle. His next stop was an underpass about five minutes from his present location. It was where druggies and homeless hung out after dark. He was looking for one particular young man whom he had approached months earlier. Charles thought the fellow seemed reliable, as long as he got to him before he was spaced out. No names were ever mentioned between the two men, but when the young man saw the stranger coming, he was on his feet and walking towards him. The young man grinned knowing that he was finally going to earn some money.

Charles asked, "You still up for that small job kid?"

"You know I am. What do you want?"

Charles handed him the paper bag. "Don't open it now. There's a burner phone inside. When I call you later tonight, answer it. The rest of the contents inside will be self explanatory. If it's done on time, I'll be back tomorrow with a fifty dollar bill." Charles already knew that he wouldn't be back tomorrow as he would be long gone by morning. He did however, put the fifty dollar bill inside, but didn't tell the kid. The money was worth every penny knowing that Bill would be dead.

"You can count on me."

Charles returned to his car and headed over to Jenny's house. She was Tom's wife, although he wasn't quite sure what his brother saw in her. Tom had been a mechanic at the local gas station and had gone to a small coffee shop daily to visit one of the waitresses. He had become totally smitten with her and the two were married a year later. Jenny had few skills, but Tom liked coming home to find her in the kitchen making his meals and cleaning their house. She was devastated when, in a weak moment, he tried drugs and everything they had worked towards was gone. He had killed a woman who he thought was attacking him, and no one could change that fact. Tom was upset at what he did, but shocked when he was sent to prison for twenty-five years: It was an accident, after all.

Charles parked one block away and walked towards her house. He never parked in front of Jenny's place; the neighbours were suspicious of anyone coming or going there after hours, especially after Tom's conviction. They were nosey and he didn't trust them. Remaining under the radar was important, at least until this was all over.

Walking along the sidewalk to her house, he noticed that the atmosphere in Blue Ridge had already changed in the short time since he arrived in town. It was now damp and chilly and the town was blanketed with low clouds and a fine misty rain that left his surroundings enshrouded in gloom. He pulled his hood up over his head to keep his hairless head warm. Glancing up, he noticed a break in the clouds. The moon appeared bright in the sky, sending down a slight glimmer of hope that tomorrow would be a brighter day. Charles already knew that the day would be brighter because Tom would be free. He guessed that most people were probably glad to be indoors watching television with a cup of hot tea on their laps or sipping on a mug of beer.

As Charles walked up the path to Jenny's house, he kept mumbling under his breath about murder and revenge and appeared to be very agitated and delusional. These sudden changes of personality were a part of his everyday life. He could go from zero to ten in a matter of a few seconds. When a doctor told him of his condition and that he needed a prescription to control his outbursts, Charles thought that if anyone was crazy, it wasn't him; it was the doctor. He thought of himself as eccentric, but normal, quite ordinary.

He ascended Jenny's steps and quietly tapped on the door. She opened it and moved aside so he could enter.

"I'm not here for a social visit. Let's go. We don't have much time."

Jenny pulled on her heavy jacket. "Where are we going?"

"Tonight's the night that we get Tom out of jail."

Hesitantly, she followed him out to the car and slid in the passenger side. "How're we going to get him out?"

"You leave the details to me. My plan is fool proof. Let's just say that by 8 a.m. tomorrow morning, you'll be reunited with your husband and the two of you can live happily ever after." He cackled, "This is just the beginning."

CHAPTER TWO

FIVE HOURS EARLIER – 5:00 – 10:00 P.M.

Bill had his head buried in the last file to be scanned for the day when the cell phone beside him chirped. Reaching for it, Bill glanced at the screen. No number was displayed. He answered, "Hello, Bill Smithe here." He paused when he heard someone on the other end breathing; but no one spoke. The person on the other end hung up, so Bill did too. It was quite common for him to get wrong numbers coming through his phone as his number was close to several businesses in the community. He returned to the file in front of him and studied the contents.

There was a time when B and E's were a serious problem in town, but this one was the first case to pass Bill's desk in several months. If it wasn't dealt with early, Bill knew it could mushroom into something more serious. He would pass the file onto Bob Billings. Bob had been in the local precinct for several years. His contribution to the community was with youth activities. Officer Billings had taken the bull by the horns and started a mixed hockey team to keep the youth occupied and give them a sense of purpose. Hockey was definitely his forte, so starting up a team was a goal that was up and running in a matter of a few months. At first, the youth either didn't show up for practice or were late, but eventually they started having fun so took it more seriously. It seemed to have had a positive effect on reducing petty crimes. Bill recalled that Bob mentioned the team needed a few more players to complete the line-up. Recently, Bob had said he did now have two lines, but was hoping to have enough for a spare line. Although the team had more males than females, the ladies could hold up their end of the game. Closing the file, Bill rose from his desk to leave for home. He left his office unlocked in case the night shift workers needed access to confidential files.

On the way out, he glanced at his day shift workers. The precinct was full of well experienced officers, some having been there over twenty years, and each officer had their own specialty. Don Wilson was an expert in drug control who often gave seminars several times a year for parents and visited schools frequently. Jack Spencer was excellent with domestic disputes. He could often calm down a situation and did follow-up visits after every incident. The precinct was top heavy with male officers as the only female in the force was Debbie Mozer, and she was on maternity leave. She had joined the team less than a year ago and was a police technician. She followed up on assignment cases, issued citations and directed traffic at accident sites and crime scenes. Her male officers were more than happy to cover for her until she returned to work.

Bill dropped the file on Bob's desk before leaving the building. "Found a new hockey player for your team."

Bob opened the file. "Good, I need a spare right defence man." He glanced at the file and commented, "Guess I may as well add another B and E player to my team. I haven't had one of these for a while."

Bill smiled. "I hear they're quite a good team. Will have to come out one evening and watch them practice."

"You're more than welcome. You might be surprised how well they play. As long as they're tired at the end of the practice, I know they're too tired to get into trouble." He closed the file then added, "I know then that I've fulfilled my mission."

Bill announced to all the officers. "I'm heading home."

Don Wilson turned to him and smiled. "Another short day, boss?"

Bill turned and responded, "I start work way before you come in so I should be able to leave before you. If you want to leave at the same time as me, I'll call you in the morning so you can arrive at the same time. Then we can leave for home at the same time. It could be a bonding moment for us."

Don grinned. "That's okay. I'll stick to my schedule. It works for me, but I thought we'd already bonded. Am I wrong?"

Bill tapped his desk. "Real buddies."

Eight Hours

Bill enjoyed a peaceful ride home. He loved living in Blue Ridge. It was a quiet town with minimal excitement. The crime rate was down and his days were filled with family get-togethers and peaceful evenings with his wife Beatrice. Fall was his favourite season of the year. The trees were just starting to change so in a matter of a few days, the maple leaves would be bright red and lining the streets with much needed colour. The roads still had a shimmer from the earlier rainfall, which made them appear glassy. He drove with the car window down, as the earlier afternoon rain seemed to clean the air and leave a fresh scent. Looking up, he saw a break in the clouds with patches of blue peeking through. Off to the right was the hint of a faint rainbow.

It had been six years since the earthquake and tsunami had hit Blue Ridge. The catastrophe had devastated the shoreline and left all the businesses on the lower part of town buried in mud several feet deep. Bill was proud of how the locals had come together to do the massive cleanup. It took almost a year and a lot of volunteer hours to get the businesses up and running again, but the town survived with no fatalities. He recalled how lucky Richard and Kimberley were, and all the diners who were trapped in the Panorama Room that night. He also remembered Beatrice collapsing into his arms as they watched the dining room cover with water. They had both felt so helpless that night knowing the people trapped inside could very well have drowned. The memory of the drive to the dining room that night was still as sharp as if it had happened only a few months ago. What a relief when they found everyone huddled together for warmth while they waited to be rescued. There had only been a few minor injuries among the frightened and saturated people.

As Bill drove home, he saw several people out walking and enjoying the last few hours of the day before darkness closed in on them. He knew almost everyone in town so he waved and greeted them all. Some were holding hands while others supervised their children in the playground. Fall was in the air and people were out enjoying it before winter set in.

Bill pulled into his driveway and saw Beatrice at the kitchen window where he thought she was likely washing dishes. He waved to her and when she waved back, her hands were covered in bubbles. Some splashed on the window so she smiled and wiped them off with a tea towel. Leaving her apron on the counter, Beatrice met Bill at the door. He gently kissed her, then suddenly stopped in his tracks, saying, "The air outside was so refreshing that I drove home with my window open. It was heavenly, but not as good as the smell in here. What's for dinner?"

Beatrice smiled and led him into the kitchen. "Just a roast with roasted potatoes and carrots. Hope you're hungry."

Bill grinned. "Starving. Do I have time to get out of my uniform?"

She smiled. "Lots of time, darling."

Bill went upstairs to the bedroom and slipped out of his uniform, neatly folding it and placing it on his chair so he could wear it tomorrow. He returned his weapon to the safe inside their closet before heading back downstairs.

Beatrice was in the process of opening a bottle of red wine.

"Let me do that Beatrice. It'll be my contribution towards dinner."

Beatrice smiled and handed him the corkscrew, then turned to serve their dinner. Once they were at the table with their plates full, Beatrice asked, "How was your day?"

He happily replied, "Uneventful, just the way I like it. And if anything did happen I couldn't tell you anyway. How was yours?"

She beamed from ear to ear, but before she could say a word, he cut in.

"Oh yeah, you were babysitting Claire. I can't imagine that going well."

Beatrice scowled at him. "Don't make fun. She's a beautiful baby and I'm babysitting so Kimberley can still keep her teaching job. It's hard to believe that she's already six months old." Beatrice paused before adding, "And she's also a real joy. She is so full of smiles and giggles. Wish I could babysit her every day, but I do have to share her with Bob and Barbara." She paused again. "After all, they're also her grandparents." Before Bill could say another word, Beatrice kept going. "Oh, I forgot to tell you that Kimberley's dad is also coming this weekend, so Steve will get to see how much Claire has grown over the past month. He's so proud of his first grandchild and constantly showers her with gifts. You would think it was Christmas every time he arrives."

Bill ate quietly as he listened to Beatrice. He finally got a word in edgewise. "This dinner is delicious. I certainly married well, didn't I?"

"Thank you, dear. Glad you're enjoying it, but then, you like almost anything." She took several mouthfuls before she spoke, "Claire is so close to rolling over and crawling." With excitement in her voice she added, "I almost forgot, her first tooth just came in too. She looks so adorable when she smiles."

"I expect she does."

After dinner, the two retired to the living room to finish off the bottle of wine and watch the news. Bill could tell that Beatrice was tired as she fell asleep before her wine was empty. The news was always rather depressing for him as he had news happening every day that he was at work, but he watched it regardless as he knew it was spending quality time with Beatrice. He enjoyed watching her sleep on the sofa beside him. Getting up carefully, so as not to wake her up, Bill headed into the kitchen. Beatrice felt him move and was on her feet following behind him. She yawned so Bill suggested, "You look tired, dear. Why don't you leave the dishes for me?"

Beatrice objected, "I absolutely won't hear of it. Besides, I enjoy cleaning up with you."

Bill laughed, "Let me guess. Doing dishes is also quality time together?"

Beatrice simply smiled and let Bill wash as he disliked drying. They were both looking forward to a quiet evening.

Bill never brought his work home so once he came through their front door, he was an entirely new man. The same went for when he went to work: home life was important, but he didn't let it interfere with his work.

They both had a quiet evening watching television and talking about Claire.

Glancing over to the bookshelf, Beatrice saw two photos. One was Richard and Kimberley's wedding picture and the second one was Claire at three months old. She got up and crossed the room to pick them up. She went back to her seat and handed the two pictures to Bill. "These two events are the happiest days of my life."

Bill scowled. "So our wedding day didn't count?"

She scowled back at him. "Of course it counted." She then added, "I guess our wedding day was the first, Richard and Kimberley's wedding was the second, while Claire's birth was the third." She appeared to be thinking. "On second thought, Claire may have been the most memorable."

Bill laughed, "You're impossible. You know that don't you?"

Beatrice laughed, "You shouldn't have made me make a choice. Claire wins hands down." She looked at the wedding photo again. "Kimberley was a beautiful bride and Richard was extremely handsome. They both look so happy." She then put Claire's photo next to the wedding one. "Beautiful baby for a beautiful couple." Bill nodded his approval. She continued, "Evelyn would have been so proud of how Kimberley turned out." She felt suddenly uncomfortable and tears started to collect in the corner of her eyes. "I'm so sorry, Bill. I shouldn't have brought that up."

Bill didn't skip a beat. "Evelyn would have been very proud of her and you for how well you have raised her. Don't apologize. She was special to all of us. You certainly had your hands full. I think the most memorable time I spent with Kimberley was when she was young and I was helping her with her multiplication homework. She would come into the office and I would put everything on hold, even told Don to hold my calls. We would practice her times tables over and over. I will always cherish those moments we spent together."

Beatrice appeared to be thinking. "My most memorable moment was when I slowly taught Kimberley how to cook. I really wanted her to be self sufficient. She was a good student. Richard got himself an excellent chef. It was her idea to switch places with me when I broke my ankle, otherwise she and Richard may have never met. Her charade went on for quite some time before Richard discovered it was her and not me cleaning his house and cooking his meals." Beatrice added, "Yes wonderful memories." Glancing back at the wedding photo, she smiled at him. "It was so nice of you to let Steve walk her down the aisle."

"Why wouldn't I? He's her father."

Beatrice kissed him on the cheek and returned the photos to the bookshelf. She yawned and conceded, "I'm tired. I think I'll go up and take a bath before bed. Come up when you're ready." She paused then added, "There's no rush."

Bill got up from his chair. "I'll be up in a few minutes. Just want to check that the doors are locked."

It was ten o'clock by the time Beatrice had climbed out of the bath and crawled into bed beside Bill. She fell asleep in his arms within a few minutes. She looked so peaceful when she slept.

He kissed her on the forehead and whispered, "I'll always be here to protect you, my darling." He grinned and settled in for the night. Sleep came quickly for him too as his mornings started so early; plus the wine helped him to relax.

CHAPTER THREE
12:00 − 12:15 A.M.

Bill awoke to his cell phone buzzing on the end table beside his bed. He glanced at the clock before grabbing his phone, and then quietly snuck out of the room. His cell phone going off in the middle of the night could only mean trouble, and his mind was racing as he left the bedroom and quietly closed the door. Once in the hallway, he pushed the talk button. Without waiting to hear who was on the other end, he queried, "Okay. What's broken now?"

There was a long pause before the person at the other end of the line responded, "Nothing's broken, sergeant. At least I don't think so." There was a slight pause. "Hope you don't mind if I call you at home, Bill."

Bill was puzzled. "Who is this and how did you get my number?"

There was a chuckle at the other end of the line. "Finding cell phone numbers isn't difficult Bill; you should know that. You're a policeman so probably use the website frequently. You most likely get the site free, being the big important sergeant that you are. Whereas someone like me has to pay a small fee to use it."

Bill was frustrated at being woken by a total stranger. "If you want to talk to me, call during office hours." Bill was about to hang up when he heard a deranged voice scream into the receiver.

"Don't you dare hang up on me!"

Bill was shocked and stared at the receiver before returning it to his ear. Obviously, this fellow must have a grudge, and poor Bill was at the receiving end. He was still half asleep and needed to snap to it. He had to wonder if the guy was on drugs. How did the voice at the other end of the line even know him? Bill slowly started to go downstairs then slipped into the kitchen to splash some cold water over his face. He had to wake up enough to know what this guy wanted. Bill hesitated. He spoke, "Okay. You have my attention. What the hell do you want at this time of the night?"

"I have a request."

Bill was losing his patience. "Can't this request wait until office hours?"

"No, it can't. I'm kind of on a schedule; which means you're on one too." By now, Bill had gone into the living room and was sitting in his oversized chair.

"Okay, what do you want from me?"

"You know Tom Lockman?"

Bill shifted uneasily in his seat. "Only too well. He's the scumbag who shot and killed a lady in the grocery store parking lot while high on drugs. If my memory serves me well, he got twenty-five years in prison with no chance of parole for ten years. I think the judge was very lenient with his sentencing." Bill was clutching the receiver too tight and his fingers were starting to cramp. He switched hands and stretched out his fingers, trying to relax them. "I assume you don't agree with his sentencing?"

"Probably, but that's not the point. Apparently, he isn't doing very well in prison."

"Guess Tom should have thought of that before he killed someone. Joan Wilks was out picking up a carton of milk for her family. She was innocent and Lockman shot her in the back. Her poor husband is now trying to raise two children on his own. Tom is where he belongs; behind bars." Bill was rubbing his forehead, feeling a nasty headache coming on. He was a good policeman, but when he got instant headaches like this, it could only mean bad news. "What do you want from me?"

"It's real simple. I want him released from prison and all charges dropped."

Bill was in total shock as he got up from his chair. Approaching the window; he carefully parted the curtains slightly, then glanced outside to see if the caller was out on the street. Pacing between the living room and the kitchen Bill added, "I suggest you take it back to the courts and ask for an appeal. That's all I can do for you."

The voice at the other end of the line responded, "An important sergeant like you can move buildings if given the correct push. I know it's going to happen, and you're the one that's going to make it happen!" There was a slight pause from the person at the other end of the line before he blurted, "Shut up Dad! I wasn't speaking to you! Can't you see I'm on the phone!"

Bill perked right up as he never heard anyone other than the man holding the phone at the other end. Was there someone else involved in this phone call? Bill mentally stored the stranger's comments into his memory as it could come in handy in the future. Bill continued evaluating the state of mind of the person holding the receiver at the other end. "What's your interest in Tom Lockman? You drinking buddies or what?" Bill was starting to get very agitated so inquired, "Who are you? What's your name?"

There was a slight pause. "My name isn't important."

"You're right on that point," Bill replied. "Okay, then I'll give you a name. How about scumbag two? That means you're probably a carbon copy of Tom Lockman." Bill then added, "Do you know what the definition of scumbag is?" Bill didn't even hesitate. "Never mind; let me tell you. It means a dirty or despicable person. Also, creep, dirt bag, slime ball. Do you want me to continue? I think that applies to you. What do you think?"

The caller was growing impatient. "Let's just say that someone could die tomorrow morning if you don't cooperate."

Bill felt sick to his stomach. Maybe he had pushed this guy too far. Reaching for some antacids that he kept beside his chair he asked, "What are you talking about? Who's going to die?" Laughter at the other end of the line sent a chill down Bill's spine.

"Let's just say someone very special to you."

Bill jumped out of his chair and yelled, "What do you mean someone special to me is going to die?"

Beatrice must have heard him yelling and came downstairs trying to rub the sleep from her eyes. "Who is it, Bill?"

Bill turned to her and raised his hand. "Shhh." She froze then sat on the bottom stair and listened nervously.

There was a slight pause before the man at the other end of the phone responded, "Sounds like you woke the Mrs. Aww, what a shame, please apologize for me."

Bill was upset that he had lost control of the situation. He could almost see the other man grinning as he said this. He knew how guys like him thought. He likely assumed that he was smarter than the cops, but Bill would eventually prove him wrong.

"But let's get back to business. Don't make rash decisions Bill, until you've heard all my details. I already told you that I want Tom Lockman out of jail. I'll give you until eight o'clock tomorrow morning to make it happen or someone will die."

Bill felt shocked and was trying to stay calm and keep a clear mind. He had dealt with crazy people throughout his career, but this case sounded like it was going to be personal. "You must know that I can't do it by eight tomorrow morning. Nothing is open before then." By now, Bill had placed scumbag two as a terrorist.

"I'm counting on you getting it done. Don't disappoint me."

Bill shouted, "I already told you it's impossible! Are you deaf?"

Beatrice sat quietly on the staircase, watching the expressions on Bill's face change from nervousness to outright fury. She had never seen him so upset before. It was frightening for her. What sort of conversation could make him this angry?

"That attitude will get your six-month-old granddaughter killed."

Bill froze. Beatrice watched in shock as the color drained from his face. He didn't miss a beat. "I don't have a granddaughter."

"Maybe not a real granddaughter, but a child that will probably call you grandpa when she grows up." There was a long pause. "If she grows up."

Seeing the expression on Bill's face and hearing Claire become part of the conversation sent Beatrice into massive shock. She could barely rise from the stairs and then collapsed into her chair. Tears were already streaming down her cheeks, even though she didn't fully know what was going on. All she knew was that Claire was probably in grave danger. Her eyes darted around the room not knowing where to look. She just knew that if she looked at Bill, his expression would overflow into her already breaking heart.

Bill tried to keep calm but felt like he was drowning in the deep end of a pool. He had to control his breathing before speaking. "If you hurt her, I'll personally kill you and ship your body to the prison and put it next to Tom's cell. You seem to be close to him, so then you can be together forever. Imagine spending every birthday and Christmas together; although the conversation would be rather one-sided."

"Did I hit a sensitive nerve? Oh well, anything to get your attention. It seems I'm holding all four aces in a deck where you only have kings. If he's released by eight tomorrow morning, your granddaughter will be dropped off at a location that I'll give you. Oh, and Bill, don't go calling in outside law enforcement. We don't need this to become a whole big thing. You call in outside help and the baby dies immediately."

"You're crazy. Actually, I'd put you in the category of a terrorist."

"I'm only thinking of my brother's well-being."

"Ohhh, so that explains a lot! Scumbag number one's your brother. Insanity must run in your family. Bet your parents are real proud." Bill thought about mentioning his conversation only moments earlier where the stranger implied that his dad was there, but opted to wait until he had more details.

Bill stood and crossed the room to the window again and parted the curtains. He was hoping the weirdo would be out on the street by now, watching his house, but all was quiet. Not a soul to be seen anywhere. Bill rubbed his forehead. At least now he knew that Tom had a brother. He filed that away for later use. Bill's thoughts were now racing. He was dealing with a crazy terrorist who was threatening his family. He was hoping he was dreaming and couldn't wake up, but Beatrice on the couch across the room meant it was real; all too real. He was sweating now, but had to keep his speech calm. After a brief pause, he again spoke, "Anything else you want to share with me?"

"Just one more thing. I'll call you every hour, on the hour, to check on your progress. Make sure your phone is fully charged and don't hesitate to answer. It won't go so well for the baby if you ignore me." Charles hung up his phone.

Bill hung up too and ran over to Beatrice. Her tears were almost more than he could bear. "I'm so sorry, darling, but I have to go to work."

CHAPTER FOUR

12:15 — 12:30 A.M.

Charles Lockman slammed his satellite phone on the dashboard of his vehicle and let out a string of curses that frightened Jenny. He took a few deep breaths before shouting, "Why the hell did I tell Bill I was Tom's brother?" He pounded his fist on the dashboard several more times before slowly calming down. Eventually he conceded, "Oh well, guess Bill would've figured it out before the night was over." The slight setback wouldn't have anything to do with the overall results. Tom and he would be sharing the bottle of whiskey that was stored in the trunk of the car before the night was over. Regardless, Charles was still upset with himself and vowed to be more careful in the future.

He turned to Jenny who, even in the darkness, looked frightened. "What's wrong with you? You're not going soft on me, are you?" She didn't reply. He was enraged again. "Who the hell does he think he is?" Taking a second look at her, he pointed to the bundle in Jenny's arms. "Does he think I won't kill that baby?"

Jenny started to tremble and pulled the swaddled baby closer to her body. She was horrified at the last words that came out of Charles's mouth. Feeling sick to her stomach, she tried to figure out what to do. What had she got herself into, and how could she get out of it? Jenny couldn't live with herself knowing that the only way to get Tom out of prison was to kill an innocent baby. Was Charles really capable of such a hideous crime? Jenny realized that the next eight hours were going to be a fight for not only her life, but also for the life of the small child she was holding. Charles had already told her that he would snuff the life out of this defenceless child. Jenny would have to do everything in her power to keep the baby safe.

Charles turned to Jenny and snapped, "Stay in the car. I'm going to have a look around."

She watched as he blended into the darkness. Tears ran down her cheeks and she half considered running away, but she knew Charles would hunt her down and kill her. That would mean the child she was holding would be defenceless. Running was not an option.

Charles walked around the outside of the cabin and recalled how Tom had introduced Jenny to him. His first impression was that she appeared rather frail; even delicate. She carried no extra weight and had a tired look about her. Tonight, she appeared older than he thought, maybe because she hadn't slept properly since Tom went to prison. The bags under her eyes and her greying hair pulled back into a ponytail told the true story. She had put on her best flower dress for when she was reunited with her husband. Charles guessed it was already several years old, but Tom would have never seen it. The fabric already showed signs of being worn and washed too many times. With Tom in prison, Jenny had at least gone back to work at the restaurant to make ends meet. Charles was getting tired of having to take care of her and listen to her constant whining about being lonely. He knew he frightened her when he got angry, often leaving her in tears, but if all went well tonight, he would have Tom back and the baby would be safely back with her parents. Killing the baby was only a means to an end, nothing else.

With the coast clear, Charles returned and opened the vehicle door. Just then, the baby was starting to fuss, so Jenny cuddled her and whispered just soft enough for Charles not to hear her. "Shhh, my little one, you're safe with me."

"Can't you do something with that kid?"

Jenny wanted to keep quiet, but knew she couldn't. "She's just a baby that you've scooped up in the middle of the night. What do you expect?" She then added, "If you feel like you must yell, please don't do it near the baby. This whole ordeal will run smoother if she stays asleep."

Charles didn't like to be told what to do. "If I want to yell, I'm going to yell. The only reason you're here is to take care of that baby. I'm not interested in what you think. Just prove to me that you can do the job. If not, why did

I even bother bringing you along? If you aren't working with me, then you're definitely against me. It's a long walk back to town and you aren't taking the kid with you, so make your choice now."

Jenny was in shock and remained silent. Looking out the front windshield, she saw a cabin, but wasn't quite sure where they were. It was dark when they left town and it had taken about an hour to get there. She climbed out of the vehicle and slowly walked towards the cabin. The darkness closed around her like a blanket and the trees looked as if they were strange creatures moving in the soft breeze. She held the child close to her body to protect the little thing from the cool air. She longed to be inside of the structure, protected from the cold darkness that surrounded her. Charles unlocked the cabin door and pushed it open. There was no electricity so he crossed the room and lit the single candle in the middle of the table. To Jenny, he seemed ghostly looking; maybe even possessed. She wondered just how far he was going to push this. He picked up the flashlight and announced, "I need to use the outhouse and then I'll start the fire when I get back."

When he left the cabin, Jenny recalled the day that she met him. He was the type of man that gave you the creeps and made people back off. He was average height and medium build, but it was his face that scared most people. His eyes were far too close together and jet black in color. It was like looking into two black holes, void of all feelings. His nose had been broken several times in fist fights, which he bragged he had always won. Most of the fights were defending his younger brother Tom, who was the placid one. A scar on Charles' right cheek was the result of falling on a sharp object as a child. Luckily, he was too young to remember the incident. Years later, it was still bright red, as if it was a recent accident, and it still looked inflamed. His bald head made him appear even more sinister, while his face was usually void of any emotions. His teeth were stained yellow from lack of hygiene and drinking too much coffee. He had several missing teeth that made him look downright frightening. On his back were torn and dirty clothes from living on the streets in Sidville. Tom had told her that they weren't always homeless, but when their parents abandoned the two of them years earlier, it forced them to grow up fast. After their parents had left, there was no money for rent, so eviction from their home came shortly after. They both relied on food banks and petty theft to keep from starving; and living under overpasses protected them from the wind and rain. This lifestyle had toughened up Charles, but Tom had somehow remained placid, and he always seemed to hover in his brother's shadow. Jenny had fallen in love with Tom but certainly not his overpowering brother. Tom had shared with her that Charles had talked to a local gas station manager, and practically begged the owner to offer Tom an apprenticeship in mechanics. Remarkably, the younger brother was a natural at the job. Somehow, he could fix anything, and before long he had a good career. Although Jenny was forever grateful to Charles for that, she never really felt comfortable around him, but Tom's job allowed the two of them to purchase a home and help Charles through the tough winter months.

Jenny found her way to a couch in the darkness and sat down, cooing to the bundle that she was carrying. "Don't worry, my darling. I'll protect you. I wish I knew your name." She gently stroked the baby's chubby cheek. "Soon you'll be back with your family." She got up, fumbled her way to the bed, and placed the baby on it, making sure the little infant was wrapped tightly to keep her warm. Returning to the couch, she sat down and suddenly felt sick to her stomach. Her thoughts went back to the baby sleeping soundly on the bed. She whispered, "Oh my God, what have we done?" Her thoughts were racing through her mind, trying to take control of her inner self and figure out what she could possibly do.

She rewound to several hours earlier when she was sitting in Charles' car outside a strange house. Charles had turned to her and spoke, "Get out. I need your help."

Jenny nodded. "What are we doing here?"

"If you want Tom out tomorrow, you'll follow my orders."

Afraid to speak in case she said the wrong thing, she left the car. Charles opened a back door and pulled out a crowbar.

"What do we need that for?"

"Never mind. Just follow instructions. You can do that, can't you?" They both snuck around the house, keeping their bodies close to the building. At the back of the house, Jenny watched Charles slowly approach a window. He put his ear against the glass and listened for any sounds. With everything quiet, he slipped the crowbar under the bottom of the window and pried it up carefully. Charles stopped when he heard the lock break under the force of the crowbar. Having no more use for the heavy tool, he tossed it in the underbrush away from the window. He waited again until he was sure the room was still quiet. Slowly lifting the window, he disappeared inside. It was only a few moments before he reappeared and handed Jenny a blanket with a baby wrapped up inside. She took the package and watched Charles climb out of the window, slightly lowering it before they left.

She looked at him in shock. "What the hell are you doing? This is a baby!" Jenny wanted to protest even more, but she saw the look in Charles' eyes and looked away.

Charles turned to her. "Shut up and let's get out of here."

She was shocked at what had just happened, but his snarl warned her to keep quiet. Charles climbed into his side of the car, Jenny got in her side, and they sped off. He kept looking in his rear-view mirror to make sure no one was following him. When he was sure the coast was clear, he sneered and settled behind the wheel.

Jenny finally confronted him. "What's going on? What're we doing?"

"What does it look like? We just kidnapped a baby."

Jenny was confused. "But why?"

"You want Tom back, don't you?"

"Yes, of course." She looked puzzled. "But why the baby, and who is she?"

"She's our ticket to getting Tom out."

"What are you talking about? What ticket?"

Charles was sneering as he spoke, "She's the granddaughter of the man who put Tom in prison." It was a good thing it was dark in the car, for if Charles had seen her face, he would have seen the horrified look in her eyes and the tears start to well up. Jenny had to take a few deep breaths to calm down and stop from screaming at Charles. She now knew he was capable of harming her and the baby.

Charles returned to the cabin, jarring Jenny back to the present. He was carrying an armload of firewood. The flashlight was sticking out of his mouth, lighting his way to the wood stove. He dropped the firewood into a pile then rubbed his hands together to warm them up. "Man it's cold out there."

The baby let out a soft noise and turned her head away from the sound of Charles reentering the cabin, but she didn't wakeup. Although there was soon a roaring fire, it took some time to warm the room, but at least there was a little more light, and Jenny finally got to see the inside of their accommodations for the next seven hours. Squinting around the dark room, she could tell it had been unused for some time. Although she couldn't see the dust covering the furniture, she could taste the staleness in the air. There were several windows, but no curtains, which seemed to bring the outside darkness into the room even more. The constantly flickering shadows from the wood stove sent shudders down her spine. The front door might be adequate in keeping bears out, but it did little to stop the drafts she felt whenever she approached it. Jenny moved the couch closer to the fire to keep warm. The kitchen area also had a sink with no tap and the wood stove, but upon further inspection, there was no food or even tea she could make to calm herself. She glanced at the baby who was sound asleep. Hopefully, the infant would stay that way until this was all over. Jenny could hear a train in the background. Somehow, in spite of this nightmare she was now living, Jenny found the click clack rhythm of the sound relaxing.

Charles was busy praising himself; he had thought this kidnapping through to the last detail. He carried two baby bottles full of milk and a few sample diapers that he got online. They were a free trial offer that he took advantage of. He crossed the room and dropped the bottles and diapers on Jenny's lap. She placed the diapers beside her chair then went in search of a pot to heat up one of the baby bottles. She found an old, beat-up pot inside one of the cupboards; it would have to do. Looking around the cabin, she discovered there was no water to be found.

Glancing over to Charles, she politely asked, "Could I trouble you to fetch me some water? When the baby wakes up, it would be nice to already have a warm bottle waiting."

Charles sneered at her, but took the pot and left the cabin. Several minutes later, he returned with the pot full of river water. He placed it on the stove then took one of the bottles and put it in the water. He then returned to his seat, and to Jenny, he appeared to be taking a nap.

A short time later, the baby woke up and started to fuss. Jenny picked her up and fed her the bottle. The little thing drank hungrily then fell back to sleep. Jenny once again crossed the room and placed her in the center of the bed. This time, she surrounded the child with cushions to prevent her from rolling off the bed, which also provided extra warmth for its' tiny body.

Charles glared. "Don't get too attached to the kid. By tomorrow morning, she'll either be reunited with her parents or dead."

Those words sent chills down Jenny's body. She watched as Charles left the cabin again. Tears formed in her eyes, and she knew they had done something terribly wrong. Had her loneliness for Tom sent his brother over the deep end? She walked towards the kitchen area and started searching all the cupboards and drawers. In the back of one of the drawers, she found an old rusty knife. After glancing at it, she slipped it into the pocket of her dress. It wasn't much, but it was better than nothing; just in case she had to defend herself and the baby.

Charles walked the circumference of the building, checking on his three traps. They were all still intact. He grinned at how well his plan was falling into place. Going back into the cabin and crossing the room, he glared at Claire. For a moment, Jenny thought he may be reconsidering hurting the child, then he scowled and mumbled, "It'll be a shame to have to kill her, so hopefully Bill comes through." He then plunked himself down into his chair.

Jenny studied him before speaking, "Why did you choose this location? Why here?"

"For several good reasons. First, it's close to town and the highway, so we can leave the baby here once Tom is released. Secondly, there's only one way in and one way out. No one can come here without me knowing it."

"You really thought of everything didn't you?" At this point, she knew he was crazy and that she and the baby were in the middle of a dangerous situation. Knowing she had to keep him calm, she tried to smile. "Thank you for helping to get Tom out of prison. I'm not sure how we'll ever be able to repay you."

Charles just grunted and looked at his watch. "Another half an hour before I make my next call." He closed his eyes. Jenny couldn't tell if he was resting or planning his next move. In fact, he was planning Bill's death. He knew the sergeant would come with backup, but hopefully Charles could eliminate them or at least detain them long enough to finish off Bill. If by chance the sergeant stepped into one of the traps, Charles could watch him slowly die from a distance. Yes, that would make his day. He could imagine the other officers trying to open the trap. If they did manage to get it open, and Bill didn't die or bleed to death, he would surely lose his foot.

CHAPTER FIVE

12:15 — 12:50 A.M.

Bill ran up the stairs, taking them two at a time, to their bedroom. Beatrice struggled to keep up with him and suddenly stopped at the door. She was gasping for air from the exertion of climbing the stairs and frightened from the conversation between Bill and the unknown person at the other end of the phone. Watching Bill scramble to get into his uniform told her that something was seriously wrong with Claire.

"Who was at the other end of the phone, and why was Claire's name mentioned?"

Without looking at Beatrice he shouted, "Get dressed! We're out of here in five minutes!"

Beatrice had never heard Bill's voice so demanding. She was scared and confused. "Talk to me Bill. What's going on?"

He tried to calm down, but his heart was racing, so his voice remained demanding. "Hopefully it's nothing. Just get dressed and I'll fill you in on our way to Richard and Kimberley's."

She inquired, "Why are we going there? It's the middle of the night."

Bill paused slightly and asked, "Do you trust me?"

"Of course I do. It's just you're scaring me."

"I'm sorry, darling. I'm scared too." He pleaded, "Please, just get dressed."

Beatrice looked concerned when she saw the fear in his eyes. She crossed the room and started pulling on her clothes, watching Bill the entire time. She could tell by observing him that something was seriously wrong. His body was tense and his face was deeply troubled. She had never seen him in this state before.

Bill glanced at his watch and was deeply disturbed. He picked up his cell phone and called Don at home. He half shouted and then pleaded, "Pick up! Oh God, please pick up!"

Don was groggy when he answered, "Must be serious, boss, to call me in the middle of the night. What's up?"

Bill was holding the phone on his shoulder as he finished pulling on his uniform. "Meet me outside Richard and Kimberley's house in ten minutes. Don't approach the house, just wait for me there. No lights or sirens!"

"Okay. What's going on?"

"Nothing I hope. I just got a strange phone call that I need to check into. See you there?"

"I'll be there."

Beatrice pulled the last of her clothes on as she watched Bill go to his secured gun safe and take out his weapon. He shoved several rounds of ammunition into his pocket, then loaded his gun and shoved it into its' holster.

He turned to Beatrice. She looked so frightened. He crossed the room, pulled her into his arms, and kissed her forehead. "Let's go. We can talk in the vehicle."

Once they were in the car, she turned to Bill. "Who was that on the phone and what did they want?"

Bill looked troubled. "Let's just say it's a disgruntled person who's messing with the wrong man." He half turned to her and whispered, "I'm sorry, Beatrice. I'm hoping this turns out to be a prank call, but I do have to investigate it."

There was just enough light reflecting off the console that Beatrice noticed Bill was gripping the steering wheel too tight. His fingers appeared white, and she knew if she tried to peel them off, he wouldn't let go. She also noticed that he was deep in thought.

She paused, then asked, "Of course you have to look into it, but why am I coming with you?"

"I'm not sure if you're safe at home alone." He paused. "Do you remember several years ago when a woman was killed in the grocery store parking lot?"

Eight Hours

"Of course I remember. That poor family. Those children left with no mother. You put him away."

"Well, his brother wants me to overturn the sentence and set him free."

"You can't do that. He's a murderer." She paused, "What does that have to do with Claire, and it doesn't explain why we are going to Richard and Kimberley's at this ungodly hour?"

Bill looked straight ahead, refusing to look at her. There was no easy way to tell her of Claire's kidnapping, and he could already predict her reaction. He softly spoke, "He claims he's kidnapped Claire and I have eight hours to release his brother or he'll kill her."

Beatrice shook and gasped for air as if she was having a heart attack. The last time she experienced this condition was the day her sister Evelyn had died in a car crash. She felt like she couldn't even think as her brain tried to understand what Bill had just told her. Her whole body trembled and when she tried to speak, the words were not really there. Beatrice was unable to form a sentence that would make sense, as if her brain had already started to shutdown. Her whole body shook and she began softly sobbing. "Oh my God, this can't be real!"

Bill reached across to her side of the vehicle and took her hand. "Are you okay? Don't you dare have a heart attack right now. I'm so sorry, darling, but I'm really going to need you before the night is out."

"I can't breathe. You have to find her, Bill!"

Bill tried to sound positive, but knew he was failing miserably. "I'm hoping it's just a prank call, but you know I can't take that chance. Not with Claire."

Beatrice slowly calmed down and whispered, "I know."

They arrived at Richard and Kimberley's house. Don was parked a block away. He climbed out of his vehicle and worked his way to his boss' car.

Bill turned to Beatrice. "You stay in the car and lock the doors when I leave. You don't open them for anyone. Do you understand?" She nodded. When he was out of the vehicle, she locked the doors and watched him walk towards Don. Beatrice suddenly felt very cold, so pulled her jacket tighter, not for just warmth, but also for security. She couldn't believe what Bill had just told her. No one in their right mind would kidnap a baby, especially one so small. Her body was trembling. She closed her eyes, but reality slowly set in. Beatrice buried her face in her hands and wept. "My poor Claire."

Bill and Don looked at Richard and Kimberley's house. It was dark, which was normal for this time of the night. Looking around, Bill didn't see any suspicious vehicles on the street. They both heard a dog barking and turned towards the sound, finding the dog alone and probably just protecting his domain.

Don inquired, "What's up, Bill? You were pretty cryptic?"

"I received a phone call at midnight on my cell. Do you remember Tom Lockman?"

"Sure do. He's in prison for murder. Does this have something to do with him?"

"Yes. Apparently, his brother said Tom isn't doing well in there and he wants him released." Bill's voiced choked. "He said he's kidnapped Claire and we have eight hours to have Tom released or he'll kill her."

Don froze and was speechless. "I recall the case. Didn't you say his brother was at the trial?"

Bill replied, "Now that I think of it, yes he was."

Don was trying to remember. "I think his name was Chuck or Charles. No, definitely Charles."

"That's good to know."

Don let out a sigh. "Holy crap. We need to get on this pronto. How do you want to deal with this?"

"First, I want to check out the house to see if anyone has broken in. Certainly don't want to scare Richard and Kimberley if the jerk was bluffing."

Beatrice watched as the two officers pulled out their flashlights and started working their way around the house towards Claire's bedroom window. They disappeared around the back leaving Beatrice waiting impatiently, quietly sobbing in the darkness. Seconds turned into minutes. How many minutes, she wasn't sure.

Bill and Don walked slowly around the house looking for signs of intruders. They both shone their flashlights along the path leading to the area near Claire's window. Then Bill's heart sank. It was obvious the window had been jimmied and left slightly ajar. He already felt sick to his stomach and used all of his strength not to scream or puke. No way would Richard or Kimberley leave the window ajar. Cautiously approaching the window, he directed his flashlight towards the damaged lock and then towards the empty crib. Bill's nightmare was about to begin and would only end when Tom was set free.

Don whispered, "Okay, Bill. Let's think this through." He shone his light all around the window area, then directed the beam towards the garden area close to the window. Something shiny caught his eye. "Whoever did this is pretty sloppy." He picked up the crowbar with his glove. "I'll take this to the car and be right back."

Bill knew he needed to form a plan, but he was still trying to get his head around the fact that Claire was missing. He was enraged, but knew he had to remain in control. That was the only way he would be able to work efficiently. Bill had to imagine that it was just another kidnapping case and try not to think of it as a family member.

He waited for Don to return, then said, "I think the best thing to do is to call Richard on his emergency number and ask him to meet us out front. Meanwhile, you call Jack and get him over here. I want him to dust the entire bedroom, especially around this window, and also that crowbar. We need to know how many sets of fingerprints he finds. The rest of the officers are to report to the precinct ASAP. We'll meet them there."

Don stepped aside and started making phone calls.

Bill slowly walked back to the car knowing he had to deliver Beatrice the bad news. She could tell by the expression on his face that Claire was gone. He climbed into the vehicle and cradled her as she wailed in despair.

"Bill, you have to find her. Without her medicine, she'll die!"

It was several seconds before he spoke, "I'll find her, Beatrice. I promise." He added, "Right now, I need you to be strong and let me do my job. I also need your help."

She pulled away from him and with a shaky voice inquired, "What can I do?"

"I need you to stay with Richard and Kimberley. They're really going to need you right now. It's going to break their hearts when I tell them that Claire has been kidnapped. I want you to stay with them until all of this is over. I need to concentrate on the case and not have to worry about the three of you. Can you do that for me?"

She kissed him softly. "Of course, but you have to make me a promise."

He looked at her, puzzled. "What?"

"Come home safely with Claire."

"You have a deal." Bill hoped he was not making a false promise. He dialled Richard's cell number and waited for him to pick up.

"Doctor Jackson. What's up?"

"Richard. It's Bill." He hesitated before continuing. "Don't say a word just meet me on your front porch."

Richard was confused, but replied, "I'm on my way." He hung up and slipped out of bed.

Kimberley turned to face him. "Another emergency?"

"It appears I'm needed. Go back to sleep darling." He leaned over and kissed her forehead. Richard quickly pulled on his clothes and left the house.

Bill and Beatrice were waiting on the front porch.

"What are you two doing here?"

"There's no easy way to say this, so I may as well cut to the chase." He glanced down at his watch. His time was running out. He turned to Richard. "I don't have much time. It's going to be difficult, but please try to remain calm." He continued, "At midnight, I got a call that Claire has been kidnapped. We've searched your property and her bedroom window has been pried open and she's gone."

Richard stared for several seconds before he bolted back into the house. When he entered the nursery, he felt an emptiness that shouldn't have been there. He looked around the room, confused, and started trembling.

"Where is she? What's happened to our baby?" Richard scanned the room and saw the broken lock on the window. He turned to Bill with more questions that he knew Bill couldn't answer.

Bill looked at him sadly. "I'm not sure at this point, but I'll find her. I promise."

CHAPTER SIX

12:30 — 1:15

Charles was sitting in his chair grinning, anxiously counting down the minutes before his next call to Bill. He felt confident that Tom would be released by morning as he had the apple of Bill's eye; his granddaughter. Certainly, that had to count for something. Charles already knew that Bill would do anything in his power to keep her safe. Rising up from his chair, Charles crossed the room to look at the baby, who lay sound asleep, nestled between the pillows that surrounded her. Somehow the child had wiggled her arms free of the blanket and they were spread out above her head. Charles looked at the tiny hands and fingers and the delicate face that lay in front of him. He recalled his new baby sister sleeping in the same position. Like his sister, this child was also a beautiful baby. Her clean swaddling blanket was covered with pink teddy bears and yellow kittens. It looked out of place next to the dirty blankets that lay on this half-broken bed. He shrugged off the image of her innocence. Now would be a bad time for him to grow weak, especially with Tom's freedom at stake. Glancing at the pillows that surrounded the baby, he figured out that Jenny did that in case the baby rolled over in her sleep and fell off the narrow bed. He had no idea when babies started to roll over, but obviously Jenny knew.

Charles returned to his chair and looked proudly around the cabin. Even in the dim light from the single candle and the flicker of the wood stove, he saw that his hideout was ideal. Upon looking closer however, there were signs that mice had found small holes to wiggle through, and he spotted droppings in most corners, especially around the small kitchen area. The ceiling was rather low so he could've brought out an oil lamp to suspend from an existing hook if he had seen it earlier. Reconsidering, Charles thought that while the cabin may have been ideal, he didn't want to see how dirty it really was. Living on the streets of Sidville had not been ideal, but wherever his group of homeless friends met for the night, it was always kept somewhat clean. Being homeless, he knew the downfalls, the illnesses and diseases that came with that style of living. It was so important to not only keep himself safe, but also his little brother as well. He glanced over to Jenny who appeared to be watching him.

She decided it was time to find out what was going to happen over the next seven hours. "Do you care to share your overall plan with me?"

Charles looked at her before answering. "I'll be calling Bill every hour to find out what he's doing to get Tom out of prison and brought back to us. As each hour passes, if there's no progress, I'll be upping my game."

She was afraid to ask, but had to know. "What does upping your game really mean?"

"By the end of tonight, Bill will be a wreck as he can't possibly beat me. I've spent years planning Tom's release down to the very last detail. Bill will die a most painful death tonight, either by my hands, or simply by knowing he couldn't save his precious granddaughter."

Jenny was scared. She whispered, "Do you actually plan on killing her?"

Charles gave her his deadly stare. "If I have to, yes."

Jenny turned away from Charles, trying to control the horrified look on her face. She skeptically asked, "Do you think it's fair doing this right now?" She looked at him and swept her hands around the cabin. "It's the middle of the night. What could this Bill fellow possibly do to get Tom free in the middle of the night?"

Charles was irritated. "He's a big important sergeant, so guess he'd better figure it out, besides you leave the thinking to me and keep that kid quiet. Do you really think we could've pulled this off in the middle of the day? We couldn't have possibly kidnapped that child in broad daylight. People would be roaming the streets, being nosey. Don't you think it would look out of place with the two of us carrying a baby around in broad daylight? You leave the thinking to me."

Charles glanced down at his watch and turned to Jenny. "Now shut up and listen. You're about to see a foolproof plan fall into place." Charles dialled Bill's cell phone. He answered on the third ring.

"Hello."

"Hello, Bill. Glad you didn't forget that I was calling." He paused. "By now you must know that the baby is no longer in her crib. How frightening that must be for the parents." He started laughing. "Looks like I have a lot of bargaining power, and you, incidentally, have none. How are the plans going to set Tom free?" Charles snarled.

"I'm not sure." Bill paused before continuing, "You do realize that I can't go any further in this case; it's a conflict of interest. I'm forced to hand this over to my most senior officer, so you'll be dealing with Don Wilson. Now that I've confirmed the kidnapping, it's out of my hands and into his."

Charles was livid. "Don't for a minute think that you're off the case that easy. Here are the rules. I only deal with you; if anyone other than yourself answers the phone each hour, the game is over."

"You think this is a game asshole? We're dealing with the kidnapping of a small child. If you have a beef with me, then we meet face to face and we deal with it. Involving a small child is just bad etiquette."

"You know the old bible reading; an eye for an eye, and a tooth for a tooth."

Bill sounded surprised. "Exodus 21:22-25. Didn't expect you to be a bible scholar."

"Hey, I went to Sunday school as a child; you have a problem with that? Who knows what stupid crap one remembers, but it seems to apply here, don't you think?"

"No. Guess none of that Sunday school really sunk in properly though, or we wouldn't be in this situation at all."

Charles was running out of patience. "So, now that I've put you back on the case, let's get back to business. What the hell have you done so far to get Tom released from prison? Do I have to remind you that we are on a pretty limited time schedule here?"

"You must already know that I had to confirm the kidnapping was real before I could move forward."

"Of course. After all, you're a professional." He then added, "Not sure what your skills are as far as kidnapping cases go, but guess I'll find out."

"I've been dealing with assholes like you most of my career. I follow the rules, criminals don't, but I always manage to outsmart them and put them behind bars, where they belong. You're just another crazy wacko idiot who thinks that he can outsmart me. Rest assured, I'll find you, dead or alive. You just have to let me know if you want to be put in prison next to your brother or six feet in the ground. It makes no difference to me."

Charles laughed, "Ohhh, the sergeant is trying to play the hero role. You know Bill you are trapped in a game that you can't possibly win. It's about time that you figured it out. I'm smarter than you. I get whatever I want and I always will. You can't beat me. No one can."

Bill was reminded of Charles speaking to his dad in their first conversation. "How is your dad doing?"

Charles was rather setback. "This has nothing to do with my dad."

"He must be there. I heard you speak to him on our last call."

Charles shouted, "He isn't here!"

Bill was starting to realize that Charles must be hearing voices, if indeed his father was not there. He would have to tread lightly so as not to trigger him off before he could fully assess his condition. Bill took a deep breath and laid it out for Charles. "We're both gentlemen, so we can settle this in a matter of a few hours."

Charles laughed, "Even you can't work that fast, sergeant."

"What do you even know about me? You have no idea how fast I can work when I'm really motivated. I've been known to solve cases in record time. Your timeline may be a bit tricky, but it forces my team to work faster." He paused. "Not sure how well you know my officers, but they're completely committed to closing this case, well before eight o'clock. Be on the look out, we're coming for you."

Charles laughed again. "Ha ha ha. Good one."

"Why don't you tell me the location of the baby and I'll reunite you with your brother." Charles didn't say anything. Bill continued, "I've reserved the cell next to him so you can see him everyday." He spoke in a threatening tone. "If she dies, you'll be up for murder too, just like your brother, and you'll get the same time in prison. Guess murder must run in your family.

Just think Charles. You could spend every birthday and Christmas together. That's what you want, isn't it?"

Charles let out a scream. "You idiot! You just killed your granddaughter!"

Jenny reprimanded him. "Shush. You'll wake up the baby."

Charles glared at her and hoped Bill hadn't heard that.

Bill paused, then spoke, "Oh, I see you aren't alone."

Charles grew even angrier that Bill had heard Jenny.

Bill had never heard Charles' father earlier, but this woman's voice he heard clearly. "Got a girlfriend?" He didn't skip a beat. "No, can't be a girlfriend. No one out there with a right mind would want to be within a hundred miles of you. I also know you won't kill the baby."

"How can you be so sure?"

"If you kill her now, you'll never see your brother again. It's too early in the game to throw in the towel. We're just beginning." He shouted, "Watch out, I'm coming for you Charles!" Then the call ended.

Charles jumped up from his chair. Bill had cut him off! He slammed his phone down then paced around the cabin. He crossed the room and was about to pick up Claire, but Jenny quickly responded. She sprang to her feet in an instant, gasping at him. "What the hell are you doing? You'll wake her up."

"He's messing with me. I'll show him who's boss." He pulled his knife from his back pocket and leaned over the bed.

Jenny pushed him aside and came between him and Claire. "Are you insane? If you kill her now, Tom will never get out of jail. He's our goal, isn't he?"

"I don't take any crap from anyone, especially a cop, so tell me why I have to take it from Bill?"

Jenny was panicking and had to calm Charles down. "He's just rubbing you wrong. He's playing a game with your mind. Don't let him into your head. You're better than that. You should know by now that cops play dirty. Just keep in mind that they also have rules." Her face lit up as she snickered. "You don't. Why don't you take a walk and clear your head. It'll help you to plan your next move."

Charles glared at her, but she stood her ground, so he grunted. "I'll take another look around outside." He then turned and pointed at her menacingly. "Don't you ever come between me and that baby again," he snarled at her.

As Charles left the room, Jenny whispered, "Please don't slam the door on the way out. This whole kidnapping will go much smoother if the baby sleeps through it." She was surprised when she turned around to see the door already closed and Charles gone.

Charles let his eyes adjust to the darkness then slowly walked the perimeter of the cabin again, but there was no change. His body was a mass of knots that Bill had instigated in their last conversation. He knew the sergeant was a worthy opponent. How worthy, he was about to find out. Maybe he put too much time into his escape plan for Tom, where he should have spent more time researching his rival. All he knew about him was that he was married and his only family was his wife, a niece and her husband, and their child. Having few relatives made him think Bill would do anything to protect them and keep them safe.

Charles strolled around the cabin, lighting his way with a flashlight. It was far too soon to expect anyone to come around. Bill wouldn't even know where he was this early in the game. He was startled when he heard a branch snap around the side of the cabin.

"Crap, almost scared myself there," he muttered. "Better not piss myself." He laughed, then crouched down and listened; there it was again. He cursed under his breathe. "Damn." He had left his weapon in the house. His only defense at this point was the knife in his back pocket. Maybe someone had seen the fire burning in the window or smelled the smoke that spewed into the air. Didn't matter which, he had to get rid of the intruder.

He slowly peeked around the corner, sensing a presence, but saw no one. Slowly working his way towards the front of the house, Charles clung to the building, carefully removing his knife from his back pocket. Once he was close enough to the intruder, he could kill him and dispose of the body in the woods. No one would find it until spring. Taking a deep breathe, he turned on his flashlight and lunged forward at the same time. Standing in front of him was a deer, standing like a statue, its' eyes frozen in time, not moving a muscle. Charles sprang forward and screamed, "Get the hell out of here!" He watched the deer bolt out of sight. Bushes crackled as it fled, slowly sounding fainter as it went deeper into the forest. Charles was relieved when the deer shot off into the darkness; after all, he wouldn't have wanted to kill it and drag it away, getting blood all over his clothes. He had just bought this knife and wanted his first kill to be human. It didn't matter which human, although Bill was at top of his list of contenders.

Charles was pumped up and needed some down time, so he moved towards his vehicle and opened the trunk. In one corner sat his duffle bag with all his worldly possessions, as meagre as they were. Hidden in the other corner was a brown bag with a bottle of whiskey inside. He had planned on opening it with his brother to celebrate his freedom, but right now he needed a drink. He slugged down a few mouthfuls before returning it to the trunk of the car. Looking at his watch, Charles sneered. "Time goes by when you're having fun." His watch read 1:35. He ground his teeth together and sneered again. "Round two in twenty-five minutes." He sat on the front stairs thinking. He wasn't sure about Jenny. She was in, and then she was not in. He already knew that if she got in the way, he would have to eliminate her. Tom would just have to understand. Of course, he would make it look like an accident. Most likely he would blame it on the police force. Tom already hated them for putting him in prison so why not take advantage of the situation. He could also say that Bill did it. Tom's hate would run deep and he would make it his mission to eliminate him. Charles had always thought of himself as a good planner and he could see Bill's murder falling into place. Still sneering to himself, he reached into his pocket and took out a package of cigarettes. He lit one and inhaled deeply. "I can't wait to see the sergeant face down on the ground with blood seeping out of his mouth," Charles thought out loud. He glanced around. "Now that would make my day." He dropped the half-smoked cigarette by his boot and ground it out.

Looking up at the sky, Charles noticed a weather front fast approaching the area. He could feel the moisture in the air; a downpour was not too far off. Ten minutes passed before Charles went inside. All was quiet. The baby was sleeping, and in the shadows that moved around the room from the wood stove, he could see that Jenny was sound asleep too. He still couldn't figure out what his brother saw in her. She appeared frail and weak, not at all like the woman he would have chosen for a wife. His wife would have to be strong willed, but know her place in the home. He was the head of the house and she would have to learn that very quickly.

Jenny had managed to find a blanket and was wrapped tightly in it, spread out on the couch. He could hear her snoring and thought this was his opportunity to eliminate Claire. He paused on his way to the bed and realized that maybe Jenny was right. Killing her this early in the game could mean that Tom would never be released. He sat in his chair and closed his eyes, wanting to clear his mind before his next call. Bill may have won the first round, but he would lose the next.

CHAPTER SEVEN

1:10 — 1:58

After slamming his cell phone closed, Bill took a few seconds to compose himself. He sat on the front porch, continuing to breathe in and out to calm his nerves and clear his mind. He wiped the sweat from his forehead with his sleeve. He had tried to remain calm during the call to ensure Claire's safety and prevent him from saying anything stupid.

All through the call, he had tried to analyze Charles' state of mind. He already knew he was crazy, but how crazy was yet to be determined. Bill felt he had the situation under control and had even discretely tested Charles' actions and reactions to his strategy. Experience with criminals made it possible for Bill to almost read their state of mind, and in some cases, even their next move. Although Charles was a terrorist, he had to have some weakness. Bill just needed to figure out what those weaknesses might be, and how to turn them into an advantage for him. After thinking a few moments, Bill wondered who the woman's voice was and whose side was she on. Was she in on this kidnapping or just caught up in a bad situation? No, it didn't seem reasonable that she was involved. There was too much concern for Claire in her voice, plus Charles was unhappy that she even spoke. Bill had heard her voice, but not Charles' dad. Something didn't add up and Bill would have to study Charles over the next few phone calls before coming to any conclusion. Hopefully he had made the right decision when reading Charles, knowing he had to gain the upper hand early. He had to keep Charles wondering what was going to happen next. His motto of 'good strategy' had always paid off in the past, so once again, he hoped it would be his means to a peaceful ending.

Jack Spencer arrived, carrying his fingerprint kit, and approached Bill. "What's up, boss?"

"I'll fill you in once we're inside, but first I need you to get Richard and Kimberley's fingerprints; then I want Claire's window dusted. I need to know who broke into the nursery, and we need to know whether it was more than one person." Then he remembered. "Also, Don has a crowbar in his car. Dust that for prints too." Bill choked through the next phrase. "Claire has been kidnapped and I want the bastard who did it."

Jack was stunned. "Are you serious? Who the hell would do this?"

"Someone who's pissed off with me and is looking for revenge. He's screwing around with the wrong person."

Bill and Jack went to the bedroom where they found Richard hovering over the empty crib. He was in a complete state of shock as he turned to Bill. "What's going on?"

Before Bill could answer, Kimberley heard all the commotion and came out from the bedroom, rubbing her eyes. She was totally baffled. "What's going on here? Why are–?" She froze mid sentence upon seeing the empty crib. Glancing around the room, she looked for whoever was holding Claire. With panic in her voice, she screamed, "Where's Claire? Where is she? Oh my God, what's happened?"

Richard moved next to her and pulled her to his side. Kimberley looked at him and saw the fear written all over his face. She started to tremble. Crying and gasping for air, she finally asked, "Where's our baby, Richard?" She pulled out of his arms and approached the crib, touching the mattress where Claire had been sound asleep only hours before. She turned to Bill with questions she knew only he could answer. Kimberley's imagination was going places it shouldn't. The room started to spin and the voices in the room started to sound muffled.

Richard saw that she was going to faint and rushed to her side. He caught her in mid-air and gently lifted her up, carrying her across the hall and laying her on their bed. Beatrice was right behind him.

Richard's voice was trembling as he asked Beatrice. "Could I trouble you for a cold cloth for her forehead?" She was already heading to the washroom to retrieve it. Richard softly applied the cool cloth to Kimberley's face and watched as the color slowly returned to her cheeks. Glancing around the room, Kimberley suddenly remembered what had happened only moments earlier. She tried to sit up, but Richard gently laid her back down.

"You've just fainted, Kimberley. Maybe just lay there for a few more minutes until the feeling passes." Richard turned to Beatrice. "Do you mind staying with her while I go find out what's happening?"

"Of course." She sat on the edge of the bed and gently covered Kimberley with the blankets that were thrown aside only a few minutes earlier. Taking her hand, she softly stroked it. Without hesitating she spoke, "Bill will figure this out. You have to trust him. I'm staying here, right next to you, until this whole nightmare is over. You won't be alone."

Kimberley hugged the bedding and wept uncontrollably. She felt like her whole heart had been ripped out of her chest and had left a painful void within her. Beatrice lay down beside her and held her close. Both ladies hadn't shed this many tears since Evelyn's car accident. The body wasn't designed to feel so much pain, and yet the two of them had just been thrown into another disaster that once again triggered it.

Richard crossed the hall, still in utter shock. It was important for him to stay focused, not only for Kimberley, but also for himself. His mind was overworking. He had so many questions that he didn't know where to start. "What's going on Bill? Why would anyone take Claire?"

Bill spoke softly, almost as if Claire was still sleeping and he didn't want to wake her up. "It's entirely my fault, and right now I don't have time to get into it. I'll explain later." With a tremble in his voice he announced, "I have to go." He turned to Jack. "When you're finished here, I need you at the office." Jack nodded. Bill glanced at the window. "The house is not safe with the broken latch so please nail the window shut until we can get it fixed."

Jack reassured him. "I'll do it myself."

Jack turned to Richard. "I'm going to need you and Kimberley's finger prints." Both were taken in a matter of a few minutes.

Bill gestured for Don to follow him out to the front porch. He appeared overwhelmed. "Don we have a serious problem here."

"You mean other than the fact that Claire has been kidnapped?"

Bill felt his world closing in on him. "Yes, this is a conflict of interest so I should be stepping aside and putting you in charge."

"Yes, you should, but why do I sense that's not going to happen?"

"Charles has chosen to change the rules."

"I'm listening."

"He will only talk to me. If anyone else answers the phone, Claire is dead."

"Oh crap, Bill. I'm so sorry. What're you going to do?"

Bill thought for a moment. "I'm going to answer the phone each hour, but we have to work as a team. All decisions have to be agreed on by both of us before anything happens. I have to appear to be in the background, which means the paper trail has to only lead back to you. All signed documents will only have your signature on them. I'm only here to answer the phone and communicate with the bastard. When this is all over, the creep will be dead, if I have any choice. Screw the system." Bill paused. "Sorry, you didn't hear what I just said."

"Sorry, boss, I wasn't listening. All I heard was that I'll be filling out all of the paperwork." He then added, "Of course, you already know that it's a major part of closing a case as serious as this one. It's not an ideal situation, but we can make it work."

Bill looked at his watch. It was already 1:20. He dialled the precinct number.

Daniel Straume answered swiftly. "I'm here, boss. What's up?"

"I'm on my way there. Set up a recording device so I can plug my cell into it when I get there. I want to record this bastard's voice and try to trace the call. It would save time if we got a location. He'll be calling at two o'clock so we need to be ready."

"You got it, boss!"

Bill climbed into his vehicle and was about to leave when he saw Richard running down the driveway. He jumped into the car and put on his seatbelt.

"What're you doing?"

"What do you think I'm doing? I'm coming with you."

"No, you're not. Kimberley needs you."

"I don't think so, Bill. Did you forget that you left Beatrice in charge? I trust her to take good care of Kimberley." He tried to sound nonchalant. "Those two need to be there for each other. I, on the other hand, need to be with you." He paused, his voice trembling when he spoke again. "She's my daughter, for God's sake, and whether you want me here or not, I'm not leaving!" Bill noticed a single tear run down his cheek. Richard never turned away or attempted to remove it. "You need me, Bill. You need to do your job and I need to do mine. I promise I won't get in your way and I can also keep Beatrice and Kimberley updated on what's happening." He added in a soft voice. "We need each other. I need you to find her and you need me to be there to treat her. You know about Claire's type 1 diabetes, but I don't think you know quite how serious Mellitus is. As each hour passes, Claire will start to dehydrate and will need more fluids, but will eventually go into a diabetic coma. Checking her sugar levels and figuring out her insulin dosage is going to be a delicate process. She's tiny and if not given the correct amount of insulin, she could die."

Bill knew his conversation with Richard was far from over, but he had no time to waste before his next call. He would have to explain to him that he was no longer the main investigator on the case because of his conflict of interest. Certainly, Richard was aware of the legality of Bill continuing as the lead officer, but he wasn't aware that Charles would only speak with Bill. Charles' had claimed his main purpose behind the kidnapping was to get Tom released from prison, but Bill knew there had to be more to it. An eight hour timeline told Bill that Claire was only meant as a distraction and more likely the bait to draw him in. Charles' main purpose must be to eliminate him. What else could it be? Bill could literally taste the venom in Charles' voice as he had laid out the rules of the game.

Bill's time frame to get Claire back was short, but his life could be even shorter. If he died, Claire would be safe, if he lived, then Claire wouldn't. Bill had to put those facts in the back of his mind and concentrate on the case. He had to snap out of this way of thinking and help Don work the case. He started the car, and the two were on their way to the precinct. The trip to the station was a blur, neither one saying a word. Each man was caught up in his own thoughts and feelings. Bill just wanted Claire back and Charles put away forever; while Richard wanted to save his baby. Claire shouldn't have been a diabetic, but Kimberley had developed it during her pregnancy, so it was passed down to their daughter. An emergency caesarean was performed to give their baby a better chance of survival. The two had shed many a tear accepting her condition, but were also thankful that Richard was a doctor and knew how to care for her. He slowly taught Kimberley the signs to watch out for. She was a good student and life seemed to work out for the three of them.

Bill arrived at the station to find his three nightshift workers puzzled at all the commotion around them. Sam Lawson, Greg Thomas, and Jim Banks listened as Bill filled them in on the events that had happened so far and the short timeline they had to find Claire.

Sam broke the silence. "Well, so much for a quiet shift."

Jack strolled in and hung his coat on the hook, then turned to Bill. "Only one set of fingerprints other than Richard and Kimberley's at the house. You care to guess who they belong to?"

"My guess is his brother, Charles."

"Good guess. They're also all over the crowbar. He may be a terrorist, but he's a lousy one."

Bill turned to Don. "We're lucky he's a lousy terrorist. At least we know who we're dealing with. Some cases can take hours to identify a suspect. He just made it easier for the team. We're going to need the whiteboard, there has to be no chance for error in this case."

Don got the board out of the back cupboard and hung it on the wall. "Ready when you are, boss."

"I'm not the boss, remember. You're in charge of this case."

"I know, but that doesn't mean that you do nothing. Make yourself useful and fill in the whiteboard."

Bill didn't say a word, just moved to the blank white board and wrote in big letters, 'Charles Lockman.' Next to it he wrote, 'Tom Lockman.'

Don turned to Bob. "I want to know everything about these two guys; their parents, pets, friends if they have any criminal records, anything and everything. Trivial stuff may work to our advantage."

Bob jumped in. "I'm on it."

Bill turned back to the board and put a large question mark below the brother's names.

Jack inquired, "Why the question mark? Who is it?"

Bill turned and faced his men. "On my last call from Charles, I heard a woman's voice in the background. We need to find out who she is. By now you should all have been filled in on the case, so you know that our timeline is very short. We only have until eight o'clock this morning to find her; but preferably earlier. Richard, can you fill in my men on Claire's condition?"

Richard nodded and stood beside Bill. "Claire is a diabetic, so it's imperative that we find her fast. With her body weight and condition, she will start to show signs that her sugar levels are off track by seven o'clock or earlier." He choked out the next sentence. "She may not still be alive by eight o'clock." All officers shifted uncomfortably in their seats. Richard looked away as tears started to form in the corner of his eyes.

Bob moved to the whiteboard and glanced at Bill. "Mind if I add a few details?"

"Fly at it."

Bob slowly entered the information he knew, up to this point, onto the white surface. "Okay. Tom and Charles Lockman are the children of Betty and Ted Lockman. They also had a daughter Nikki who died only six months after she was born. Father was a mechanic and their mother a waitress. Neither parent handled their daughter's death well."

Don inquired, "Do we know anything else about the parents?"

Bob replied, "At this point, no. Our files only cover British Columbia. If they moved out of province it will take longer to find out their location."

Bill was stunned and thought to himself, if Charles's father was out of province, then he must have returned to help get Tom out of prison. This still didn't answer his question of why he didn't hear the father's voice in the background. Charles was going to prove to be a difficult adversary. Bill was starting to form a mental portfolio on Charles, but kept it to himself for now. It was still too early to share his thoughts with his team.

Bob continued, "Tom and Charles both have a criminal record, but Tom's record was clean until he shot and killed Joan Wilks in the grocery store parking lot five years ago. Charles has a long record of beating up people he doesn't like; and also has a few breaking and entering charges under his belt. Interestingly enough, Tom has a wife named Jenny. I've called her house and there's no answer, which is unusual as one would think she should be home in bed sleeping."

Don smiled. "Good work."

Bill placed an arm on Richard's shoulder and said, "My men have their work cut out for them, but once they find her, the rest will be up to you."

Bill shook away the feelings that were building inside of him and studied the whiteboard. His eyes scanned all the information they had, but his eyes locked onto 'Jenny.' She must have been the lady that came to Tom's trial several times and was there for the sentencing. He vaguely remembered a distraught woman being dragged out by a man. Little had he known that several years later, that same man would appear and try to destroy his family and his life.

Above the brothers' names, he saw the parents' names and careers. Nikki's name was also put up on the board. He was unaware of the family name until the Joan Wilks' murder. He recalled the times he and Richard had to attend the trial as witnesses.

Don turned to Bob. "You have an address for this Jenny?"

"Sure do." He glanced back at his computer screen. "Number 16, Birch Crescent. I was just about to leave and check it out." The address was added to the whiteboard.

Don responded, "Do it and get back to us." He then turned to his men and appeared to be thinking. "At this point gentlemen, we are unsure of Charles overall plan. Holding Claire hostage until his brother is released from prison may not be his main objective. Hostage release time periods are rarely so tight. That makes me think that there could be another motive. He has insisted that Bill be here to answer his calls every hour. That tells me that he also knows that if we find her, Bill will be there for the takedown. Maybe Bill is the main target for putting his brother behind bars."

Bill responded, "I have to agree with you Don. Charles appears to be out for blood, mine specifically. If he wants me, he won't stop until I'm dead. The man is crazy and the fact that it's a conflict of interest doesn't matter to him. He's forcing me to be involved. I'm the only one he will speak to. If the truth be known, I would rather leave the building, but that's not in the cards. Don is going to be working closely with me until this is all over. Not an ideal situation, but it's all we have to work with right now. Don, do you want to take over?"

Don stood in front of his men. "We're obviously working blindly at this point, so this is what I want you all to do." He turned to the whiteboard and picked up the felt pen. As he wrote, he spoke to his men, adding vacant buildings to the list. Eric Simpson, the spare night shift worker, had been called in to help out. "Eric, you and Sam check all the empty buildings in town." He then returned to the whiteboard. "Jack, I want you to check the lighthouse and take Greg with you." Don wrote the next location on the board then glanced at his watch. It read 1:50. He ran his fingers through his hair and then looked around the room. Bob had just returned from Jenny's house and Don could tell from the look on his face that he had found nothing there. "Bob and Jim, you two head out to the Panorama Room. It's temporarily closed as the owners are doing minor renovations." That location was added to the whiteboard. "Keep in mind that this guy appears to be unstable, so be careful. If any of you see anything suspicious, call for backup. Don't try to be a hero."

His officers grabbed their jackets and weapons and were on the run.

Bill turned to Richard and spoke with authority. "My next call is in ten minutes." He paused. "Here are the rules. No matter what Charles or I say to each other, you are not to say a word. Do you understand?"

"Yes, but–"

"No buts. I don't have a lot of time to explain, but you must absolutely keep quiet. If you can't do that, then you should leave the room now and come back once the call is finished. I'm not sure how many rules are being broken with you being here, so if you choose to say anything at any point in our conversation, you must remove yourself from the room. Agreed?"

Richard was scared, but conceded, "Agreed."

Bill turned to Daniel. "Are we good to go?"

"Just need your phone, boss."

Bill passed it to him and watched as it was plugged in. "It's as simple as that; now we wait."

Richard paced back and forth. His mind went back to happier times spent with Kimberley and Claire. Cherished story times and laughter kept him thinking positive. Claire's first tooth had just come in and she was so close to rolling over. He couldn't imagine not watching her take her first steps. He shook the negative thoughts from his mind. Instead, he thought about how Bill and Beatrice played a big part in helping to raise her. He knew how he felt but couldn't imagine how Bill was feeling. Claire's life was literally in his hands. Richard tried to remain calm, but inside he was trembling. He imagined carrying Claire back home and giving her to Kimberley. The other option he chose to block out of his memory. Bill had to succeed.

CHAPTER EIGHT

1:15 — 2:25

Charles was nervously chewing on his fingernails and watching Jenny pampering the baby. The child responded to the attention by giggling, which irritated him to no end. This night couldn't go by quick enough. Charles wished he could somehow time warp to eight o'clock in the morning, avoiding the next six hours. The movie producers certainly could do it, so it would be nice if it worked for him too. He hated wasting time building up to Bill's demise. Charles just knew that when eight o'clock arrived, Bill would be dead, lying outside the cabin in a pool of blood. Charles was getting tired of playing this game.

Staring at nothing in particular didn't mean he wasn't thinking. If Charles couldn't time warp forward in time, at least he could return his mind to the past. His brother's court case had been four years ago, but to Charles it seemed as if it had only happened yesterday. Every little detail was stored inside his head. He constantly mulled over that day, keeping it fresh in his mind. He had to get vengeance not only for himself, but also for his brother. Five years of Tom's life was already wasted behind bars.

He and Jenny had found out the court date, and somehow managed to scrape up enough money to catch a bus to that location, which was two hundred miles away. Upon entering the court room, Jenny spotted Tom and his defence seated on the left side of the room just beyond the railing. To their right sat the prosecutor, ready to put Tom behind bars. Just behind the railing sat the victim's husband who appeared years older since his wife's death. Towards the back of the courtroom on the right hand side sat the witnesses; Sergeant Bill Smithe, Doctor Richard Jackson, and two other witnesses that Charles couldn't identify. Charles glared at the two men as he walked by them and took his seat behind his brother.

Tom spotted Jenny and the two shared a wistful smile. Glancing around the room, Jenny noticed the walls were a bright red mahogany, making the room appear very masculine. The gallery and council tables were separated with a three-foot mahogany divider wall that looked like a picket fence. On either side of the judges' bench were a Canadian flag and a British Columbia flag. The Queen's photo was centered on the wall above the judge's desk.

The clerk stood and made his announcement. "The criminal case between the prosecution and Tom Lockman, file number 446, is now in session. All rise, the Honourable Judge Ferguson presiding." Everyone in the court rose when the judge entered. Tom had chosen not to have a jury, but to rely wholly on the judge's final decision. His lawyer was convinced that this gave him a better chance so he took his lawyer's advice. Trying to convince twelve people of his innocence may have been difficult.

Jenny leaned over to Charles. "I hope this doesn't take too long, and then the three of us can catch the later bus to get home. It would save us a hotel." She had no idea how the judicial system worked; a murder trial could run on for weeks.

The judge glanced at the folder in the center of his desk and then turned to the prosecutor. "Are you ready to make your opening statement?"

"Yes, your honour." The prosecutor moved to the front of the room and glanced between the judge, and the defence. "The prosecution will prove, without any doubt that Tom Lockman may have been on drugs, but is still responsible for the alleged shooting death of Joan Wilks. Mrs. Wilks was in a hurry to pick up a carton of milk before her children got home from school. She was in the wrong place at the wrong time. The store manager has turned over a surveillance video that covers both entrances, and it shows Tom Lockman walking up to Mrs. Wilks and shooting her in the back at close range. This video has been turned over to the defence as evidence. We also have several witnesses, plus the sergeant on duty that day, and the doctor who attended Joan Wilks when she arrived at the hospital. Your honour, no matter how you look at the case, murder is murder, and a crime is a crime, whether you are on drugs or not, and the prosecution will prove that Mr. Lockman has ruined an entire family and blemished a community. He should indeed be put behind bars. Thank you, your honour." He walked back to his seat.

The judge turned to the prosecutor. "Are you ready to call your first witness?"

"I am your honour. I call Sergeant Bill Smithe of the Blue Ridge Police Department."

Bill rose and walked to the front of the court room. He stood with his right hand raised and the other resting on a bible. The clerk spoke with authority. "Do you solemnly swear to tell the truth, the whole truth, and nothing but the truth, so help you God?"

"I do." Then Bill sat in the witness box.

"Please state your name and occupation."

"Sergeant Bill Smithe of the Blue Ridge Police Department."

The prosecutor approached the witness box and asked, "Can you, in your own words, tell the judge what happened on the afternoon of July 21, 2002 at a local grocery store parking lot in Blue Ridge?"

Bill sat up very straight. "We received a 911 call that came from our local grocery store manager that a woman had been shot in his parking lot. My senior officer, Don Wilson, and I headed over to the store, and found the manager had detained the shooter and gladly turned him over to us. The weapon was still on the pavement as the store manager knew better than to pick it up. Tom Lockman was handcuffed and put in the back of our cruiser, and his weapon was placed in a plastic bag as evidence. It was fingerprinted later that day and Mr. Lockman's prints were the only ones on the weapon."

"And, sergeant, is the shooter here in this court?"

"Yes, he is." Bill pointed to Tom. "That's him."

The prosecutor then asked Bill. "Can you tell the judge what state of mind Tom Lockman was in at the time of the shooting?"

"He was very incoherent and high on drugs."

The prosecutor then asked, "Do you know how Mr. Lockman got the gun?"

"I didn't at first, but with only one sport shop in town, I was able to narrow down who it belonged to. The store manager keeps very accurate records. It was registered to Mr. Tom Lockman."

"Thank you, sergeant." The lawyer then turned to the defence. "Your witness."

The defence approached the witness box. "Sergeant Smithe, let's talk about Tom's state of mind. The fact that you say he was high on drugs, was he ever tested?"

Bill answered, "As soon as we arrived at the station, he was drug tested by a non-partisan doctor. He had high levels of LSD with a mixture of alcohol in his system."

"Sergeant, do you think he is criminally responsible for something he didn't know he was doing?"

The prosecutor jumped in. "Objection your honour. Sergeant Bill Smithe is not qualified to make that kind of judgment. The defence is trying to discredit my witness."

The judge thought for a moment. "Overruled. I'll allow the witness to answer the question."

Bill hesitated then answered, "I believe everyone should be accountable for their actions. Just because a person chooses to do drugs doesn't mean they have the right to shoot an innocent woman, and I might add, an unarmed one. There has to be accountability."

The defence stared at Bill. "No more questions your honour."

Bill returned to his seat next to Richard.

Charles was quickly brought back to the present when Jenny touched his shoulder. He shot out of his seat and started swinging, thinking someone was attacking him. "Are you crazy? I could have killed you. What do you want?"

Jenny was frightened, but pointed to her watch. "It's almost two o'clock. I just didn't want you to miss your next call."

Charles still had five minutes before he had to call Bill. He glared at Jenny. She looked too comfortable holding the baby and that irritated him to no end. He shifted topics as he spoke, "Did I ever tell you about how my nose was broken; at least the first time?"

Jenny looked up, not sure what to say. "No. How did it happen?"

"Tom and I were at school and it was lunch time. I went outside to meet up with him and found him laying on the ground surrounded by half a dozen kids who were laughing at him and kicking him in the head. They were calling him a weakling. That really pissed me off. I ran towards the group and broke through their circle and started to pick Tom up. One of the students attacked me from behind. I turned in retaliation and started swinging. Before too long, all six of them had bloody noses and went snivelling to the principal." He then added, "I picked up my brother and took him home. When my parents saw Tom, they were horrified. I explained what happened and do you know what my father said?"

Jenny was afraid to ask. "What?"

"He approached me and threw his fist into my face and broke my nose. He said I was supposed to protect my brother. The way he hit me, I knew my nose was broken. It swelled up pretty fast and was hard to breathe, also hurt like hell, but I never flinched. I didn't want my dad to think I was weak so I waited for him to leave the room. My mother was scared, but never approached me to see how I was. She also left the room, which devastated me. I thought my mother loved me, but after that incident, I had my doubts. Tom was the only one who cared how I was. That day, I learned how to reset my nose. It was painful when I snapped it back into place." He paused a bit, then continued, "Did you know that once a nose is broken it breaks even easier the second and third time." He half laughed, "Maybe I should have become a doctor." Charles shrugged. "To make matters worse, the school called my parents and we were both suspended for two weeks."

Jenny wasn't sure how to respond to what she had just heard. "I'm sorry, I didn't know that."

Charles glanced at his watch and punched the number for Bill's cell, unaware that his call would not only be recorded, but also traced.

"Lose track of time Charles? You're two minutes late."

"Mine says two o'clock on the dot."

"You surprise me, Charles."

"How's that?"

"For someone as efficient as yourself, I would have thought that your watch would be correct." He paused. "Not to worry. Oh, by the way, how's Jenny?"

There was a slight hesitation in Charles' voice. "Jenny who?"

"Come on, Charles. We already established that the woman with you isn't a girlfriend so she's probably the only other woman in the picture." He inquired again. "Is Jenny doing okay?"

Charles screamed, "Where's my brother?"

Bill kept his cool and sounded calm. "Come on Charles. Don't tell me this is your first kidnapping. You should know how it works. I need proof that the baby is okay before we even consider releasing him."

Charles crossed the room and looked at the sleeping baby. "She's pretty small." He sneered. "She's sound asleep, but I guess I could pinch her and you can hear her scream."

Bill didn't trust Charles so he had to take a chance on Jenny. Her earlier concern for the baby made Bill more comfortable talking to her rather than Charles. "That won't be necessary. Put Jenny on the line and she can tell me herself."

Charles was livid. "Sorry Bill. That isn't part of our agreement. You only speak with me."

"Don't be offended Charles, but I don't trust you. I'm not even sure if I trust Jenny, but I'll take my chances with her."

Charles hesitated. He hadn't planned for the tables to be turned around on him and he seemed to mumble to himself, but Bill couldn't understand anything he said. Charles glanced at Jenny. His brother's wife looked frail and weak, not just physically, but also mentally. Was she able to hold her own against Bill? Letting her talk to Bill seemed the only immediate decision he could make. Charles covered the mouthpiece and whispered, "No tricks. Just say that she's okay and sleeping." He then reluctantly passed the phone to Jenny.

She took it and spoke to Bill. "The baby is fine."

Bill spoke quickly. "Listen Jenny. Her name is Claire and she has a serious medical condition that requires her to have medication soon. Without it she will die."

Jenny looked at Claire. "She's sound asleep. She's okay."

The phone was ripped out of her hand. "What did you say to her?"

"I just told her the baby's name is Claire."

Charles returned to his seat and started to fidget with the arm of his chair. He found a lose thread and started pulling on it, literally ripping a foot-long tear in the fabric. No way would he let Bill take control of the conversation this time. As fast as he sat in his chair, Charles shot out of it and started pacing the cabin. He felt trapped within the confines of the walls. He looked at Jenny who sat on her couch nervously watching him.

53

"Where's my brother?"

"Well, truth be known, he's still in the Edmonton Maximum Security Institution." Bill added, "I've talked to them and it isn't standard procedure to release prisoners in the middle of the night. It won't happen before nine o'clock."

"That's not good news, especially for Claire. Nice name by the way. Is she named after a family member?"

"No. The name means bright or clear, but thanks for asking." Bill paused and added, "I looked up your name. Have you ever wondered what Charles means?"

"Cut the crap and tell me what I want to know about Tom."

"Surprisingly enough, it means freeman and strong."

"What kind of bullshit are you playing with me?"

Bill continued, "Oh, there's more. My name means resolute and protector; which means that I'm firm and determined. Sounds to me like you might think you're free and strong, but my name means I'll never give up until I have Claire back and you're behind bars. Sounds like a win-win to me."

Charles was still somewhat agitated, but he had calmed himself a bit and spoke firmly. "I don't see it that way. I feel that I'm the winner because I planned this down to the last detail."

"I'm not finished, Charles. Your bother's name means twin. Guess the two of you are alike. Both scum bags. Hope your bags are packed because by eight o'clock, I'll have Claire back and you'll be eating lunch with Tom. Now, I have work to do." Bill hung up the phone.

Charles was like a possessed demon. He appeared to lose control, slammed down his phone and stormed out of the cabin. He screamed a most deadly sound. "Ahhhhh!"

Jenny went to the window and saw Charles raging as he punched tree after tree. She suddenly became concerned for Claire's well being. She wasn't sure how to protect Claire, or herself for that matter. Feeling inside the pocket of her dress, the rusty knife was still secure. With trembling hands, she hoped she wouldn't have to use it.

Walking to the bed, Jenny looked at Claire. The baby still slept quietly, but Jenny did wonder what Bill meant about her needing medicine or she would be dead by morning. She started pacing around the cabin too. Jenny wanted to go outside and get some fresh air, but that wasn't possible with Charles still rampaging. She needed to stay indoors to watch over Claire.

Charles suddenly felt extreme pain in his hands. Looking down, he saw his knuckles covered in blood and bark embedded in his flesh. Cursing, he slowly pulled out the bark; flinching as each piece was extracted. He couldn't alter his plans now. His goal was not only to get Tom out of prison, but also to eliminate Bill. If he couldn't do that, then Plan B was out of the question. This so-called Doctor Jackson was his next target. He had also testified against Tom in the court of law, so he had to be eliminated too. Remembering the whiskey in the trunk of the car, he opened the bottle for the second time and slugged back a few gulps. It would help to ease the pain. He hated wasting the alcohol, but poured a small amount over his bleeding hands, flinching with pain. He took a few breaths then went inside, dropped into his chair, and glared at the fire.

"What have you done to yourself?" Jenny asked, "Do you want me to look at it?"

He glared at her and shouted, "Stay away from me!"

He looked at his watch. It read 2:25. He vowed that if Bill hung up on him one more time, he would kill both Claire and Jenny just because she was interfering. She was weak just like his brother and he was tired of covering for them both. Bill was like a thorn in his side, that he couldn't remove. The damn cop was in Charles' head and messing with his plan, but the last laugh would be his as he could visualize Bill obliterated from society and no longer on this earth. He simply had to be removed so he didn't try to put Tom back in prison for a second time. Charles looked across at Jenny. "What're you looking at?"

Jenny looked at him sadly. "Nothing."

CHAPTER NINE

2:10 — 2:40

Bill hung up his phone and turned for an update from Daniel, who was busy pushing buttons and appeared overwhelmed. He glanced up at Bill, not knowing if he was allowed to pass on any details without Don being there. What he had to share wasn't revealing anything that Don would disapprove of, so he looked at Bill and spoke, "We got the recording, but unfortunately, we weren't able to trace the call."

Bill looked confused. "What do you mean you couldn't trace the call? We do it all the time, so what happened this time around?"

Don came over and joined the conversation. "Any luck?"

Daniel answered, "Yes and no."

"I'm going to need clarification on that statement."

"We got the recording, but were unable to trace the signal from his phone, which means he's not on a landline."

Don was as confused as Bill, so asked, "We have all this advanced equipment and we can't trace a simple call?"

Daniel looked at both men. "First of all, if this was a simple call, I would already know where it was made from." Both men still looked confused. "Okay, this is how it works. When tracing a call, it becomes a game of elimination. The call didn't trace because it wasn't made from a landline. Our system is able to pick up signals from landlines and cell phones only. If both of those fail, then it becomes more difficult. Let's hope we have better luck the next time around. This Charles dude thought of everything." Daniel paused. "I'll listen to the tape and see if there's anything useful on it."

Don pulled Bill aside and stated, "We need as many officers on this case as possible, so I took it upon myself to call in our two new rookies. They should be here any minute."

Bill responded, "Good call. I haven't officially met them yet since their shift doesn't start for a few more days. They were both hoping to have a few days off to finish moving before they started work. How do you plan on utilizing them?"

"I thought it would be wise to set up a stake-out at Jenny's house. If Jenny is involved in the case, they may return there. Charles has to know that we would've already cased the place out, but he might not expect us to keep officers on the location. If there's a slight chance he could return, hoping to stay under the radar, we want to know about it."

Bill responded, "Good thinking." He then pointed to the door as the two new officers entered the building. Bill crossed the room and shook each man's hand. "Thanks for coming in on such short notice. I'm Sergeant Bill Smithe and this is Don Wilson, my go-to guy."

The first officer introduced himself. "I'm Eli Watson." Bill and Don both shook his hand.

The second officer then introduced himself. "I'm Muhammad Salomar." Once again, handshakes were exchanged, then the men got down to business.

Eli inquired, "We're both ready to start, so what's the big emergency?"

Don pulled both men aside and filled them in on the case, while Bill went to stand in front of the whiteboard, carefully studying it.

Don continued, "A child was kidnapped around midnight and we have to get her back before eight o'clock or the terrorist is going to kill her."

Both men were stunned. Muhammad replied, "I thought moving to a small town would get us away from the big city crimes." He continued, "I guess not."

Don added, "The child that was kidnapped is Bill's granddaughter, and to make things worse, she has a serious medical condition. If we don't find her before eight o'clock she will most likely already be dead."

Muhammad responded, "Wow. That doesn't give us much time. What do you want us to do?"

Don closed his eyes for only a second then spoke to both men. "When was the last time either one of you were on a stake-out?"

Eli answered, "As a matter of fact, not that long ago."

Muhammad also confirmed, "Same for me."

"The house you'll be watching belongs to the terrorist's sister-in-law, and at this time, we're not sure how involved she is." He then added, "Bill has a call every hour from our terrorist, so keep us updated at least once an hour. Anything suspicious and you call it in."

Eli answered, "Just need the address and we're off."

Muhammad asked, "By any chance does the force have a spare pair of binoculars? Mine are somewhere in a number of boxes that are still packed."

Don turned to his desk and opened the drawer. He donated his pair to them. "Address is 16 Birch Crescent." Eli was given the keys to an undercover vehicle and both men set off to their location.

Bill looked around the room and spotted Richard sitting in a corner looking rather lost. Thinking that he may need a friend right now, Bill made his way towards him. He made a detour to the coffee machine and filled two mugs. Bill handed Richard the coffee and suggested, "Why don't we head into my office and get away from the noise. I think we both need to give the officers some breathing room." Once the door was shut behind them and the two were seated, Bill glanced at Richard. "You got something on your mind?"

"You mean, other than the fact that this kidnapping is tearing Kimberley and I apart? We simply can't lose her Bill, it's not an option." Richard looked up from his coffee mug and asked, "Do you mind if I ask you a question?" He tried to laugh, but it came out more like a tearful plea. "Actually, more than one question."

"We have the whole room to ourselves, so let's talk. It'll be good for both of us."

Richard sounded defeated as he stated, "I feel totally helpless, and I have lots of questions that I need to get out in the open."

Bill dreaded what Richard might be about to ask him, but he was prepared to be truthful, dodging the subject would only create a lack of trust. "We've got an hour, so let's talk and clear the air."

Without hesitating, Richard asked, "Was it smart to hang up on that Charles character? Wouldn't that put Claire at a greater risk?"

Bill looked across his desk at Richard. "Let me try to explain how this negotiating tactic works in simple terms. Right now, Charles has the upper hand because he's holding Claire at ransom. He may not be asking for money, but he's in complete control of the situation. She is his means to getting his brother out of prison. My job is to switch his focus from Claire to myself. In order to do that, I have to piss him off enough that I become the main target, thus taking Claire out of the picture. He will be so enraged with me that Claire will not even exist in his eyes."

Richard looked worried. "But won't that put you in danger?"

"Definitely, but better me than Claire. He will keep her alive just long enough for us to find him, then try and eliminate her in front of us. That would create the most damage and he still can kill me at the same time. My team won't allow that to happen. We just need to find out where he's hiding, then we can arrest him or kill the son of a bitch. Either way works for me." Bill paused. "There's one thing that I've learned over the many years of being a policeman, and then a sergeant: be patient and eventually you achieve the upper hand."

"But how does hanging up prove that he's in control?"

"Good question. By turning off my phone, Charles immediately thinks that he's breaking me and I'm hanging up out of frustration."

Richard replied, "Well I'm pretty frustrated right now. Aren't you?"

"Frustration is a state of mind. You can either take control of it or you can drown in it. I've chosen to take control of it until Claire is safely home."

Richard looked puzzled as he studied Bill. "Have you been involved in lots of kidnapping cases?"

"Lots when I was living in Vancouver, but not so many since moving here. Bigger cities mean bigger crimes."

"Were they all happy endings?"

"Richard, thousands of children are kidnapped each year, some parental kidnappings, a divorced couple out to hurt each other, while others are as simple as wanting ransom. Each case is different depending on the circumstances."

"Will we get Claire back in time?"

Bill shifted in his chair. "My team is well aware of the timeline that's set in front of them. They're a great bunch of men who all take their job seriously. Let's let them do what they do best, and we'll be there on site, when we're needed. Every decision and every move the team makes will be carefully planned. Claire is their main concern so all I need to do is let Charles think that he's in complete control. As long as he thinks that, Claire is safe. My officers are the best that Blue Ridge has and every one of them knows what's expected of them. You have to trust them, and in turn trust me. The only disadvantage that we have at this point is our timeline."

Richard responded, "I do trust you, but I'm really scared right now."

"We all are." Bill managed a weak chuckle. "Good talk there, Doctor Jackson, now may I make a suggestion?"

Richard simply nodded.

"I think right now you should be calling Kimberley and Beatrice and filling them in on our progress."

Richard looked puzzled. "What do I tell them? I don't see any progress?"

Bill hesitated. "Follow me." The two left the office and approached the whiteboard. "We've made a world of progress. We have Charles' complete family, including Tom's wife Jenny and her address. No one at her house, so that confirms she is most likely part of the kidnapping, whether she knew about it in advance or not is still undetermined. Those two officers that just arrived are going to be staking out Jenny's residence just in case they return there. I feel confident that I have established an ally with Jenny."

"How can you be so sure of that?"

"She may not have any children, but now she knows Claire's name, and has held her. I'm convinced that as the hours pass, Jenny will protect her."

"Another one of those feelings?"

"Yup, starts in the stomach and slowly works its' way to the surface. I just need a few more chances of talking with her to find out where she is on this." Bill glanced at the whiteboard again. He then added, "Right now officers are out there scouring the neighbourhood, and hopefully will find Charles's hideout, or at least eliminate locations in town where Claire isn't. That's a big move forward."

Richard's voice broke. "Those few more calls could put Claire in a dangerous situation. I don't have to tell you that she's tiny. The only positive thing is that her diabetes develops slowly over several hours, which will work to our advantage."

"Good to know. You just have to trust me and my team. I would never let anything happen to Claire and right now it may not look like it, but before long we will have the upper hand. Charles just doesn't know it yet." Bill's voice cracked. "This whole night sucks and it's my entire fault that this has happened. I'll make it right. I would rather die saving her than lose her."

Bill turned to Daniel who had headphones on and was listening to the recording. He glanced up and gave Bill the thumbs up. Richard saw the signal and inquired, "What does that thumbs up mean?"

"It means you need to go make that call to the ladies and Don and I need to get back to work." Bill then crossed the room and took the seat across from Daniel. They waited for Don to join the group. Bill inquired, "You okay if I sit through this?"

Don nodded and asked Daniel. "What've you got?"

"I'm not totally sure." He passed two sets of headphones across the table. Bill and Don placed them on and listened.

Daniel waited then asked, "What do you make of this sound?"

Both men heard a faint sound, but couldn't identify it. Don spoke first. "I'm not sure. Can you replay it?"

The three officers listened several times and still came up with nothing. Daniel finally made a suggestion. "Maybe if I play around with the soundtrack a little more, we would have better luck." He moved dials around and they kept listening until Daniel thought he couldn't do anything else to improve the sound.

Bill ran his fingers through his hair. "I need a coffee, how about the two of you?" Both men nodded and Bill left, soon returning with three mugs of the steaming hot beverage. He was slowly sipping his mug and secretly hoping the caffeine would give him the boost he needed. Exhaustion had started to set in, and Bill knew he had to keep alert or his body would start to shutdown. Shift work had taken its' toll on his body years ago, so his latest promotion to sergeant meant a nine-to-five day job. Bill's head hurt and the office was starting to close in on him. "I need some fresh air. I'll just be outside."

The outside air was chilly, but it was just what Bill needed. Right now, he knew that darkness was his best friend, and finding Claire before the sun rose was imperative. He worried about Kimberley and Beatrice. The news Richard was about to give them wasn't much, and the team still didn't have the breakthrough they needed. Bill wished he could slow time down or, even better, turn back the clock. If he could have foreseen this event, his family wouldn't be going through this horrific night. No point in beating himself up for something he had no control over. He didn't own a crystal ball so he had to bite the bullet and deal with it.

He was startled when he heard Daniel shout, "I think I have it!"

Bill ran inside to Daniel's desk and found a wide grin on Don's face. "You figured out the sound?"

Daniel nodded. "I think so. See what you think."

Bill listened, but was still baffled. "Maybe I'm just over tired. I still don't know what the sound is."

Daniel grinned. "Don't you think it's the crackling of a fire? It's faint, but I think I'm right."

Don responded, "It's definitely a fire."

Bill closed his eyes and listened carefully. He realized the sound was indeed a fire. "Good work guys." He ran to the whiteboard and wrote, 'sound of crackling fire on tape.' Bill knew it wasn't much to work on, but one more word on the board meant the team was that much closer to finding Claire.

Don came over and stood next to Bill. "Once our three teams of men have finished their ongoing search and heaven forbid find nothing, we need to look at places where there are fires. Campsites stand out at the top of my list. I have to ask you, Bill. I sure hope I'm doing things correctly, your shoes are hard to fill. Please, at any point, if you think I'm not doing everything in the right order, let me know. I will take care of the paperwork, but I need you up front for your expertise. Your qualifications put mine to shame."

Bill turned to Don. "I have an old saying that's got me through many difficult cases. Keep positive, keep positive."

CHAPTER TEN

2:30 — 2:45

Entering Bill's office, Richard quietly closed the door behind him and took a seat against the wall next to the filing cabinet. He wasn't quite ready to call the ladies yet, as he wasn't sure if what he had to say would sound like progress to either one of them. He needed time to himself, to regroup his feelings. Richard sighed, rested his head against the wall, and looked up at the ceiling. His mind went to places it shouldn't have gone. He could visualize Charles glaring down at his beautiful daughter with intentions of hurting her. He could also see arriving at the mysterious location to find her already deceased. He would carefully pick her up and cradle her lifeless body. If Charles was still alive at that point, he would break his neck out of revenge. He had to shake those emotions from his mind and remember that he was a doctor pledged to saving lives; not eliminating them. It wasn't long before the tears were streaming down his face, but he didn't wipe them away, instead he let them flow freely. Hopefully the tears that seemed never ending would be a form of cleansing for him. Richard couldn't even imagine not being able to hug or kiss his daughter ever again. He also knew that Kimberley, the love of his life, would never be the same. The two would have scars that would never heal and could never be removed. The tears started once again, and this time Richard wiped them away.

Being a doctor, he knew how to treat Claire's condition. When she was old enough, he had planned on teaching her to not be afraid of her diabetes, but learn how to treat herself. He only had to protect her until then, but now that things had changed, he felt like he was letting her down. She should have her whole life ahead of her and this Charles was trying to steal it away from her. His tears turned to anger.

Years earlier, when Bill was doing his job and had arrested Tom Lockman for murder, he never guessed that today it was going to come back to bite him. Why was Charles so full of hate and vengeance, especially towards an innocent child? Richard turned his attention to Bill, trying to imagine what he was going through. He wasn't prepared to put on Bill's shoes, as he knew they came with guilt and uncertainty. Bill had shared that he was willing to sacrifice himself for his granddaughter and that meant a great deal to Richard, but hopefully Bill was going to be able to not only save Claire, but also himself. Turning the tables around on Charles and making Bill his main target and moving Claire into the background was heroic in Richard's eyes, but also concerning. It was imperative that both of them survive. Richard glanced around Bill's office and noticed several diplomas behind his desk. Richard was sure they had always been there, but he hadn't noticed them until now, so he got up to take a closer look. All three certificates were in a black satin frame, all at the same height, almost as if a level had been set on top of each one before hanging them.

The first one was from the Police Academy in New Westminster. The bold letters at the top read JIBC which Richard discovered meant, Justice Institute of British Columbia. Bill's name was scripted in black letters underneath the title, and the year on the bottom left corner read 1980. The second certificate was from Vancouver and the bold letters on it were AGP for Advanced Geographic Profiling. Bill's name once again stood out in black letters. Reading further down the certificate Richard noted, 'trained to handle complex violent crimes peacefully.' The year Bill got this specialized certificate was 1982. The last was from the CPC, the Canadian Police College; a negotiator certificate, which once again had Bill's name scribed beneath its' title. This let Richard know that Bill was qualified in having hostages released peacefully through negotiating. The third and last certificate was dated 1983. All certificates were signed by the same official, but Richard was unable to read the name. Richard returned to the chair he had sat in earlier and took another look at Bill's degrees. "I never should've doubted him." He waited several minutes, trying to figure out what to tell the ladies. Finally, he gave up and dialled the number, hoping he could sound positive for their benefit.

Kimberley answered on the first ring. Her voice was panicky, but also had a hint of hope in it. "Richard. Do you have her?"

Richard softly spoke, "Not yet sweetheart, but Bill is getting closer." He could hear her crying in the background and he already knew that Beatrice was next to her.

"Is he going to find her in time?"

"Sweetheart." Richard ran his fingers through his hair and closed his eyes, wishing this whole night was over and Claire was back in her crib. "Can I ask you something, Kimberley?"

She took control of her emotions before answering, "Of course, what?"

He looked across the room at Bill's certificates. "How many times have you been in Bill's office?"

There was a slight hesitation at the other end of the phone. "I don't know exactly, but probably hundreds of times. Why do you ask?"

"I was just sitting in here looking around when I noticed his impressive certificates hanging on the wall. Did you know that he was a trained profiler and also a negotiator?"

"No, I didn't."

Richard sounded very excited and he asked, "Do you know what this means?"

"I could make an educated guess. He must know what he's doing?"

"Exactly, he may have not done this for some time, but he knows not only what to do, but also how best to do it. We have to put our full trust in him." He didn't share the part about Bill placing himself in danger to save their daughter. That would only put Kimberley and Beatrice under more stress.

"I always have. He's been my rock since he came into my life, so yes, I trust he'll do everything possible to find her. My big concern is whether he finds her in time." Tears were now flowing down Kimberley's cheeks and she was speaking in gasps. "Richard, they have our baby."

Richard covered the mouthpiece of the phone and took a few deep breaths to compose himself before speaking. Knowing he had to be strong for her, he replied, "I know. Is Beatrice there?"

"She's not left my side since you went with Bill." She started to half cry and laugh at the same time. "She's been feeding me cup after cup of tea. I don't have the heart to tell her that enough is enough." With puffy eyes she glanced at Beatrice.

"Can I talk to her?"

Kimberley passed Beatrice the phone.

"Hi, Richard. How are the two of you holding up?"

"Well, if the truth be known, I'm a wreck. Bill on the other hand is calm and professional, but he does look a bit tired. I'm sure it has been hard for him to turn the reins over to Don, but he's still involved with a lot of the decisions being made. It's kind of nice to watch his team at work, just wish he wasn't under so much stress and circumstances were different. I thought we were getting nowhere when he pointed out to me just how much progress he and his team were making." He got up from his seat and walked to the window. All was dark outside, but he was glad of the darkness, because like Bill, he knew that if it was daylight, then Claire's time was up. Richard's voice broke, "Thank you for being there with Kimberley."

"Where else would I be?"

"I need you to do me a favour."

"Of course. What can I do?"

"I need to be here when they find Claire's location so I can also be on site to treat her. Help Kimberley realize that I want to be with her, but at this point I can't. Also, I'm not sure how often I'll be able to call, but I'll do my best to keep you updated."

"Of course, Richard, I know she understands."

"I'm heading to the hospital after we hang up and getting all the equipment that I need once we find her."

Beatrice's voice trembled. "Thank you, Richard."

"For what?"

"For being a wonderful husband to Kimberley, father to Claire, but mostly a doctor who can treat Claire once you find her."

"I'll call you soon with an update." Richard hung up and went back to the communal area. "Bill, do you have a minute?"

"Sure. How did your call go?"

"Surprisingly well." He then added, "I really need to apologize to you. I should never have questioned your strategy; especially after seeing all your certificates on your office wall."

"Apology accepted, but they're just framed papers with my name on them. I had to put something up there to break up the otherwise bland wall space."

"They're more than that Bill, and you know it. Like your office, I also have certificates on my wall, but mine are medical diplomas. We're two different people with two different gifts and right now yours are the most important." He then asked, "Any chance I can I borrow your cruiser?"

Bill looked puzzled. "Sorry, it's illegal for a civilian to drive a police car. Why do you need it?"

"If you recall, I came here with you so have no wheels. I need to get to the hospital and pick up supplies so when we find her, I'll be prepared."

Bill replied, "Okay, I can drive you, but we have to be back here before three o'clock. Just one more thing, Richard. Just remember that you're the only one who can treat Claire, so when we find her, you'll stay in the vehicle until Charles is in handcuffs. We can't take any chances that you get injured."

"You have a deal."

Bill headed towards the door with Richard in tow. "Let's go get your kit."

CHAPTER ELEVEN

2:00 — 2:45

Eric and Sam slowly drove through the dark streets of Blue Ridge, scanning all the homes, parks, recreation buildings, and parking lots looking for any clues that could help them solve this latest case.

Eric turned to Sam. "Bet none of us saw this coming."

"Not in a hundred years."

Eric thought for a moment before he replied, "At midnight, when I got Don's call, I was barely awake, but I knew instantly that something was seriously wrong. I could tell by his voice, but it was his lack of information that scared me the most. It was the urgency that told me to get moving, that I was needed at the office." He paused. "You know, I've never heard that tone in Don's voice before. He portrayed both fear and urgency. As I was driving to work, I speculated what might have been wrong, but I was way off track." He added, "You know that every officer with a long career has had to deal with kidnappings, but this has to be the worst. What does this Charles hope to accomplish by eight o'clock? Certainly, he can't expect to get his brother out in that short time."

Sam answered, "If you recall, Bill said that he thought that he was the actual target, Claire was meant to be a distraction. Getting Bill on his own allows him to get his revenge, and there's a strong possibility he may still remove Claire from the picture as double revenge."

Eric shuffled in his seat. "I was surprised at how many officers were called in to help with the kidnapping. Knowing the conflict-of-interest issue Bill was facing must have pissed him off. He's the one with all the terrorist training and Don is the most senior officer. Don must have been overwhelmed taking over the case, but Bill assured him that he'd be in the background overseeing all decisions. That must have made Don feel better."

Sam replied, "Bill must have full confidence in Don or he wouldn't have chosen him."

"He has the most seniority and experience so was a very good choice."

While glancing from house to house, Sam thought a moment then inquired, "What're we actually looking for out here?"

"Any homes with lights on that look suspicious. One would assume that at this time of night, all houses should be dark, but if Charles is inside one, the lights would be on all the time. He can't take the chance of falling asleep and missing his next call."

Sam hadn't worked too long at the station, but even in the short time since he joined the team, he had discovered that his fellow officers were a very close-knit group, constantly watching out for each other. They were like a well-oiled machine. Sam was proud to work alongside his fellow officers. Although Bill was an excellent leader, Don was a good fill-in for the time being.

While scanning their surroundings, Eric asked Sam, "So, what do you think of this whole nightmare? Do you think the rescue is doable?"

"It's complete bullshit, but we have to find her, not only for the family, but also to put the scumbag away for a long time. For now, I'm trying to keep my mind on the job and not the struggling families involved." Sam shrugged his shoulder then added, "Guess this nightshift just got busier because of some psycho maniac. It's going to be crazy, but we'll all get through it. This Charles character is going to find out just how good our force really is. He won't know what hit him, but rest assured, he'll be safely behind bars by eight o'clock if not before."

Eric glanced across the vehicle and looked at his partner for the night. "Amen to that, brother." He then continued, "I have a daughter about the same age as Claire. I can't imagine what the family is going through. My little girl is my pride and joy. I love my wife dearly, and I know that she loves me too, but if the tables were turned and it was our daughter who was taken, I'm not sure if our marriage could survive it. They're so innocent at that age and completely dependant on an adult. I sure as hell wouldn't trust a crazy psycho with her life. I wouldn't even ask questions when I found her, I'd just shoot to kill."

Sam looked across at his partner. "I feel the same way, but that's not how the justice system works."

"But what if the kidnapper is proven innocent and released back into the general population? He would be laughing at the police force and going on as if nothing had happened."

Sam responded, "I'd set up surveillance and nail the bastard if he even sneezed too hard. Everywhere he turned, there would be someone watching him. He would be so scared of us that he may even turn himself in and want to be behind bars."

Eric sighed and added, "That sounds like a fairy tale ending, but let's just hope this case turns out well for all the families involved."

As they cruised down each street, both looked for anything out of the ordinary. There were a few houses that had lights glowing in their windows, but none of them alerted Eric or Sam to any suspicious activity. Eric knew most of the families living in this section of town, so guessed that a child inside either needed a glass of water or a visit to the bathroom. The streets were deserted at this time of night, with not a soul to be seen. The odd dog barked as their vehicle passed by and a few cats cut in front of their vehicle. Luckily, none of them were black, as Eric was very superstitious.

Sam noticed Eric was uneasy as a cat darted across their path and he inquired, "You okay?"

"Cats, I just hate cats, especially black ones. Nothing turns out well when they cross in front of you. Since we're sharing, I also hate walking under ladders. With my luck, a gallon of paint would land on my head."

Sam laughed, "Not superstitious, are you?"

"I guess it shows."

"Maybe a little, but tell you what, you watch my back and I'll watch yours. Those sneaky black cats won't get anywhere near you." Both men laughed.

"I appreciate that, but it does sound like you're making fun of me."

"Maybe a little."

Once the two were satisfied there was nothing to be concerned with in the downtown and residential areas, they headed for the only empty warehouse in the commercial part of town. It was an old cannery building that had closed six years ago, after the tsunami hit their town. Fishing decreased dramatically after that event and the business was forced to close, putting about fifty men out of work. Turning the last corner, before the warehouse came into view, Eric pulled over to the side of the road and killed the headlights. The two sat for a few seconds to let their eyes adjust to the darkness. As if the early morning couldn't get any worse, a streak of lightening shot across the sky, followed by a clap of thunder. The heavens opened and rain poured down in sheets, making visibility almost nil. Eric turned on his windshield wipers to clear the glass that separated them from the storm. The two of them took a final look at the building in front of them before leaving their dry vehicle. They looked at each other then slowly opened their doors and stepped out into the puddles. Eric locked the vehicle and the two men ran towards the building. They were soaking wet before they even got close and huddled together under the overhang. The building was overgrown with brush and weeds, but off to Eric's left, there was a slight red glow coming out of a dirty window. Sam turned to Eric. "Do you see that?"

"Sure do. Looks like a red flutter of light coming from that window."

Eric moved quickly away from the building, stepping back into the rain, and looked up at the roof. He quickly ducked back under the eaves. "Smoke's coming out of the chimney, so someone's inside and looks like there's a fire. I'm going to call it in." Eric pulled the radio out of his inside pocket and clicked the talk button.

"Daniel here, what you got?"

"We're at the warehouse and it looks like there could be someone inside."

Daniel responded, "Do you need backup?"

"Negative. Sam and I are going in for a closer look. I'll get back to you." Eric then added, "And no, we won't do anything stupid."

"Copy that."

Both officers worked their way toward the window. When Eric squinted through the cracked, dirty glass, he noticed that the light was in fact, a fire, but it seemed to be contained. He turned to Sam and whispered, "Window is too dirty to see much, but there's definitely a fire inside."

"Where there's fire, there has to be someone who lit it."

"This looks like a hell hole. Sure hope this isn't the hostage site." Eric moved away from the window, turned his flashlight on, and scanned the full length of the warehouse.

"Looks like there are three doors. We may as well try them in order."

The weather had turned uglier with a high wind blowing the rain directly into their faces. Both men bent into the wind in hopes that it would help to keep them dry. The storm was relentless and came with a chill that seemed to pass through their jackets and sent them into shivers, but the two officers trudged forward. Once at the first door, Eric turned the handle, but the door appeared to be locked so they moved to the second one, which was also locked.

Eric leaned towards Sam and said, "Third time lucky?"

"Sure hope so. I'm soaking wet and miserable. We need to get out of this weather."

"I agree." Eric added, "I hope we don't have to kick the door in. It would definitely ruin our element of surprise."

At the far end of the building, the two officers approached the last door, which Eric noticed was in the same condition. Upon further inspection, he noticed it was probably not locked, but rusted shut. He knew that pushing on the door would cause the hinges to squeak, not only giving away their location, but also warning the people inside of their presence. Hopefully the distance between this door and the burning fire inside was enough to allow them to enter the building unnoticed. Eric turned off his flashlight and tucked it back into his jacket pocket. Both drew their pistols. Eric took a deep breath before pushing gently on the door. He whispered, "Here goes nothing."

"Right behind you partner."

Eric might as well have been scratching his fingernails on a chalkboard. The squeak of the hinges sent shivers down both their spines. Eric opened the door just enough for the two of them to slide through and push their backs against the wall. Both men waited to see if anyone had heard them. All was quiet so Eric retrieved the flashlight from his jacket pocket and turned it on. Neither one of the two officers was prepared for the swarm of bats that suddenly set upon them. There were hundreds, maybe even thousands of them. Both men were ducking and batting their arms trying to protect their faces from this massive colony. The squeaking, clicking sound was deafening as they seemed to be attacking both men from every angle. Eric covered his head and moved away from the door. Sam followed his lead. Both officers turned their flashlights towards the tiny opening of the door, lighting an escape route for their attackers. The nocturnal creatures found the small opening and a steady black stream of bats left the building, the clicking sound slowly decreasing. Once their attackers were gone, both men turned off their flashlights.

Eric slowed down his heart rate before saying, "Hey man, thanks for not shooting me."

"Was too busy trying to survive." Sam took several breaths. "Guess there goes our element of surprise."

"No doubt."

It was obvious that whoever was in the building now had to know of the intruders. They waited for a few minutes to see if anyone would come looking for them, but no one came to check, so they proceeded. It was difficult for the two officers to see in the dark room as there were very few windows, so they once again turned on their flashlights, fully aware that they may have to turn them off in an instant. They separated with one walking down the left side of the room and the other down the opposite side. The corrugated walls were covered in rust from missing fasteners, allowing the rain to seep in. The cold metal walls offered no warmth for the two soaked and already frozen men. The floors were covered in garbage and they could both see their breath as they walked from one room to the next. Being an old cannery, both men could smell the putrid odour of rotting fish. At the far end of the second room were cartons of unused tins, which would have been used to process the fish. Rats were constantly under their feet, so both officers had to dodge to avoid stepping on them. The rodents scurried around them and dashed into small, rusted openings at floor level then quickly disappeared outside.

There was no warmth at this end of the warehouse and as much as the two officers wanted to barge forward, they had to be cautious. They passed through several more rooms before they found the one with the burning fire. It was contained in the remains of an old stove with a chimney running about fifty feet up to the roof where the smoke was able to escape. Both men holstered their weapons as they spotted about half a dozen homeless people huddled around the stove, trying to keep warm.

The half dozen men slowly turned to see who was behind them. One of them spoke, "We ain't doing any harm here officers so what do you want?" He then added, "We heard the bats making all that noise, but thought whoever came in would have fled in fear. I guess having a gun helped, although you never fired a shot. Guess there would have been no point as there were thousands of them." He seemed to study both men in front of him. "We never go down to that section of the building because of the bats." He waited a few seconds then asked, "You looking for someone?"

Sam started to approach the men. "Mind if we join you for a few minutes. That's if you'll share your fire. Horrible rainstorm outside caught us both off guard."

The homeless man looked at the two soaked officers and nodded. "Don't mind at all." He then studied Eric. "I think I know you."

"That could be. I've lived here for a long time. I like the small-town atmosphere, more personal than the big city life."

"You're the officer that goes around to the schools and speaks about drug abuse."

"No, that would be Officer Don Wilson, but we're often mistaken for each other." He was chuckling when he added, "We're both kind of good looking."

The homeless stranger continued, "He's helped a lot of teens in this town." He paused. "We may be homeless here, but we don't do drugs. The only thing we're doing here is trying to keep warm over the winter."

Eric and Sam joined the men huddled around the old stove extending their hands and rubbing them together to warm them up. Eric noticed that old furniture and large chunks of wood had been stacked a short distance from the fire. The pile was big enough to last at least a week. He turned to the man who appeared to be the spokesperson of the group. "We're wondering if any of you have seen anything out of the ordinary in this area. Any people who shouldn't be here?"

"We've never seen a cop here, let alone two cops, so that's out of the ordinary."

Eric laughed, "I meant other than us."

"Nope, haven't seen anyone in days until you two came around."

Eric glanced at the group of men. "Are you here full time or do you just come here at night?"

"Pretty much full time. The building is vacant so we're not disturbing anyone. Found a big pile of cardboard that we place on the cement floor to sleep on, keeps the chill off our bodies. As luck would have it, one of the offices had a pile of old coats and blankets stashed in a cupboard." The man added, "It may not be the Ritz Hotel, but it's dry and warm."

Eric and Sam would've liked to stay longer, but their case had to take precedence. Eric added, "Thanks for sharing your fire." They stayed for a few more minutes before leaving the warehouse and returning to their cruiser.

The walk back to their vehicle was even worse than when they first left their cruiser. Eric unlocked the door and both men jumped inside. Eric picked up his radio. "There's nothing here, Daniel, just some homeless people trying to keep warm. We're coming in."

Daniel answered, "Copy that."

CHAPTER TWELVE

2:00 — 2:45

Jack and Greg slowly drove out towards the lighthouse. The road was twisty but there was almost no traffic, so both men had time to consider the events that had happened over the past few hours. Earlier, Jack had left work at the end of his shift, had a quick bite to eat, and was looking forward to a quiet evening. He was already in bed when the call came, so his sleep was cut short. Getting a call at that time of the night meant it was serious, so he carefully listened to Don's voice at the other end of the phone. Once he hung up, Jack was out of bed in a shot, pulling on his uniform and out of the house in record time. His mind came back to the cruiser and keeping his eyes on the road, Jack commented, "It's going to be a long night."

Greg responded, "Probably more for you than me, I slept half the day away. I was in the middle of my coffee when all hell broke loose in the office."

"Guess we'll both be sleeping tomorrow." He then added, "Wonder who'll be holding down the fort then?"

Greg answered, "I heard Don on the phone earlier talking to the force at Sidville. He's made arrangements for two of their officers to come and cover tomorrow's day shift." He then added, "Now that's what I call planning ahead." He squinted out the front window and announced, "Looks like there's a storm moving in."

Jack slammed on the breaks as a shadow passed in front of his vehicle. The car came to an abrupt stop. Half of the vehicle was on the pavement while the other sat on the gravel shoulder. Jack was shaking uncontrollably. He killed the headlights, shut off the engine, threw off his seat belt, and then fumbled for his weapon. "Did you see that? Someone just walked in front of our vehicle. He must be crazy, I could have killed him!"

Greg tried to calm him down. "There's no one out there, Jack."

Jack wasn't convinced. "Didn't you see that, he passed right in front of us?"

Greg watched as Jack's head looked between the rear-view mirror, both side mirrors, then the road in front of him.

"Trust me, there's no one out there, and stop turning your head like that. You look like a bobble-head police doll stuck on a cruiser's dash."

Jack turned to Greg. "Okay, Mr. Know it all. How do you explain what we both saw, that is, if in fact you saw it?"

Greg started to explain, "I guess you've never heard of fog ghosts."

"Stop messing with me. That's something you just made up."

Greg continued, "No they're real, I've seen this phenomenon only once before, that is, until tonight. It only occurs when the weather conditions are ideal. It has to be a wet, foggy night, headlights on, no street lights and with some sort of a pulsating light that can cross in front of a vehicle. Even though we're still a mile away from the lighthouse, the light from the beacon passes in front of our vehicle and reflects off the road into the fog. The first time I saw it was when I was driving at night up a steep hill near the airport. The airport beacon light crossed the road in front of me and I saw the same thing that we just saw tonight."

"You're pulling my crank and it isn't funny."

Greg nervously suggested, "First, why don't you put your weapon away?"

Jack hesitantly put his gun back into its' holster and turned to his partner. Greg then asked, "Do you trust me?"

"What do you mean, trust you? I have to, you're my partner, at least for tonight."

"Turn on your headlights and then wait for the light to pass in front of us again."

Jack turned them on and waited. When the light once again passed in front of the vehicle, the same image presented itself before the two officers. "That's so weird. I wouldn't have believed it if I hadn't seen it with my own eyes."

Greg thought he would have a little bit of fun with Jack, so he slowly spoke in a haunting voice, "Woohahaha. Gotcha."

Jack jumped at the sound and then returned to reality. "Cute, but we have a lighthouse to search, so let's get on with it."

Luck wasn't on their side tonight. When Jack started the vehicle, the rain also started to spit, but soon turned into a real downpour. He quickly switched on the windshield wipers, which had a hard time keeping up with the torrential downpour. This was just a freak storm that no one knew was even coming. Both men looked up at the sky and saw only darkness. When the lightening hit, the dark sky lit up for a split second before the bolt shot out to sea. The flash disappeared as quickly as it had appeared and was soon followed by the sharp crack of thunder which trailed off into a low rumble out over the sea. Both men looked at each other, still mesmerized from the light show they had just witnessed.

Jack took a few seconds to recover from what the two of them had just experienced. Squinting through the window he spoke, "Now that was crazy and frightening, and so unexpected. We're so close to the lighthouse, let's continue on. How close do you think we should get before we start to walk? We don't want to alert anyone of our presence."

Greg responded, "Halfway down the causeway should be safe." He studied the storm surrounding them. "Looks like we're going to get wet tonight, but we can't waste any more time. Let's do it and get the hell out of here."

Within a few minutes, the rain had slowed down, so Jack parked the vehicle along the side of the causeway's gravel road. Both men remained in the vehicle for several minutes, letting their eyes adjust to the darkness outside. The flashing light on the lighthouse spun like a well-greased wheel at the top of the tower, taking about a minute to make a complete rotation. There was always a flash of light first, followed by eight beams, which sent rays at three hundred and sixty degrees, lighting up the circumference of the building and the water.

Greg looked at the lighthouse with amazement and appreciation. "This lighthouse saved my cousin's life several years ago. The navigation system on his fishing boat failed and he was lost at sea for several days. His family was worried sick. The night stars safely led him back to the coast and the lighthouse helped him stay away from the rocks. His family was so relieved to hear that he was back on land, safe and sound."

Jack admired the building in front of him. "Did you know that Greece actually was the first country to build a lighthouse? Alexander the Great can take full credit for that innovation. Unfortunately, it was damaged in an earthquake and is no longer standing. At one point, it was considered one of the Seven Wonders of the World in ancient history. It was built in 280 BC, but was destroyed in the 1300s."

Greg looked at his partner. "Aren't you just a walking encyclopedia?"

"Hey, I just find them fascinating."

"Sounds like trivia to me."

Jack conceded, "Maybe. Guess that puts me into the dork category."

Both men waited for the rotation to finish. The rays lit not only the ocean, but also the landscape, giving Jack and Greg a quick look at their surroundings. Both men waited for several seconds, observing and listening, but nothing seemed out of the ordinary. The storm that had battered them fifteen minutes earlier had subsided and only a drizzle remained. Jack turned off his vehicle engine and both men got out of the car. After locking the cruiser, they slowly worked their way towards the lighthouse. The walk was challenging as neither man wanted to turn on their flashlights, so that meant stepping in puddles was inevitable. If this was the hostage location, neither officer wanted to give the abductor a heads up. The darkness was their greatest ally, apart from the flash that lit up their surroundings for a split second, making them both sitting ducks.

Jack scanned his surroundings as he walked. Greg followed him, turning occasionally to check behind them. The gravel beneath their feet crunched, causing both men to worry the noise would give them away. The overcast sky still provided the officers with some protection. Once they got closer, both men knew they would have to walk slower, cutting down the noise their feet made. Their ears were tuned into any sounds or movements around them, but all they could hear was the squawking of seagulls and the crashing of waves on the causeway walls. The sound of the water was soothing, but they weren't there for relaxation. Jack whispered, "Hopefully this is where we'll find Claire and her abductors."

"That would be nice. Then you could go home and back to bed, and I could finish off my shift."

"You must be from another planet. If we find her here, there will be tons of paperwork to fill out."

Greg shrugged. "Maybe Don will let us fill it out tomorrow?"

"Do you know what would give me great satisfaction right now?"

"What?"

Jack replied, "To call the precinct and have the full team backing us up as we all saved her. It would be better to find her early and get her to the hospital for treatment than to find her too late."

Jack pushed that idea out of his mind. Too late wasn't an option. They had to find her, not only for Richard and Kimberley, but also for Bill and Beatrice. He also wouldn't mind if he and Greg were the heroes of the night.

The odd splash was heard as fish broke the surface then dived back below the water. With their weapons drawn, both men walked slowly forward. Closing in on the lighthouse, they both ran and plastered their backs to its' walls. The concrete was not only cold, but also soaking wet from the earlier downpour. Pausing for several seconds, the seagulls and waves were still the only sound they heard. The lighthouse was octagonal, so each side could pose a danger for them. When Jack got to the door, he turned the handle, but as expected, it was locked. He placed his ear against the door, listening for sounds of anyone moving around inside, but all was quiet, so they continued around the next corner. They both carefully moved towards the back of the building, pistols ready just in case. If there was a vehicle on the site, this was the most likely place for it. From the causeway, it would be hidden, so could only be seen from the water.

Jack cautiously peeked around the corner and whispered, "I see a vehicle and it looks like it could be empty." The two men cautiously moved closer, one on each side of the car. Once in place, both men turned their flashlights on to peek inside. They were both shocked to find a young couple in the back seat making out. The couple were both horrified and embarrassed. They had been meeting there for several months and had never been caught before. Jack tapped on the glass and the young man put down the window. Jack spoke, "I think before things get too heated in there, you should both head home." He then inquired, "How long have the two of you been here?"

The young man sheepishly answered, "About an hour."

"Have either of you seen anyone else around here?"

"No one, officer. Are we free to go?"

"You are and get the lady home safely."

Slightly embarrassed, the young man answered, "Okay, officer. Sorry."

Jack responded, "Don't apologize to me, maybe you should save that for the young lady's parents."

The couple left and both officers laughed. Greg commented, "I remember those days when the wife and I snuck out after dark. The only difference is we never got caught."

Jack laughed, "Let's get back to the car and call it in." The walk back to the vehicle was easier going as they were able to use their flashlights, thus avoiding the mud puddles. Both men turned around to take one last look at the lighthouse, convincing themselves that it was all clear.

Once back inside their vehicle, Jack picked up the radio. "Jack here. Lighthouse is a bust. It's locked up and secure, just a young couple making out in the back of their car. We caught them off guard. I think they were surprised, but mostly embarrassed, to see anyone out there, especially two officers. We're on our way back to the station."

Daniel replied, "Copy that. See you back here."

CHAPTER THIRTEEN

2:00 — 2:45

Bob recalled having left work earlier that night. He'd had a quick bite to eat before meeting up with his hockey team and was pleased at how well they were playing, reminding him of when he was that young. Oh, the energy he had back then. Those were the days. These kids needed a distraction from their delinquent activities and hockey was a good substitute. Bob was able to raise enough money, from local businesses, to buy good quality equipment for his players. Practice was once a week and an hour long, and by the end, Bob was exhausted, and he was hoping the young players were too. Coaching was tough after working a full shift, but he thoroughly enjoyed doing it.

He recalled saying to the team earlier that evening. "Before you guys leave, I think you're ready for your first competitive game so I'm going to set it up with the Sidville team, and I know that you're going to knock them off their skates." The hockey team was beaming from ear to ear. They had worked hard and were more than ready to see how they measured up to other teams. "Go straight home and see you next week." He shook all their hands as they left. He arrived home and popped open a cold beer, then flopped onto the sofa next to his wife Sandy.

She was sipping on a glass of wine when she asked, "How was practice?"

"I'm really proud of them. They're so ready to kick ass."

She looked at him sternly. "I hope you don't use that kind of language in front of them."

Eight Hours

"Of course not," he then added, "My job requires me to be professional in everything that I do, including my language. I just like to vent a little when I get home."

"Fair enough, just don't do it in front of Jason. Lord knows he'll learn those words soon enough, but I prefer they didn't come from your mouth."

He leaned over and kissed her. "I promise." They finished off their beverages and then headed off to bed.

Bob shot up when his phone rang just after midnight. The caller ID showed it was work. "I'm here. What's up?"

Don answered, "We need you at the precinct ASAP." Bob knew better than to ask why because ASAP told him it was an emergency.

"I'm on my way."

Sandy rolled over. "An emergency at work?"

"Sounds like it, dear. Go back to sleep." He then kissed her forehead before dressing and leaving his house.

Upon arriving at the precinct, he saw the nightshift workers, plus all the dayshift men sipping on mugs of hot coffee. He went to his desk and grabbed his cup to fill it up. With the coffee pot empty, he put on another pot for later in the shift. When he saw the whiteboard on the wall, he instantly knew that something horrific must have just happened. Bob waited patiently beside his fellow officers, who were huddled around Bill and Don, anxiously waiting to find out what was going on. Bob listened as Bill laid out the earlier events leading up to this point, but the short timeline sent the entire room into shock. Never had any of them experienced such an unrealistic demand. He felt sick to his stomach as he comprehended the full reality of the situation. Bill then threw coal on the already burning fire when he announced that Don would be in charge of the case, and he would ride right wing. The kidnapper would only talk to Bill, so he had to be on site, but only for the hourly calls and Don had taken the lead. They also heard that the perpetrator warned them not to call in outside help or the baby would die.

Dr. Jackson was then called forward to fill in the men on Claire's condition. The room was dead silent while Dr. Jackson spoke, and everyone in the room sensed the doctor's concerns for his daughter, while Bill's expression was also visible to all the men. Eight hours was not a long time to find the child and the team had already lost two hours. Tensions were high, and that meant their expectations were also high. There was absolutely no room for error. They looked at each other before turning to Don for leadership.

Bill had moved to the whiteboard and let Don take the lead. Nervously, Don stood in front of his officers, then split them up into three teams, giving each of them locations to search. Bill wrote the search locations up on the whiteboard as Don mentioned them and placed two officers' names next to each site. Once finished, Bill moved to the back of the room, becoming a spectator, which was out of character for him. He had always been in control. Charles must know that Bill wouldn't be able to run the investigation, but would have to be on site. The kidnapper made sure that Bill would be sweating and anxious to take control, but Charles had no idea that Bill trusted Don one hundred percent.

Don looked at his men, then added, "This Charles is very dangerous and can't be trusted. No taking chances tonight gentlemen. You call for backup if you think you need it." Before he said another word, his men were grabbing their jackets, weapons, and were leaving the building.

The drive to the Panorama Room was slow as it was an overcast night and there were no streetlights outside of the city. The drive in the daylight was spectacular as the road ran beside the inlet, with each corner displaying another breathtaking sight. However, at night, everything was entirely different. The road was twisty with lots of corners to manoeuvre. Oncoming headlights often would blind you for a few seconds before they passed by, but luckily the traffic was light at this time of the night.

Bob glanced at his partner. "I've never worked with you before, Jim, so it's a pleasure to be alongside you tonight."

"Thanks, feeling's mutual." He then added, "This case is so bizarre. What can we possibly do in five hours? It'll take a miracle to find her in time."

"You're not giving up already, are you?"

"I'm trying not to, but we have zero leads. It's hard for me to think positively right now, but I guess it's still early in the game. I can't imagine what Bill and the doctor are going through. It has to be hell for them."

"It probably is, but if we look like we're giving up, it will shatter both of them. Right now, we can't let one minute slip away." Bob then inquired, "You like the nightshift?"

Jim responded, "Yeah, I do. I was finding that shifting from days to nights was too hard on my body, so I chose the nightshift. I have a girlfriend who's a teacher so by the time she's off work, I'm out of bed."

"A teacher, eh. Does she know Kimberley Jackson?"

Jim replied, "Yes, they both teach at the same school just different grades."

"What grade does your girlfriend teach?"

"Grade six, but she also fills in as the librarian."

"I think Kimberley is kindergarten plus a multitude of other courses."

Jim laughed, "I hear you. No such thing as teaching one subject anymore."

The wind had come up and fog slowly crept in, which forced Bob to slow down. The usual fifteen minute drive was now turning into twenty-five minutes. As luck would have it, Bob was relieved when no oncoming vehicles were on the road. Between town and the Panorama Room, there were two marinas and a fishing shop. All was quiet at the three locations. After the tsunami had hit the dining room and cracked the foundation, the building had to be taken down and rebuilt. It took the owners just over a year to reopen. It was a slow time for the business right now, so they closed for several weeks to allow their staff to use up their vacation time. Don must have thought there was a possibility that Charles could be hiding out there. It was secluded and well off the beaten track. Several miles short of the Panorama Room, the skies decided to open up and slow down their progress. The streak of lightening that lit up the sky and the sharp crack of the thunder surprised both men.

Bob swerved to avoid a boulder on the center line and hit the side of the road hard. The next sound both men heard was the tire slowly deflating under the weight of their vehicle. Bob was mad and carefully pulled to the side of the road. "I'm dead." He slammed his fists on the steering wheel before shouting, "Can anything else possibly go wrong?"

Jim responded, "Don't beat yourself up. I'll call the office to let them know the situation, and then we change the tire and get back on track." Jim picked up the radio and called their dispatcher.

"Daniel here, do you have an update?"

"It's Jim and our update isn't what you're expecting. We just got a flat tire so will be delayed possibly fifteen minutes while we change it."

"Copy that."

He hung up then turned to Bob. "Rock, paper, scissors; loser has to change the tire, and winner gets to hold the flashlight." He grinned. "It's fair. As I see it, we're both going to get soaking wet."

Bob finally admitted, "This is my fault so I'll change the tire and you can hold the light." Both men got out of the vehicle, walked to the trunk of the car, and took out the spare tire and jack.

Bob was busy jacking up the vehicle when he suddenly froze and yelled, "Get back in the car now!"

Jim wasn't sure what was going on, but the urgency in Bob's voice told him to move fast. Both men jumped into the vehicle and slammed the door shut. A few seconds later, a grizzly bear was on the hood of the vehicle, pounding on the windshield. Both men were in shock. The bear was capable of smashing through the glass and tearing them to pieces. The second blow of the massive grizzly paws cracked the windshield, sending spider-like cracks across the glass. Jim started to climb over his seat towards the back of the vehicle. Bob immediately hit the siren and flashing lights, hoping that would scare the creature away. The bear was snorting, but jumped off the vehicle and disappeared into the brush across the road, while two small cubs followed behind it.

Bob's voice was trembling as he tried to speak, "Shit that was close."

Jim was speechless as he rested his head on the back of his seat, waiting for his heart rate to slow down. "What do we do now? We have to change the damn tire or we can't investigate the Panorama Room."

Bob thought for a moment. "Okay, the cruiser lights and siren sent the grizzly running and the cubs were in tow. Obviously, we came between the mother and her babies, not a good scene, so we keep the lights on and siren going until the tire is changed. I'll do the tire and you'll keep watch."

"How long do we wait before we move from the vehicle?"

"We have no time, so we go now."

Both men nervously left the vehicle and were on alert until the tire was changed. No conversation passed between either of them as they were listening for any sign that the bear would return. Both officers were soaked and cold by the time the tire was changed. Bob slipped behind the steering wheel and started the vehicle. Although the windscreen was damaged, Bob was still able to see through it enough to drive. First thing he did was jack up the heat to thaw the two of them out. Upon arrival at their destination, Bob turned off his headlights. The two officers stayed inside their vehicle, observing their surroundings.

Jim was the first to speak, "Looks pretty quiet here."

"I agree. Let's just have a good look around to be sure." Once their eyes had adjusted, they got out of the car. Both officers took out their flashlight, but didn't turn them on.

Jim looked at Bob who appeared to have his eyes closed. "You taking a nap, partner?"

"No. It's an old trick that a friend taught me years ago."

"What trick is that?"

Bob explained, "This friend of mine was injured in an accident several years ago and lost his eyesight."

"That must have been horrible."

"It was, but he taught me a life-saving tip."

Jim was intrigued. "What was that?"

"There are five basic senses of the body. Smell, sound, taste, touch, and sight. When he lost his sight, he taught his body to compensate for the loss."

"How did he do that?"

Bob continued, "Easy. When his sight was taken from him, he learned to listen more. You can train your body to compensate for a loss. He became more sensitive to sounds knowing he no longer had sight. You try it. Close your eyes and listen. What do you hear?"

Jim closed his eyes and cleared his mind. "I hear water splashing as the tide comes in. Also seagulls, but they seemed to have calmed down for the night. In the distance there are seals barking and making eerie wailing sounds. A slight breeze is rustling the trees around us. Some animal is scurrying in the bushes; maybe a squirrel. I also think I hear a boat in the water. That's amazing. How did I do?"

"Surprisingly well."

"Is that how you heard that grizzly back there?"

Bob answered, "It is. Definitely a good survival tip, don't you think?"

"Sure is. Let's have a good look around." Both officers turned on their flashlights and approached the building. Bob tried the door. It didn't surprise either of them that it was locked, so he shone his flashlight through the window. There was nothing to see there, so Jim shone his flashlight though the dining room section of the building, which was also empty.

Bob jumped when a sound startled him. Both officers drew their weapons, crouched down, and shone their flashlights towards where the noise came from. The rustling in the bushes indicated that a bear had been watching them.

"Looks like we're doomed to run across bears tonight."

Jim commented, "It appears so, but I need to work on my listening skills, as I didn't hear that first bear until you mentioned it."

When the two officers were convinced that the bear was nowhere to be seen, they put their weapons away and finished checking out the location. With the water on one side of the dining room, they weren't able to go completely around the building, but both were satisfied that there was nothing to report, so they went back to their vehicle.

Both men slipped back into their side of the car, and calling the precinct, Bob reported, "There's nothing at the Panorama Room."

Daniel responded, "Copy that. Good to hear back from both of you. Obviously, you were able to change your tire and get back on track."

"Except for the minor delay when we were attacked by a grizzly bear while changing the tire, and just now a second bear was close by. I think one of us may need a shower." Bob paused. "You may want to tell the boss that our cruiser needs a new windscreen."

Daniel sounded concerned. "Okay, glad you're both safe. See you two back at the office."

The drive back to town was uneventful. Both men sighed when they came to the area where they had encountered the grizzly bear, relieved that it had all ended well. They still had to deal with the fog, which seemed to have set in thicker, slowing down their progress back to the station.

CHAPTER FOURTEEN

2:45 — 3:00

Bill was standing at the back of the room with the whiteboard directly in his line of vision. He slowly watched Don put a line through the old warehouse, then the lighthouse, and finally the Panorama Room. He turned away from the board with frustration, knowing that time was moving faster than he was comfortable with.

Bill spotted Don from across the room and pointed for them to meet up in his office. Don motioned for Jim to join them. The three men closed the door behind them, but none of them sat down.

Don turned to Jim. "This bastard has to be getting around somehow. Look into any reported stolen vehicles in the past few days. Keep most of your search within Blue Ridge, but just to be safe, check Sidville too."

"On it, boss." Jim then left the room and closed the door behind him.

Don turned his attention to Bill and asked, "Okay, if you're my boss and I'm now covering for you, what's my position?" He didn't wait for an answer but chuckled, "I must be boss two." The two laughed, but soon got back to business. Don then turned his attention to Bill. "Sorry, it would've been nice if one of those locations panned out, but don't give up." Bill nodded, but it was hard for him to hide his disappointment. Don continued, "We have a serious problem, Bill."

"Okay, spell it out."

"Just one word, Richard."

It was just a matter of time before the topic of Richard came into play. "I know, but what can I do or say to him? He's backed me into a corner. He needs to be there when we find Claire, and he promised me that he'd keep out of the way and keep the ladies updated."

"Yes, he does have to be at the rescue site, but this office is not open to civilians. There are highly classified files on site, and while I know that he wouldn't be snooping around, the rules are the rules. It's not ethical that he's here."

Bill moved to the window and looked outside. "You're right, I'll deal with it after my next call."

"No, you won't," Don said. "I'll handle it. You just concentrate on your next call, which is in about fifteen minutes. I'll make sure he's delivered back to his house safely. He should be with the ladies offering support to them rather than hanging around here doing nothing. You have my word that once we find Claire, Richard will be picked up by one of our cruisers and taken to the hostage site so he can treat her."

"Thanks, Don."

Both men returned to the common area and Bill watched Don talking to Richard. Bill and Richard's eyes locked onto each other, from across the room, and both sets were filled with disappointment.

Richard moved towards Bill. "I knew this would happen at some point." His voice broke as he added, "Find our baby, Bill, and I'll be there to treat her." Richard picked up his medical bag, knowing it wouldn't get left behind if it was safely in his possession.

"I will." Bill hoped he wasn't making false promises. He had so much on his mind and somehow, he had to filter through the important facts of the case and throw all the miscellaneous stuff into the trash bin. Finding Claire was priority number one and putting Charles behind bars was priority number two.

Richard waved to Bill as he left the building with Greg. Bill returned the gesture but felt somewhat guilty. He put his thoughts aside and mentally prepared himself for his three o'clock call. He ran his fingers through his hair and rubbed his forehead, noticing another headache was hitting him with vengeance. He went back to his office and took two more Tylenol. Once back in the common area, Bill noticed Daniel calling him over.

"We'll find her, Boss, but right now, I need your phone again. It's almost time for your next call." Daniel set up Bill's phone so the call could be recorded. The tracking device was also ready; he just had to push both buttons once the call started.

Bill glanced at his watch, then turned to the whiteboard and glanced at Jenny's name, whispering, "Oh God, Jenny, please be on our side." No sooner had the silent prayer escaped his lips, when a flash of lightning hit right outside the precinct, lighting up the entire room, followed immediately by what sounded like a cannon shot of thunder. The storm that had hampered his officers earlier in the evening was now over the town. Rain was pelting the roof and the wind forced the rain against the windows. Seconds later, the office was thrown into complete darkness. Computers shut down in a flash while officers cursed. They all fumbled for flashlights or anything that could afford them some light. The office was soon in complete turmoil.

Bill instantly started to panic. "Damn it, guys, my call is in less than ten minutes. Is there anything else that could possibly go wrong?" Bill was starting to feel that he was losing control. "We've got to get the auxiliary power up and running fast!"

Bill had to slow his heart rate down, so he lit up the whiteboard with his flashlight, more as a distraction than anything else. Somehow, he had to block out the noises going on around him and concentrate on what he wanted to extract from Jenny on the next call. It was vital that Bill discover whether she was a willing participant or not. In the last call with Charles, Jenny's voice had an air of softness about it, so Bill was hoping that she was also trapped in a bad situation. He could visualize her cradling Claire and protecting the baby. At this point Bill decided that Jenny may be Claire's only hope. Bill was reminded of his previous conversations with Charles and hoped to God that the scumbag never picked Claire up, however Bill recalled the Jackson house several hours earlier and remembered that Charles' fingerprints were all over the crowbar, window sill and also the crib. He had been the only intruder in the room so Charles had to have at least picked Claire up and then handed her through the open window to a waiting Jenny. Bill was so full of anger against Charles, but knew he had to pull himself together. Cradling a small child and consoling her didn't fit the kidnapper's profile. He thought that Charles must have brought Jenny along to take care of Claire.

Bill was startled when Don yelled, "Who the hell knows where the auxiliary power box is located?"

No one responded, so Bill grabbed his flashlight and slowly worked his way towards the stairs leading to the prison cells, one floor down. He was frustrated. "I'll reset it myself!" Don was embarrassed but followed behind him. Bill mumbled under his breath sounding rather annoyed. "So many officers working here, and not one of them knows where to find the auxiliary power? That's crazy."

Don agreed, "When this is all over, we need to take them all on an orientation tour. What would we have done if you weren't here to save us?"

Once Bill was one floor below the offices, he turned to the right and entered a storage area. Don had been in this room many times before, picking up supplies, but had never ventured any further. He was as guilty as the officers he was criticizing. Bill zigzagged his way along a few unfamiliar corridors that Don was not aware of and approached the generator. Flipping the switch, the machine turned on and the lights eliminated the darkness around them. They both extinguished their flashlights and ran back upstairs.

Once back upstairs with the computers online again, Bill called Don into his office. "We don't have much time, but there are a few things you should know about Charles."

"Okay, let's hear it."

"For me, dealing with a terrorist like Charles is like reading an open book. In some aspects, it's helpful, but in others, it's frightening. Because of my training, I'm able to think like a criminal. If that doesn't blow your mind, nothing will. I'm able to get into their heads and predict what their next possible moves might be before they even happen."

Don looked shocked but inquired, "What are you telling me?"

Bill answered, "Where are we as far as locating Charles' parents?"

Don shook his head. "So far no luck."

Bill responded, "This is only a theory right now and only between the two of us."

Don nodded, "Anything you can share will be helpful."

Bill took a seat behind his desk and motioned for Don to take a seat across from him. "On my first conversation at midnight with Charles, he yelled to his dad to shut up."

Don responded, "So his father has to be there and part of the kidnapping."

"No I don't think so. I never heard a man's voice in the background, just Charles shouting." Bill got up from his chair and moved towards the window. "Charles was very irritated; somewhat unstable. In my opinion, I don't think his father was there."

Don looked puzzled. "What are you suggesting?"

"I think Charles may be delusional, also he could be experiencing hallucinations."

Don asked, "So you think there was no one in the room with him."

"I wasn't sure, but then on my second call I definitely heard a woman's voice."

Don was slowly putting two and two together. "Okay, so that's where Jenny enters into the picture."

"That's what I think. Personally I'm not sure he's thinking rationally. Don't get me wrong, Charles is definitely a threat, but so far, I'm able to make him think that he's in complete control. That tactic will ensure Claire and Jenny's safety if she isn't involved in the kidnapping. I need to test Jenny on this upcoming call to get an idea whose side she's on. I also need to evaluate Charles' frame of mind. A lot can be learned from a person's voice, their stress levels can tell the whole story."

Don responded, "He's like a walking time bomb. How do we beat someone like that?"

"We work as a team and take it one step at a time, but also by treading lightly."

"No, I mean, how can you remain so calm?"

Bill half laughed, "Do you honestly think that I'm calm? With each hour that passes, we're losing our advantage. I'm just as frustrated as the rest of the men. If we don't get a concrete break soon, I'm not sure what the outcome will be. Time is running out for Claire. Somehow, I need to convince Charles to move the time from eight o'clock to nine o'clock. Adding another hour would make a big difference. Sometimes cases that have been lost in the past would have fared better with a little bit more time. Somehow I need to convince Charles to give us that extra hour."

"You realize that Charles' brother is a murderer, so there's not a chance in hell that they'll let him go. Canada doesn't negotiate with terrorists. You said that yourself."

Bill seemed to be thinking. "That is, unless I can convince Charles that the warden has agreed to his release."

"Have you talked to the warden?"

"No, but Charles doesn't know that." Bill glanced down at his watch and paused. "I need a few minutes alone before he calls. Do you mind?" Don quietly slipped from the room, shutting the door behind him. Bill had always been on top of things, but right now, he appeared to be a fish out of water; floundering and gasping for air. He was glad that Don had taken over the case, although it didn't exactly relieve Bill's stress level. He took several deep breaths before returning to the common area. All the officers were sitting at their desks, watching the second hand on the wall clock count down to three o'clock.

Jim approached Don. "No stolen vehicles reported between Blue Ridge and Sidville for the past two weeks." He then added, "If it was stolen last night, the owner wouldn't know until tomorrow morning."

Don got up from his desk. "Thanks, Jim, it was worth a try." According to Bill's watch, it was 2:57. The next few minutes seemed to be never ending. He approached Daniel's desk, sat down, and waited. When his phone finally rang, Bill jumped from the sound. Daniel hit both machines in front of him before Bill answered.

CHAPTER FIFTEEN

2:50 — 3:30

Jenny watched Charles from across the room. He appeared to be asleep. Upon further inspection, she could see that Charles was mumbling under his breath, but she was unable to hear what he was saying. She slowly rose and quietly approached him. The whispers that came out of his mouth sent chills down her body. He kept repeating over and over. "Step in it," followed by a terrifying sneer, then again. "Step in it," and that awful looking sneer again. She nervously returned to her couch and sat down, while still watching him.

Charles was in the midst of a most wonderful dream. It was as if he was stuck in a happy place where he was able to rewind his vision over and over again. When any other person was in that condition, it often meant they had a very high temperature and were delusional, but not Charles. His visions were perfectly clear. He was outside the cabin and Bill was slowly approaching him, no weapon, no backup, and asking, "Where is the child?"

Charles laughed and motioned for Bill to follow him. He was led right up to one of his traps. He turned to Bill laughing. "Step in it!"

Bill was shocked. "No way! Are you crazy?"

Once again, Charles repeated, "Step in it!" Charles shot out of his chair and glared at Jenny. "I just saw how Bill is going to die. He's going to step into one of my traps that I've placed around the cabin."

Jenny was terrified at what she just heard. "They're traps around the cabin. When were you going to tell me about them? I could have headed to the outhouse and stepped in one."

"If you're going to the outhouse, there aren't any in your way. They're set up in the forest to protect three sides of the cabin. Quite clever if I might say so."

Jenny wished he would stay asleep longer as he looked so innocent when his eyes were shut, but once they opened, he was like a wall of fire. The stress of Jenny being in such an awful situation that she had no control over made her feel as if the cabin was filling up with smoke and choking her. However, Jenny and Claire's rescuers wouldn't be firemen, but the police force overtaking the cabin. She feared the rescue would most likely not be in her favour. Jenny turned away from Charles so he wouldn't notice the tears running down her cheeks. She wished that she hadn't shared her loneliness with Charles. He always listened to her constant nagging about being left alone and not being able to go and visit Tom. She knew that Charles went to see him, not that long ago, but all he said about the visit was that he had everything under control. Jenny let that comment slide, but now she knew what having it under control really meant.

Jenny heard the rain outside and she jumped when the lightning struck and the thunder rumbled. It was too close for comfort. She got up, looked out the window, and saw in the dim light that puddles were already filling the tire ruts Charles' borrowed vehicle had made hours earlier. She turned to see Charles glaring at her again. Feeling uncomfortable, she smiled, hoping it would change his threatening look. "I don't recognize that vehicle, where did you get it from?"

Charles answered with a wide grin on his face. "Borrowed it from a friend. If I stole one, the police would be able to track it down. It's also our escape vehicle, so we needed to remain under the radar." Charles glanced at his watch and commented, "It's show time."

Jenny had always looked away from Charles when he dialled Bill's number, but this time she kept her eyes on him. She was surprised when he only touched one button. That could only mean one thing: Bill was on speed dial, but what number did Charles touch? Maybe she could warn Bill of the traps. It would be risky and she couldn't afford to get caught or Claire would be left with no one to protect her.

Once again, there was a pause before Bill answered, "Hey Charles, how're you doing?"

Charles responded, "I must have woken you up."

Bill replied, "Why do you say that?"

"Come on, three rings. You're not playing games with me, are you?"

"In case you're not aware, a massive rain and lightening storm has just passed over Blue Ridge and we lost our electricity. We had to scramble to reset the auxiliary power, but we're up and running again. In the confusion, I misplaced my phone and had to hunt it down."

"That sounds like a bullshit story to me. We never lost our power here."

Bill made a mental note to add that to the whiteboard, if Jenny confirmed that they were indeed not in town.

"Let's forget about the small talk. What're you doing to get Tom released?"

"Come on, Charles. You should know by now how this works. First I talk to Jenny and get an update on Claire."

He shouted, "Claire's fine!"

"Hope you aren't offended, but I don't trust you, however, I do trust Jenny."

Charles practically threw the phone to her. He was upset that once again Bill trusted Jenny more than him. "All you say is the baby's fine."

Jenny took the phone and placed it next to her ear. "Claire's fine. She's sound asleep."

Bill quickly asked, "Are you anywhere in town?"

She didn't hesitate as she knew her time was limited. "No."

Charles snarled and quickly grabbed the phone and shouted, "What the hell did you ask her?"

"I just asked if either she or Claire were hurt. Fair question, don't you think? I just needed to know, because when I find you, I'm not sure if I should bring an ambulance with me."

Charles exploded. "Where the hell is my brother?"

"I already told you that he can't be released before nine o'clock. I'm just a sergeant of a small town and unfortunately, I have no pull in Alberta. Their prison system isn't the same as British Columbia's."

Once again, Charles was pacing the cabin, going between his chair and Claire's bed. He was like a caged tiger, pacing and snarling as he looked for an escape from his own prison. His cage bars were closing in on him and Jenny felt she had to do something, so she got up from her couch and whispered, "I'm going to change her diaper. By now she must be soaked." She slowly removed the blanket that covered Claire and changed her, hoping Charles would move back to his chair. She then picked up the baby, took her over to the couch, and cradled her.

Charles sat down and grinned, sure that he had the upper hand this time around. "Your time's running out Bill. Don't for a minute think that I won't kill the baby."

"Her name is Claire, remember?"

Charles snarled and slammed his phone on the desk beside his chair. He glared at Jenny, then turned his attention back to his phone.

Bill had obviously heard the bang at the other end of the line. "Oops, Charles, did you drop your phone?"

"Keep in mind that you're on borrowed time, Bill." He repeated in a threatening voice. "Yes, you're definitely on borrowed time."

It was a few seconds before Bill spoke again. "I have another deal for you, and this will be your last one."

"Unless it means Tom will be released, I'm not interested."

"This is even better." Charles didn't respond so Bill continued, "You tell me where Claire is and as soon as I have her safely in my arms, I'll give you a one hour head start, then I'll hunt you down like the animal that you are. Talk to you at four o'clock. Hopefully, you'll accept my latest offer." The call ended.

Charles glared at the phone in disbelief. "The Bastard hung up on me again!"

Jenny spoke in a soft voice, not only to calm Charles down, but also to try not to disturb Claire. "Can't you see what he's doing to you?"

He glared at her. "He's driving me crazy!"

"He's trying to convince you that he has the upper hand, where, in fact, you have it. He's running out of time so he's panicking. You're still in complete control so keep Tom's release as your main focus."

Outside of the cabin walls there was an agonizing growling sound coming from within the forest. Charles was instantly irritated. "Damn bears, one must have stepped into one of my traps!"

Jenny covered her ears to protect herself from the sounds of the suffering animal that was snared and in great pain. "Charles, please go out and put the animal out of its' misery. Please, I beg you!" Jenny watched Charles get ready

Eight Hours

to leave the cabin but she had to wait for the right moment to call Bill. She felt like she was trapped in a horror movie and there was no remote to fast forward or turn the television off. The animal was still howling, but once she no longer heard it that would be the moment she would try to contact Bill.

Charles cursed as he left the cabin. "That trap was meant for Bill. I'll enjoy watching Bill die if the damn bears don't trip them all. I don't even think I'll bury his body. I'll let the animals take care of that."

Charles went directly to the trunk of his car and removed the whiskey bottle again. Several swigs later, he noticed that the alcohol was half gone. In frustration, he took another long swig and slowly swallowed, allowing the alcohol to warm his throat and calm his nerves. He glanced down at his scabby knuckles. They didn't look too bad, in fact, they didn't even hurt that much. They had, however, started to seize up slightly, so he stretched them out to try and keep them limber. His hands were no good to him if he couldn't hold a gun and shoot accurately. He knew that getting drunk could hamper his reflexes, so he returned the bottle to the trunk, vowing not to touch it again until Tom was back home. Turning on his flashlight, he strolled around the circumference of the log cabin again, already knowing that no one was around. Approaching the suffering animal that had stepped into his trap, he pulled out his gun and shot it in the head.

When Jenny heard the shot, she immediately jumped into action. She flew across the room and picked up the phone. She touched the number one and lifted the phone to her ear.

Bill picked up at the other end. "Hey, Charles, did you reconsider my last offer?"

Jenny immediately spoke, "Three traps." She hung up the phone, making sure it was exactly where Charles had left it. She started walking back to her seat. When she turned, Charles was standing in the doorway glaring at her.

"What are you doing?"

Frightened beyond measure, she quickly composed herself. "I need to get some exercise. My legs are cramping up."

"Go outside and get some fresh air."

Jenny half laughed, "Not too many people know this about me, not even Tom, but I'm actually petrified of the dark. I find it frightening, must be the insecurity of the unknown. You know when you sit around a campfire and you can only see a few feet beyond the fire, but anyone standing further away can see anything and everything you do. That's really scary for me."

Charles seemed satisfied with her explanation. "I killed the bear."

"Thanks."

"I'm going to be busy for a short time removing the animal and trying to reset the trap."

"Be careful. I'm going to put the last bottle of milk into the water in case Claire wakes up hungry before this is all over."

Charles left the warm cabin and headed towards the trap he had to reset. Once he arrived, he had to put the flashlight into his mouth to light up the surrounding area. Charles attempted to open the trap, thinking he could haul the dead animal away by dragging it behind his friend's vehicle, discarding it out of sight, and then reset his trap. He wasn't happy losing one of the three traps, leaving a section around the cabin unprotected, but no matter what he tried, it simply wouldn't release. He grabbed his knife from the back pocket of his pants and proceeded to cut the paw free from the jagged teeth that were embedded deep into the bear's flesh. With having to use so much force to get through the bone, Charles' injured hands started to throb, but he was finally able to separate the leg from the shackle. Removing the stake that he had earlier driven into the nearby tree was even a bigger challenge. Not having anything to use for leverage, he was forced to pull with all his might, cursing the bear the entire time. One final pull and it released, sending Charles into a heap next to the dead bear. He jumped up and moved away from the body, wiping the blood from his shirt. Now Charles was making some progress as he slowly tried to open the trap. It opened easily, but automatically sprang shut again. Charles almost lost a hand tying to reset it. It was far too damaged from the animal pulling on it, making it useless. In retaliation, he kicked the trap, then the head of the animal. He managed to hurt his foot in the process.

"Damn, stupid animal." He limped away mumbling under his breath. "Serves you right, you shouldn't have been snooping around here. You got what you deserved." Charles then checked the other two traps, which were both still intact. He returned to the cabin and sat outside on the porch to have a smoke. As he slowly drew on his cigarette, he looked at his package, upset that there were only four left. Not wanting to run out, Charles knew that he had to smoke them sparingly, which meant only one an hour, and then he could buy another package when he got back to Sidville. Finishing his smoke, he went inside the cabin and found Jenny asleep with Claire resting on her chest. He crossed the room and placed more wood on the fire before returning to his chair.

He mumbled to himself. "I sure hope you're right about Bill, Jenny." As each hour passed and each call was made, Charles felt he was holding all the aces, but by the end of his last call, he thought Bill was once again victorious. That frustrated him to no end. He then closed his eyes and rested too.

Jenny had heard Charles coming into the cabin so she had pretended to be asleep. She heard him add a few more logs to the fire and then return to his chair. Sneaking a peek, she saw that Charles was already seated and appeared to be resting. Glancing down at Claire, Jenny studied her for the first time, noticing that her cheeks were chubby and soft to the touch. Stroking them made Claire softly whimper and the baby snuggled in even more, looking for more attention. The infant's hair was a fine blonde color and when Jenny moved the blanket slightly away, she took Claire's tiny hand in hers. The infant immediately took hold of her finger and Jenny watched in amazement as this little baby, whom she had never met before, latched onto her. Tears started to run down her cheeks, and for the first time, Jenny felt the full impact of Claire's kidnapping. She really wanted Tom back, but not at the expense of this innocent baby. She thought about sneaking out of the cabin and trying to find help, but she knew Charles would hunt her down like an animal, and most likely kill her. There was nowhere for her to hide. She rewrapped Claire and propped the child against her shoulder, then tried to calm herself down. The knife she had found in the kitchen cupboard was still hidden in her pocket, but suddenly, it didn't offer her much security. She hoped that calling Bill would give the police force a heads up if they did find the cabin. Most certainly they would position themselves well into the bushes, but also have a clear vision of the cabin and its' surroundings. Jenny didn't know the location of those traps, but was also too afraid to ask. For her to ask that question of Charles would put her and Claire in grave danger. When it came down to the final hour, Jenny had to figure out a foolproof plan that would keep her and Claire safe. Her own conclusion was that either Charles was dead or she was. She hugged Claire even closer as her tears stained the baby's blanket.

CHAPTER SIXTEEN

3:00 — 3:30

Don was sitting at Daniel's desk, listening to the entire conversation going on between Charles and Bill. Although Bill seemed to be very calm, the look on his face painted an entirely different picture. His forehead was furrowed with creases that were not there moments earlier. Don couldn't even imagine what was going through Bill's mind. He mentally asked himself how he would've handled the situation if the tables were turned and he was the negotiator. Bill had told Don that he had taken extra courses, as it would not only advance his career, but also train him in handling difficult situations. Bill always liked a challenge, but this case was just a little too close to home. This case must have made Bill feel like he was thrown into the deep end of a pool with no swimming experience.

Don was amazed by how slick Bill was, always able to extract small pieces of information from Jenny with each call. He believed Jenny was determined to protect herself and Claire with her life. Hopefully, it wouldn't come down to that. Even the smallest clue could narrow down their search site. Charles always seemed to be tense and very quick to lose control, while Bill seemed to know just how far he could be pushed. Little did Bill know when he took those intense courses years earlier, he would be forced to use them to protect his own family. He always appeared to be in control, but his body language revealed his true feelings. Watching closer, Don could see Bill's shoulders tensing up and several times he ran his fingers through his already messy hair. He was gripping the phone far too tightly and his eyes were constantly locked onto the whiteboard. Don also observed that when Bill thought the time to end the call was to his advantage, he'd snap the phone shut and cut off the call.

After doing so this time, Bill turned to Daniel. "Please tell me you've got something?"

Daniel responded, "Yes and no."

"I don't like the sound of that."

Daniel turned his attention to Bill. "I've got the recording, but the tracking device is still a no-go." He then added, "Charles isn't using a cell phone either, which must mean he's on a satellite phone. They're almost impossible to track. Guess we'll have to find him the good old-fashioned way, with skill and leg work."

Bill appeared to be thinking. "Okay, if he's using a satellite phone, then he's probably somewhere off the grid."

Daniel responded, "That's a good possibility, however, satellite phones also work in towns, so we still have to keep that in mind. He told us he never lost power, but that could've been bullshit and he's actually nowhere near town."

Bill rose and approached the whiteboard. He picked up the pen and wrote 'not in town.' Bill then returned his attention to Don. "According to Jenny, they aren't in Blue Ridge, but at this point, we can't eliminate Sidville or anywhere in between."

Don agreed. "You're right. He would want to be close, but then again, not too close. He would want to make a clean escape once this is over. Sidville has four exits, two by road, one by train, and the last would be the airport. Certainly, he wouldn't be stupid enough to book a flight, but it wouldn't hurt to check with the airlines."

Jack overheard Don and interjected, "I'm on it." He then picked up the phone and called the airport. With only two airlines flying into their remote area, it didn't take Jack long to eliminate that possibility. He turned to Don. "Negative for the airport, no ticket was purchased under Charles Lockman. I also talked to the head of the airport and there aren't any small private planes scheduled to leave for several days. He will let us know if that changes." He then added, "At this point, we're safe to eliminate his escape by plane."

Don looked at Bill. "I still want a roadblock set up just before the airport to cover the two road exits, the airport, and the train."

Jack walked over to Don's desk. "I already checked the train station and there's no one by the name of Charles Lockman holding a ticket for the next several days, however, he could still buy a last-minute ticket. I was assured that if he appeared, we would be notified." He then added, "However, if he travels under an alias, we're screwed."

Bill was deep in thought. Don watched him for a moment before asking, "You have something you want to share with us?"

Daniel hadn't checked the recording from Bill's last call with Charles when the cell phone on the desk rang. He quickly hit the record button and Bill shifted back into his negotiating skills.

"Hey Charles, did you reconsider my last offer?" Bill was shocked when it was a woman's voice and he realized, it must be Jenny talking. She only said two words. 'Three traps!' and the line went dead. Bill panicked. "Is that you, Jenny? Hello! Hello!" He realized she was gone.

He looked at Daniel. "Tell me you got that."

"I did." Daniel pushed the replay button several times before they comprehended what she had actually said. Daniel looked at Bill. "Three traps. The son of a bitch has set up three traps, but where is he and where are the three traps?"

Bill was beside himself. "I swear I'm going to rip Charles' heart out of his chest and feed it to the birds." He sounded frustrated. "Why the hell does he always seem to be one step ahead of us? This short timeline is killing me." He then turned to his officers and yelled, "If I want to shoot the bastard, not one of you better get in my way!"

Don glanced at Bill sympathetically. "Okay, Bill, that's your heart speaking, not your gut. Put that aside, we all need you thinking straight right now. We need your expertise; or should I say that I need your expertise. This case is personal to all the men here. They're pulling every string they know of to get Claire back."

Bill shook his head several times and conceded, "Sorry. Thanks for the quick wake up call." Bill crossed the room and entered three traps onto the whiteboard. He then looked at Don. "Jenny has to be on our side. Why else would she tell us about the traps?"

Don replied, "I agree. That took guts for her to call us. She told us about the traps, and then immediately hung up. Charles had to have been out of the room just long enough for her to make that call. If he caught her, she's already dead."

Bill tried to collect his thoughts. "Maybe she was afraid to stay on the line too long and is still alive. We have to keep positive. I think I need some fresh air. I'll just be outside for a few minutes to gather my thoughts."

Don watched Bill put on his jacket and leave the office. The cool air outside helped to clear his head. Glancing up at the sky, he could see the odd star peeking between the clouds. His thoughts went to Jenny. He remembered seeing her at Tom's trial. She was a tiny woman who would be no match for Charles if he found out about her call. She was the only person who could protect Claire right now.

Bill whispered, "Be safe, Jenny, and please protect our baby." Tears streamed down his face. He couldn't imagine what she must be going through. His imagination went wild as he visualized Jenny and Claire in some far away location that his team couldn't possibly get to in time if they kept losing hour after hour without a single solid clue.

Bill felt his world falling around him. It seemed like eons ago when Bill's life was just perfect. He had passed his police academy courses with excellent marks and was well established in Vancouver. Then all hell broke lose when his sister Jeannine died of cancer. He couldn't seem to get his head around the fact that she was gone forever. His good friend Glen grieved with him. Both men threw up their hands in defeat and decided to get away from the big city. Bill heard that Blue Ridge was looking for a sergeant, so he bit the bullet and applied. Glen moved up after him, but had chosen to take some time off, maybe just do some odd jobs to try and stay busy. Bill still wasn't really over the tragic event, and he thought of her daily. When he met Evelyn, his world started to feel like it had meaning again. They were engaged to be married when tragedy hit him for the second time. Her death from a car accident threw him into despair once again. He wasn't convinced that he could ever pick himself up again, and then Evelyn's sister, Beatrice came into his life. She felt the same loss that Bill did when Evelyn died, and they shared the loss together. They grieved together, cried together, and then picked up the pieces and carried on. That's when Bill realized that he loved Beatrice and was willing to take a chance at loving once again.

Bill shook his head to clear it and wiped the tears from his eyes. Once he was somewhat composed, he returned inside the precinct.

Don shook his head. "You okay, boss?"

Bill replied, "I'm good. The fresh air really helped."

Don looked at his team. "Let's get back to work." He then turned to Bill. "What would you do next, boss?"

"I think we need to try to form a timeline, but also acknowledge that it could be very sketchy, maybe not one hundred percent accurate. We aren't really sure when he kidnapped Claire, but I got my call at midnight. Let's assume that when he called, he already had Claire and was at their present location, which is likely the hostage site. Let's also assume that he would stay at that location the entire time. It wouldn't make sense for him to move around. Richard and Kimberley don't go to bed before ten o'clock, and I also assume that Charles wouldn't try to kidnap Claire unless he was sure that both adults were fast asleep."

Bob interrupted, "Sorry to disturb you. The roadblock will be set up in half an hour. I told them to keep it there until they hear from us."

Don responded, "Thanks Bob." He tapped the tabletop as he thought. "Okay, so let's say the kidnapping happened at eleven o'clock, which would give him an hour to go wherever he was planning on holding out."

Bill nodded. "That's if we're right."

Don looked around the room and spotted Jack. He signalled for him to join them.

"What's up?"

"Any chance you can find us a topographic map of this area?"

"No problem." Jack was already heading to the basement to find one.

Bill looked at Don. "You have a plan?"

"Just an idea that I hope will be useful." Jack returned a few minutes later and, knowing Daniel's desk was already covered in electronics, he placed the map on Don's desk. Don had a felt pen in his hand with a string attached to it, which held a tack at the opposite end. "Let's assume this Charles character travelled one hour after he left the Jackson's house, at a speed of between sixty to one hundred miles an hour, depending on road conditions." He placed the tack in the center of Blue Ridge, and then stretched the string to the approximate distance Charles would have travelled in an hour if he was going

Eight Hours

sixty miles per hour. He then drew a circle around the tack, followed by a second circle in case Charles was going one hundred miles per hour. He was left with two circles staring back at them.

Bill took the pen from him and drew a line along the coastline. "I've never heard water in the conversations I've had with him, so that eliminates the ocean side of Blue Ridge. Also, Jenny said they weren't in town, so we can move our tack outside of Blue Ridge."

Don turned to Bill. "Where do you suggest that I place the tack?"

"Let's try just on the edge of town. I know it doesn't sound like much but we're able to eliminate about two miles."

Don drew a third circle and this time Sidville was included in the possible search area. He looked at Bill. "Our search site now is between here and Sidville, so a roadblock close to the airport means we won't find him if he's in town."

Bill nodded his agreement. "I know, but let's leave it there for now until we get more information from Jenny." He let out a long sigh mostly from frustration, but also because he was exhausted. There weren't enough words in the dictionary to explain how he felt, but beaten and defeated had crossed his mind.

Bill needed a few minutes to regroup, so he returned to his office, wondering what their next move should be. For the first time since this nightmare started, Bill wished the next hour would fly by quickly so he could extract another clue from Jenny, but he also knew that every minute counted to ensure Claire's safe return before her diabetes took hold of her. He had to hang onto every minute that was available and concentrate on finding her in time and putting Charles away forever. He breathed a sigh of relief knowing that Jenny was on his side. She must have been frightened when she made that call. Bill prayed that Charles wouldn't find out about it. Bill returned to the common area and studied the whiteboard in front of him.

Don approached him. "Are you thinking the same thing that I am?"

"Not sure, but if it involves sending out two squad cars to search the campsites, then we're on the same wavelength."

"It's the only clue facing us that hasn't yet been addressed." Don watched Greg returning from taking Richard home and he signalled for him to join Bill and himself. Don then turned to face his co-workers. "Okay, Jack, Jim, and Bob, I need you over here." Don tapped the words 'sound of crackling fire' on the whiteboard and paired Greg and Jack together. "I need the two of you to go to the Rock Creek campsite and have a good look around." He then turned to Jim and Bob. "You check out the Municipal campsite. Both teams will be looking for any trailer, fifth wheel, or other closed camping unit with its lights still on and signs of a campfire. If you find anything, investigate, but call it in if necessary." Both teams picked up their gear and left the building.

CHAPTER SEVENTEEN

3:10 — 3:45

Eli and Muhammad's vehicle was positioned just beyond Jenny's house, but still within sight, so if anyone should approach the building, they would see it. Eli turned to his partner for the night and said, "I've always felt that stakeouts were not only to watch a location, but also to get to know your partner better." He paused. "So, tell me about yourself."

Muhammad responded, "How far back do you want me to go?"

"We've got lots of time, so you tell me."

"My father was a Canadian soldier based in Ethiopia, where he met my mother. Amazingly enough, the two fell in love and were married there a year later. Once they tied the knot, my mother told my father that she had always wanted to be a teacher, but opportunities for women there were unachievable. My father saw how worthless she felt in her own country, so he transferred back to Canada. Many tears were shed by her mother's family at losing their only daughter to a Canadian soldier. My wife's family wasn't wealthy, and they already knew their daughter would most likely never return to her birth country. My father told my mother that Canada was the land of opportunity. They chose Edmonton as their new home and my mother was able to go to university and eventually became a teacher. You could say that when I was born, I was an Islamic Canadian." He paused slightly before continuing, "I was able to attend the police academy there and worked with the Edmonton force for some years, then when the job opening came at Blue Ridge, I jumped at the opportunity to spread my wings and make a difference in this community."

Eli inquired, "So are you married, have any children?"

"Happily married, but no children so far, however, they're part of our overall plan. How about you?"

Eli responded, "I'm also married and we have two children, one boy and one girl. My wife works from home so is able to take care of the children while still having an income. She's in telemarketing so her hours are flexible. We heard about the opening here and also jumped at the opportunity, leaving the cold Winnipeg weather behind us."

While both men spoke, they observed not only Jenny's house, but also the surrounding residences. Eli was more interested in the neighbour's house than he was of Jenny's. He asked his partner. "Have you noticed the house next to Jenny's?"

"Sure have. It must be a nosey neighbour. There's always one on every block. They probably think they're the neighbourhood watch. She's certainly well aware of our presence." Muhammad added, "Why wouldn't she be in bed at this hour?"

Eli replied, "Maybe she's part bat. Did you know that they're nocturnal?"

"I did know that."

Both officers were shocked when she disappeared from the window and reappeared on her front porch. She was shaking her fist as she yelled, "There's nothing to see here boys, so move on! Find another street to scope!" She then added, "I've got your licence number and I'm calling it into the police right now!" She then went back into the house and purposefully stood in front of the window with the phone in her hand.

"What do we do if she reports us?"

Eli answered, "Guess the force will get the call and send someone out just to keep her happy. They'll most likely let us know if that happens so we can move until they've searched the area. Why don't we move partway down the block, out of her immediate vision?"

"Good idea. I'll call it in." He radioed the station once again. "Muhammad here, nothing to report out of the ordinary, but a nosey neighbour has spotted us so we've moved down the block slightly, but we can still see Jenny's house."

Daniel responded, "Copy that."

Once they had moved a few doors down, they both spotted a man wearing dark clothing working his way towards the house. Eli picked up the binoculars and observed the man walking into the yard. Both men jumped from their vehicle and ran towards the house. Muhammad yelled, "Freeze!"

The man was instantly scared. "What do you want?"

Neither officer drew his weapon as the young man didn't appear to be about to run. Muhammad moved closer and shouted, "Turn around!"

The man immediately turned and saw the two officers standing in front of him.

Eli asked, "Who are you and why are you here?"

The man was now trembling as he answered, "I'm Joseph Marks and I live here with my girlfriend. We rent a room from the lady who owns the house."

The front door to the house opened and a young lady wearing a nightgown and slippers on her feet ran outside to find out what was going on. She shouted, "We live here. What's going on?"

Eli answered, "Sorry for the scare, we had a report of a disturbance in this area and we thought it may have come from this house."

Joseph responded, "I just got off work and was returning home."

Muhammad repeated, "Sorry for the scare." The couple went into the house and closed the door.

The officers spotted the nosey neighbour watching them again as they both returned to their vehicle and called the station.

"Daniel here. What's up?"

Eli answered, "Just had a false alarm. Young man approached the house. When we confronted him, we were informed that he and his girlfriend are renting a room from this Jenny."

Daniel responded, "We weren't aware of that. Thanks for the update. I'll get back to you." He then hung up.

Muhammad and Eli sat quietly for several minutes, watching Jenny's house. It wasn't long before the lights inside the home were turned off.

Eli inquired, "What do you think the chances are that this Charles character is going to return here when there're other people living inside the house?"

Muhammad responded, "I would say almost nil, but we can't make that call. If he is indeed a wacko, who could possibly know what he's capable of doing." He then added, "Looks like neighbourhood watch lady may have gone to bed."

"It's about time." Eli reached behind the seat and pulled out a thermos. "You want any coffee?"

"That would be great."

Both officers were startled and drew their weapons when a creepy person pressed their nose up against the window and glared at them. She had a baseball bat in her hand and was about to smash their front windshield.

Eli shouted, "No, we're police officers!" He immediately pulled out his badge and flashed it at the old lady. Upon closer inspection, he knew it was the neighbourhood watch lady. So much for thinking that she'd gone to bed.

She paused for only a slight moment and glared at both men. "You better not be lying because I already called the police. They're going to be here any minute." Muhammad reached for the radio to call the station. The mystery lady lifted her bat and was about to smash the windshield. "Freeze, you bastard. Until I know who you are, I suggest you breathe slowly, because if I even see your chest moving, I'll kill you with my bat. I was a very good baseball player so I'm perfectly capable of taking you out."

"Okay, lady. My name is Officer Muhammad Salomar and my partner here is Officer Eli Watson. We're here on a stakeout."

The lady was rather rude. "I don't care if you're the Prime Minister of Canada. Until the police arrive, you're criminals."

A jogger was out for his early morning run when he saw a lady standing next to a suspicious car holding a bat. Unsure if she was in distress, he called to her before approaching. "Hey lady, is everything okay here?"

She took a quick glance at him, not taking her eyes off the two men in the vehicle for too long. She answered, "Just two guys who claim to be officers on a stake out."

The jogger slowly approached the lady. "Have you called the police yet?"

"Sure have. They should be here any minute."

The jogger glanced inside the vehicle and looked at the two men who were frozen like statues. The force had already lost one windshield tonight and they didn't want to lose another. The jogger smiled at both men as he knew who they were.

"Hey guys, how's it going?" The jogger turned out to be one of the workers who helped unpack the moving vans for both officers.

Eli replied, "It was good up until now."

The jogger turned to the woman. "I can verify that these two men are officers, so you can put down the bat and go back to your house."

She immediately turned on the jogger and yelled, "You're probably one of them. Get away from me!"

A police vehicle with flashing lights and a siren sped around the corner and approached the distraught lady. Jim Banks got out of his vehicle and told the woman to stand down. These men were indeed officers who were undercover.

The couple inside Jenny's house drew back the living room curtains and looked outside to see what was going on. They came onto the front porch and the girl inquired, "What's going on?"

Jim replied, "Just a misunderstanding. Sorry we woke you up."

The girl shrugged. "Seems to be a lot of that going on tonight." The couple went back into the house.

Jim spent some time trying to talk down the neighbourhood watch lady, but once she was convinced they really were police officers, she retreated. Jim called after her. "Thank you for your concern and phone call. I'm glad you didn't try and deal with this on your own."

The lady just snarled, "Stupid idiots. I should have been informed if the place was under surveillance."

"That's not standard procedure lady."

CHAPTER EIGHTEEN

3:10 — 3:45

Greg pulled to a stop outside Richard's house. The doctor made sure that he grabbed his medical bag before leaving the vehicle. "Thanks for the ride."

Greg replied, "You're welcome. I hope you know that we're going to find her."

"I sure hope so." He watched as the cruiser sped down the street and disappeared around the corner. He waited on the sidewalk for several moments before slowly climbing the stairs and unlocking the front door. Richard stepped into the entrance and set his medical bag onto the floor. Kimberley ran into his open arms. She was crying and babbling between sobs. Richard held her close and let her talk, even though he didn't have a clue what she was saying. He did, however, have a good idea of what she was trying to ask him. Unfortunately, he wasn't able to provide her with the answers. He spotted Beatrice standing in the living room so he indicated for her to come over and hugged her with his free arm.

"Kimberley, give Richard some breathing room. I know you're worried, but at least let him close the front door."

Kimberley stepped aside. "I'm sorry darling, but we've both been beside ourselves with worry." She then turned to Beatrice. "Let's go into the living room to talk."

Richard sat next to Kimberley, but across from Beatrice. "First of all, Bill sends his love and wants you to know they're working as fast as they can."

Beatrice was rubbing, pulling, and twisting her fingers nervously. Richard observed her fidgeting and noticed that she looked tired and almost seemed to have aged since he last saw her. Beatrice said, "Is he doing okay?"

"He's doing as well as can be expected. His body is probably in overdrive right now, but he's holding his own. Let's just say it's a pleasure watching him at work. Every officer in that building is giving one hundred and ten percent." He then added, "I'll be here from now on. I won't be going back to the station."

Kimberley looked worried. "Why not? You need to be there when they find her."

"It's not standard procedure to have a civilian hanging around inside the precinct. Bill has assured me that when they find her, I'll be picked up immediately. I even brought my medical kit with me. I don't want the officers to forget it in all their haste."

Kimberley's puffy eyes looked directly into his. "Are they any closer to finding her?"

"Bill told me before I left that new tips are coming in constantly, and the team is searching numerous sites, not leaving anything to chance. That sounds positive don't you think?" Richard really wanted to change the subject so he asked Beatrice. "Do you think you could please make me a cup of tea? The coffee at the station is too strong for my liking."

"Of course, I'll be right back."

Richard pulled Kimberley closer to him. "I know you have lots of questions, but right now, I'm not sure I can answer any of them. We just need to put our trust in Bill. I don't think that office has ever been so busy before tonight. Every officer there is running around constantly. I thought at first it was rather chaotic in there, but I realized it's organized chaos."

Beatrice came back carrying a tray with a teapot and three mugs. Kimberley declined a cup so Richard and Beatrice slowly drank theirs. Richard's body slowly started to relax. He wasn't aware of how stressed he was until then. He wanted to scream because of what was happening not only to his daughter, but also to the rest of his family. Remaining calm made him appear in control, which he wasn't, but he had to put on a front for the ladies' benefit.

Beatrice asked a second time. "Is Bill going to be okay?"

"He's an amazing man, and we should all be very proud of him. Yes, he's under great stress, but it's truly an honour watching him at work. Not one detail goes by without him sending his officers out to investigate it." He then added, "I thought my job was stressful, but his puts mine to shame."

Kimberley laid her head on his shoulder. "I'm not sure what to do with myself. I feel so helpless."

Richard moved his arm around her. "I'm here now, so the three of us will get through this together. You know, sweetheart, baking relaxes you so why don't you and Beatrice whip up a batch of cookies for Claire's coming home party? I know the officers working on the case would appreciate them."

Kimberley looked stunned. "How can you think of cookies, when our daughter has been kidnapped?"

"I merely mentioned it as I know it helps you to relax."

Beatrice agreed, "You're right Richard, maybe Kimberley and I will do that. Who doesn't like cookies after closing an important case like this one?"

Richard suggested, "I really like those raisin ones that you make."

Kimberley laughed, "They aren't raisin, they're chocolate chip, and you like any cookie."

"Guilty as charged."

Beatrice turned back to pose more questions about Claire. "Can you at least tell us what's going on? This one phone call every hour doesn't tell us much."

"From a doctor's perspective, I see little progress." Kimberley started to hyperventilate. "Please, darling, let me finish. Whenever I doubted the progress, I needed only to consult Bill; he sees things that I don't. He knows things that I don't and he has gut feelings that I don't. And the list could go on. He reassured me that before long, they would have a positive location. I'm convinced that losing is not an option for him." Richard then asked, "What have the two of you being doing to pass the time?"

Beatrice sighed. "Well, lots of praying for Claire's safe return, but also for the safety of Bill and his team. They're working so hard and must be exhausted." She grinned. "I'm also praying for a dash of good luck for Bill and his team." She sighed and got up from her chair. "I'll leave the two of you alone for awhile. I know that you both have lots to think about and talk about." She left the room, carrying the tray with the teapot and used mugs into the kitchen.

Kimberley whispered to Richard. "I'm really worried about Beatrice. Is there anything you can do to slow her down? I'm worried about her blood pressure; it must be off the wall."

Richard laughed, "You really expect me to slow her down? What planet are you living on?" He conceded, "Okay, I have an idea. Let's just sit back for a while. When she makes the next pot of tea, I'll need you to make a slight distraction."

Kimberley eyed him with skepticism. "What're you planning on doing?"

Richard headed towards the bathroom and closed the door. He then opened the medicine cabinet to take out a container of Extra Strength Tylenol, putting two of them in the pocket of his shirt before returning the container behind the mirror. Richard glanced into the kitchen on his way back to the living room and found Beatrice bent over the sink and gasping for air. He immediately ran to her and guided her towards a kitchen chair. Kimberley knew something was terribly wrong when Richard had bolted toward the kitchen, and she wasn't far behind him. Kimberley looked worried as she spoke, "Are you okay?" Watching Beatrice gasping for air scared her. "Richard, can you do anything? What's going on?"

Richard ran for his medical bag, pulled out his stethoscope, and listened to her heart beat. It was dangerously fast but he talked softly and it helped to calm her down. A few minutes later, he checked her again. Her heart rate was slowly going back to normal.

Richard told her. "I know you're under a lot of stress, but maybe we should talk about it. Trust me, it'll help."

Beatrice looked at both of them before speaking. Her voice was a mere whisper, "I just realized," she paused. "The possible outcomes that Bill will have to face when this is all over."

Kimberley froze knowing that she was right. "Let's all try to think positive thoughts right now, okay?"

"Have either of you heard of the term 'domino effect'?" Neither responded so Beatrice continued, "Tom commits a horrendous crime years ago, now his brother Charles is out for revenge. He's probably planned to kill Bill over that entire time."

Kimberley interjected, "Let's not think about that now."

"Why not?" Beatrice replied, "There are four different scenarios to consider."

Kimberley looked puzzled as she replied, "I only see two and right now bringing Claire home is the only option I'm going to consider. Not bringing her home is not on the table."

Beatrice explained. "You have to think outside the box to see the full picture. The first option is bringing Claire home, and we all want that to be the outcome. Second, Bill is unable to save her and has to deliver the news to us that he failed. He will be a destroyed man, unable to face us with the feeling that he failed. Earlier this evening, Kimberley, we were sharing memories and Bill said his special time with you was when he was teaching you your times tables." Kimberley smiled as Beatrice continued, "I'm sure he was planning on also helping Claire with hers. If Bill fails, he knows that doing that is not going to happen, plus he'll no longer be able to bounce her on his knee. The third option is he dies trying to save her. And fourth, he may not be able to look us in the eyes again and may leave Blue Ridge forever. I can't imagine the weight that he's carrying on his shoulders right now. If he loses her, he'll never be the same man. He'll have lost his confidence." Tears were now flowing freely from her eyes. "I'll have lost the man I fell in love with and married."

Richard and Kimberley both hugged her. Richard said, "For now, Beatrice, let's keep thinking inside the box. It's easier to deal with right now. Let's not worry about the other options right now; after all, they may never happen. Kimberley, I'm going to put a pot of tea on, maybe settle Beatrice in our bed."

Beatrice protested, "I'm not going to bed."

Richard smiled. "You don't have to go to sleep, but a little rest will do you some good. I won't take no for an answer."

When both ladies left for the bedroom, Richard took the two tablets from his pocket, crushed them between two spoons, and placed the powder into Beatrice's mug. Pouring the hot tea into the cup, he stirred it until the tablets were dissolved. He then took the cup to the bedroom and placed it beside the bed. Kimberley had Beatrice propped up with a few pillows so she was able to drink her tea. Both Richard and Kimberley stayed by the bed until the cup was empty and Beatrice was drifting off to sleep. The two of them then quietly returned to the living room.

Kimberley asked Richard. "Do I dare ask what you did?"

"Just helping her to relax. It's only tea laced with Tylenol."

"Thank you, she really needed to get some rest." The two held each other and Kimberley finally fell asleep in his arms.

Richard was puzzled that she could fall asleep so easily. He felt emptiness within his own home, and suddenly very lonely. He hugged Kimberley tighter, but not enough to wake her up. He so wanted to protect her, but wasn't sure how. He recalled the two of them in the Panorama Room that night when the earthquake hit, and the impending tsunami. They were both sharing a slow dance when the room around them started shaking and the cement floor under them cracked. The events that followed were still vivid in his mind. Everyone in the building was scared and needed leadership. Richard seemed to be the only one who stepped forward and took control. Already knowing that the earthquake was large enough to cause a massive wave that could possibly cover the entire dining room, he had to come up with a solution to protect the people, and he had to come up with it fast.

He had already guessed that the windows might offer them protection, but was not one hundred percent convinced they would hold up against the pressure that could be put upon them. He had to figure out a way of protecting everyone. Using their belts to attach couples together around a post seemed like a quick solution. Whether it would work or not was another mystery. When the wave hit and the windows broke, covering everyone in saltwater, he feared the worst. Once it receded and he saw that Kimberley wasn't breathing, he panicked. He loved this woman and had to save her. When she finally started breathing again and the saltwater left her lungs he felt a sigh of relief. He had untied himself from her and reattached her to the post so he could attend to an injured person in the room. He remembered Kimberley yelling his name, telling him that the second wave was coming. He quickly took the clip from his cell phone and attached himself to the injured man's belt and held on tightly. When the second wave hit, it was much smaller than the first one, so only came up to their waists. The strong undertow, however, would have pulled Richard out to sea if he hadn't secured himself. He almost lost the love of his life that night and he wasn't prepared to lose her or his daughter to this Charles character. He really wanted to come face to face with him and tell him he was a coward and a mean, vengeful person.

His thoughts went to Beatrice who was sleeping soundly in the bedroom. He really did worry about the pressure that Bill was under but hadn't considered the four different outcomes he was facing. He was so concerned about himself and Kimberley, he hadn't even thought about Bill in that way. Richard needed some fresh air, so he gently moved away from Kimberley, left the house, and sat on the front porch. He was really worried about Claire. Not just about her diabetes, but also if Charles was hurting her. Richard had to wonder why someone would do such a horrible thing to a family, his family specifically. He glanced up at the sky and wished he could slow down time just enough for Bill to find her. The door behind him opened and he turned to see Kimberley standing behind him. She crossed the porch and sat next to him on the top step. "You okay?"

Richard had to be honest. "Not really. I feel so helpless right now. They need to find her and soon."

Kimberley leaned her head against his shoulder. "They will, darling. I feel it inside me. Bill is always saying that he feels it in his gut. I never really thought about it but now I know what he was saying. I feel it too."

"I sure hope so. Let's get inside, just in case Beatrice wakes up. I don't want her to feel abandoned."

Kimberley softly kissed her husband, and the two went inside the house.

Beatrice woke up shortly after, forgetting where she was. Dragging herself into the living room, she found Richard and Kimberley comforting each other on a couch.

Kimberley inquired, "How did you sleep Beatrice?"

"Like a baby. Hope I didn't miss anything."

"No. We're still waiting for an update from the precinct."

CHAPTER NINETEEN

3:30 — 3:50

The anger Charles felt towards the doctor who testified against Tom was deep, but not as deep as what he felt for Bill's testimony. His hate for both men was obsessive, and although murdering both would be simple, getting away with it would be another thing. Once the sergeant was eliminated, the doctor would be his next and final target, and Charles' revenge would then be complete. When he was younger, Charles would beat someone up, just to prove that no one screwed around with him. He would do a number on them and then send them on their way with either a bloody or broken nose. Bill knew that Charles was coming after him but wouldn't expect Richard to be his next victim. He flashed back to the trial when the doctor testified against his brother.

The prosecutor called his next witness. "I call on Dr. Richard Jackson."

Richard walked to the front of the room and faced the clerk. Placing his hand on the bible, he listened as he was sworn in.

"Do you solemnly swear to tell the truth, the whole truth, and nothing but the truth, so help you God?"

"I do."

Richard sat in the chair and the prosecutor approached him. "Can you state your name and occupation?"

"Dr. Richard Jackson, Medical Practitioner, and Surgeon at the Blue Ridge General Hospital."

"Dr Jackson, can you tell me what happened that day when Joan Wilks was allegedly murdered?"

"I was on duty that afternoon when the hospital emergency room received a call that there was a shooting and requested an ambulance to the local grocery store. Not being aware of how extensive the gun shot wound was, I was prepared for the worst. When the ambulance arrived, the victim was already deceased."

"And can you tell me how the victim died?"

"She died from a single gunshot wound to the back, which passed through her heart. She would have died instantly."

The prosecutor then asked Richard. "What did you do next, doctor?"

Richard shifted uncomfortably. "I had to deliver the bad news to her husband, who was pacing around the emergency ward very distressed. It's never easy to have to pass on such shocking news to the next of kin."

"Thank you, doctor." He then turned to the defence. "Your witness."

The defence approached Richard and studied him before asking, "Doctor, is it your professional opinion that someone who is not aware of what he's doing should be accountable?"

The prosecutor immediately stood up. "Objection, your honour. The witness is a medical doctor, not a psychiatrist."

The judge paused and appeared to be thinking before he responded, "Overruled. I'm interested in the doctor's opinion."

Richard paused then said, "Are you asking me to get into Tom's head and try to figure out what he was thinking in the moments before he shot Joan Wilks?"

"Exactly."

"I'm not fully qualified to do that, however, drugs in a person's system react in different ways, depending on what is ingested. Add alcohol to that and you're playing Russian roulette, not only with your body, but also with everyone who comes in contact with you. It's a pretty risky game. Mixing drugs and alcohol plays tricks on the mind, including hallucinations. These often turn into aggressive behaviours, forcing the body into survival mode, and I'm sure that is what happened to Tom Lockman."

"So I repeat my question once again. Is it your professional opinion that someone who is not aware of what he's doing should be accountable?"

"Yes, he should be held accountable. My problem with letting him off is that anyone down the road could murder someone and always know they could get a get-out-of-jail-free card. Sorry, that doesn't work for me. Joan's husband is now left to raise their children alone, always searching for daycare while he's at work, and still trying to keep a household running. That doesn't fly with me."

That was not the answer the defence expected. "No more questions, your honour."

Charles' mind came back to the cabin, and he recalled how several months earlier, he had been walking the streets of Blue Ridge, looking for a specific man to do a special job for him. He came across a group of men huddled under a bridge trying to stay warm. Charles studied the men and then chose the one that looked the most respectable.

He approached the man, asking, "Is this where you hangout?"

"Maybe, who's asking?"

Charles was somewhat put off. "Look, kid. I'm searching for someone who can help me with a specific job. Are you the fellow I need or not?"

The half spaced-out kid immediately pushed himself up from the rough ground and tried to rub the wrinkles from his well-worn clothes. "Sure. I can do it, but what's it that you want me to do?"

"When the time is right, I'll come looking for you."

"I'll be here, but when are you going to need me?"

"I'm not sure yet, but soon." If the kid was already dead from an overdose before he needed him, he would find a quick replacement.

The young druggie knew the fellow didn't live in Blue Ridge, but asking fewer questions meant there were fewer answers. There was absolutely no way the two men could be connected, and it was safer that way. As days turned into weeks and then into months, he became frustrated, thinking that maybe the man didn't remember where he was, or worse, gave the job to someone else.

Months had passed since the two men had crossed paths, and the druggie was starting to think the man no longer needed him, when he miraculously appeared that evening, carrying a paper bag with instructions not to open it until he heard the phone inside ring. He was tempted to sneak a peek, but knew that doing so could be risky. A verbal contract had been set up between the two men and the druggie felt he would be in danger if he broke that trust. The no-name policy between the two men meant that if either were arrested, they couldn't turn the other man in. The young man had hit rock bottom and thought that if it worked out between them, there would be other jobs down the road. He had never bought drugs before, but somehow, they would appear among his new friends and inevitably end up in his system. He wasn't proud of himself, but wasn't sure how to turn the situation around. This job could turn into a clean start for him, a brighter future.

Charles mind came back to the present and he was seated in his chair, glancing between Jenny and the baby, studying her closely. He knew that Tom's freedom would be exhilarating for the three of them, but more so for Tom.

Jenny smiled at him. "Almost there. Tom and I will never be able to repay you for what you've done for us."

Charles glared at her. "Maybe try to stay out of trouble; that would help. I'm not coming to your rescue again." He added, "I suggest you sell your house and move. No one is going to want to live in the same town as you anymore."

Jenny's smile turned to tears. She hadn't thought about not being welcome in Blue Ridge anymore. Charles seemed to slip into one of his meditation modes once again, happy at the many months he had put into planning Bill's death. Charles was starting to feel cheated that it would all be over in a matter of hours. Hopefully, in the end, he would feel satisfaction. He had one more wrench to throw into the works, that Bill wouldn't see coming. Charles pulled a used napkin from his shirt pocket. Squinting at the paper, which was already fading, he entered the number written on it into his satellite phone. Charles waited for the young druggie to answer; remaining patient for the first couple rings as the kid had been told not to open the paper bag until the phone rang. But too many rings had passed and Charles was starting to think the kid was either spaced out or had already opened the bag and was off buying drugs with his money.

Hearing the phone ringing, the young man emptied the contents of the bag on the ground beside him. His eyes lit up when he saw the fifty dollar bill staring back at him. He quickly shoved the money into his pocket, hoping no one around him saw it.

He answered after half a dozen rings. "Hello."

Charles was relieved. "You're on kid. Don't let me down."

"Not a chance. That fifty dollar bill in the bag is more than enough pay for what you might want me to do."

"Your instructions and everything you'll need are in that bag." He then added, "You won't hear from me again, so when we hang up, destroy the phone." Charles then ended the call.

The kid studied the contents of the bag that lay on the ground beside him. A piece of paper had an address written on it: 30 Maple Crescent. He stuffed the paper into his pants pocket. Also in the bag were a package of firecrackers and a book of matches. He put them in his oversized jacket pocket to keep them dry. A second piece of paper had instructions on what he was supposed to do. He read the note then stuffed it into the same pocket next to the address. The druggie looked at the phone and wondered if he should keep it. Destroying it seemed a waste of a good phone. But he knew he shouldn't cross the man who may need him for jobs in the future. Against his better judgement, the kid smashed the phone on the rocks and tossed it into the river.

The young man had lived in Blue Ridge his entire life and had lost his job years earlier when the cannery had closed. His bad luck and the loss of his home had driven him into the streets, living among the poorest of poor. In spite of it all, he had made friends with the other unfortunate people that slept under the bridge beside him.

He staggered out from under the overpass and walked the streets to the address printed on the piece of paper. As he worked his way to the house, he wondered why the stranger had targeted that particular home. Obviously, the residents within the building had upset him enough to seek revenge. The kid was not a vindictive person, but having said that, the stranger hadn't asked him to do anything illegal. Setting off a few firecrackers on the front porch of the house wouldn't hurt anyone. He carefully opened the gate and entered the yard. There were several lights on inside the home, so the intruder slowly crept onto the front porch and glanced into the front room window. He wondered why lights were turned on at this time of the night and why the people inside were not in bed. Two women and a man were sitting on the couch comforting each other. The young man wondered if there had been a death in the family. If that was the case, then setting off fireworks on their porch would be mean and cruel. He was starting to have second thoughts, but he also knew the man who paid him could return, and it would not go well for him if he didn't finish the job. He quietly moved towards the front door and took out the package of firecrackers and matches, then lit them. His descent down the stairs was much faster than his approach. He was through the gate before the first bang from the firecrackers exploding.

Although his job here was done, he still wondered why this particular house was targeted. His curiosity got the better of him, so he hid behind a tree across the street, waiting to see who came to the poor people's rescue. The three residents huddled together, not only in fear, but also in a state of shock. The man sent the two ladies out of the room, probably to hide in the bathroom behind a locked door. He cautiously crossed the room and peered outside, then moved so he had a view of the front porch. He saw the last of the firecrackers sputter before extinguishing.

CHAPTER TWENTY

3:30 — 4:00

Greg, Jack, Bob, and Jim were geared up and ready for their next assignment. Don glanced at the whiteboard in front of him, knowing that his team of officers were waiting for further instructions. His eyes were drawn to one unchecked clue at the bottom of the board. The word 'Fire' stared back at him. Don immediately turned to his officers and paused before saying, "In Bill's second-to-last phone call, we heard the crackling of fire in the background. It may not be much of a tip, but we're going to investigate it regardless. We just can't afford to leave any clue on the back burner. Until we get the big break we need, we keep pushing forward, searching for anything and everything." He paused for a few seconds before speaking again. "Okay, two teams, two sites to check out. Jim and Bob, you check out the local municipal campsite, while Greg and Jack, you go to the Rock Creek campsite."

Eric and Sam had not yet been assigned anything, so Eric inquired, "What do you want us to do boss?"

Don rubbed the sleep from his eyes and spoke to Eric first. "Okay Eric. We are still nowhere as far as Charles' parents are concerned. Dig up anything you can find on the two of them. They didn't just drop off the face of the earth. If we can't find them in B. C. then widen your search to the rest of the provinces. Let's just hope we don't need to look south of the border. That would really complicate matters."

Eric responded, "On it boss."

Don then turned to Sam. "Bill and I are very concerned about Charles' state of mind. See if you can find out if he has a physician and if so, give the doctor a call. If he resists, tell him the urgency of the case. Maybe he'll cooperate and talk to you, if not, call a judge and acquire a search warrant for the files. My guess is the good doctor would rather be in bed than dragged into his office in the middle of the night."

Sam was already turning away to get started as he responded, "You got it."

The four other officers picked up their gear and left for their next search locations, while Eric and Sam returned to their desks and started making calls.

Greg called to Bob. "See you back at the station. Good luck."

"We're going to need it."

Bill looked across the room to Don and nodded, indicating that they should meet in the sergeant's office. Both men entered the room and closed the door. While Bill chose to sit, Don decided to stand. Being the boss and replacing Bill had Don feeling awkward.

"Please don't tell me I screwed up." He shook his head. "Do you have any idea how hard your shoes are to fill?"

"I didn't call you in here to criticize; I wanted to let you know that I approve of how well you've taken on the leadership role. I would've sent the men out to investigate the campsites too. Until I talk to Jenny at four o'clock, we can't eliminate the surrounding area of Blue Ridge. It won't take the teams long to eliminate the campsites as not many people will be camping this time of the year."

Don asked, "How do you do it?"

"Do what?"

"Always stay so professional and on the top of every case, knowing each move before it happens?"

"It comes with years of experience. Every criminal makes the same mistakes. In order to defeat them, you have to start thinking like them, get in their heads and then outsmart them. It can be scary at times, but it's also necessary to catch them. Just remember, at the end of the day, you have to shut down, go home, and forget the case until the next day. If you can't do that, you'll burn yourself out."

"Makes sense, but if I'm going in the wrong direction, I expect you to intercede and set me back on the right track. I can't afford to screw up this case."

Smiling, Bill added, "You're doing great. As clues come in, we check them out. I have to wait for my next call at four and try to extract another clue from Jenny."

"Do you have any idea what you're going to ask her next?"

"Not really. Need to wait and see what happens at the campsites."

"Fair enough. I need to get back to work." The two men went back into the common area, impressed by the officers busy trying to put this case to rest.

***

Bob and Jim were barely five minutes from the municipal campsite when Bob broke the silence. "What do you think we'll find at the campground?"

"I'm not completely sure, but since there was an indication of a fire burning on one of the recorded messages, we have to investigate it. We can't leave any stone unturned."

"I agree. Being the middle of the night, most people will already be in bed. The fire could easily have burned out by now."

Jim responded, "That's true, but to be efficient, we'll have to only look at camper units or trailers. There's no way they would be holed up in a tent. If Claire is inside one of them, then the lights would still be on. Charles couldn't afford to fall asleep and miss his next call."

"Good point."

Once they arrived, they found the main gate locked and secured for the night. The check-in building just beyond the gate was empty and enshrouded in darkness. They parked their vehicle close to the gate, got out, locked the cruiser, and walked around the barrier. The night was cool and the sky was completely overcast with clouds from the recent storm, which made seeing in front of them difficult. They put on their night vision goggles, drew their weapons and slowly started the search. The rainstorm that had hit the town earlier had left the ground saturated. Both men had to dodge puddles, but both still ended up with wet feet.

Bob inquired, "Do you know what would really make me happy?"

"Don't keep me in suspense. What?"

"A happy ending to this nightmare would be nice. I think Bill and his family shouldn't be going through this just because Charles thinks that his murdering brother should get off scot-free."

"You're right of course. Fingers crossed that it ends here and now."

Sixty campsites were a lot to search, but almost half of them were empty as the season was coming to a close. The rest of the campsites had either RVs or tents hidden in the darkness, but so far none of the trailers had any lights on. They heard the constant scurrying of squirrels, but stopped dead in their tracks when they heard a new sound and thought a bear was close by. Their night vision goggles revealed a large black bear crossing the road in front of them. They lost valuable searching time as the bear was in no hurry to move on. When the bear finally wandered off into the bush, they were able to get back on track. In the distance, a campfire was burning brightly, but once they got closer, they saw it was only a group of teenagers partying. They were laughing loudly; obviously slightly drunk. The group froze when they saw two men approaching. Bob and Jim removed their night vision goggles and holstered their weapons before approaching the group of teens.

One whispered to the fellow next to him. "Someone must have reported us." Then he turned to the two policemen and said, "Sorry, officers. Were we being too noisy?" He also inquired, "Did someone report us?"

Bob answered, "No one reported you. This is just a standard walkthrough. Maybe think about cutting the noise down a few decibels; after all, the other campers are trying to sleep." He scanned the group then added, "I hope all of you are over nineteen years of age. Consuming alcohol in a public place as a minor is a criminal offence." A few froze and looked away. The officers noticed those two people and ignored it. They had bigger fish to catch that night and arresting minors would only slow down their investigation. "Please be respectful for the other campers and keep the noise down."

"Sorry, officers. We were just having fun and weren't aware we were that loud."

"Just keep in mind that voices carry at night."

The two officers left the campsite, put on their goggles once again, and drew their weapons for a second time, continuing their search, but coming up empty handed. With no luck, they worked their way back to the cruiser. Both men placed the night vision goggles on the back seat and climbed into the vehicle. Jim radioed the station.

"Daniel here."

"Hi Daniel, it's Jim. Nothing to report at the municipal campsite." He then added, "Sorry."

Daniel sounded frustrated. "Okay. Come on in. Maybe Greg and Jack will have better luck."

"We're on our way."

***

Greg and Jack were talking about the case and the clues they had so far while driving out to Rock Creek. Greg was the thinker of the two men, while Jack was the planner.

"This whole case is Tom Lockman's fault," Greg said, "If he hadn't killed Joan Wilks, this wouldn't be happening. He got what he deserved."

"I know, but Charles is a lowlife scumbag kidnapping Claire. Did he honestly think that he could get away with it? Bill will hang him out to dry. He'll wish he was never born. I wouldn't want to be Charles for all the money in the world if we don't find Claire in time. Our team will hunt him down and gladly kill him. Won't even waste the taxpayers' money on a trial."

Greg glanced at Jack. "This Jenny never had any children so I really wonder if she's on Charles' side or ours. She might do anything to get Tom back."

"That part really scares me. Would she let Charles kill Claire? If Jenny does, she's an accomplice so will be up for murder too. Hopefully, she has thought this through. Jenny did however, warn Bill about the traps, so she may not be a willing participant."

Greg responded, "Let's hope she has some compassion for a small defenseless baby. They definitely kidnapped the wrong child, and also were not aware of her impending medical condition. We've had no luck with the local buildings, so hopefully it'll pan out here or else we're back to square one. We really need a break."

"A miracle right now would be nice."

Greg and Jack reached the Rock Creek campsite, and like the municipal one, the gate was locked for the night. The two left their vehicle, locked it, and put on their night vision goggles. With their weapons drawn, they slowly took the two to three minute walk to the first campsite, which was up against the water. A small campfire was burning and a man appeared to be playing a guitar. It was well after quiet time of 10 p.m., but no one was around for him to disturb. The two officers holstered their weapons and took off their night vision goggles, and walked over to talk to him.

Greg spoke, "You sure know how to make that guitar sing."

The man was startled, not only because he didn't hear anyone approaching, but also because the two men were police officers. Looking nervous, he responded, "Sorry, but you scared me half to death. Was I playing too loud?"

"Not at all. You come out here often?"

"I always come here this time of year. I can have my pick of almost any campsite around. I like this one because the river lulls me to sleep. The earlier storm caught me off guard so some water leaked into my tent, leaving my sleeping bag damp. I would rather huddle around a campfire and play my guitar than try to sleep in a damp sleeping bag. I enjoy hiking and there's no shortage of trails in this area." He then added, "Don't remember officers patrolling this area before. You looking for someone?"

Jack answered, "As a matter of fact, we are. Have you seen either a trailer or motor home with a couple and a small baby?"

"Not here. It's too late in the season for families to come out here. They monopolize the campsite in the summer, that's why I come out now. No crying babies, barking dogs, or bears rooting through trash. The river is too high for fishermen right now, so I have the best of both worlds."

Jack replied, "Thanks for your help and try to stay dry."

"That's my plan." He then started picking his guitar as the two officers left his campsite. There were only fifteen sites, most of them empty as fall was ending and winter was approaching. They placed their night vision goggles on again and drew their weapons, continuing their search, but all was quiet.

Greg was frustrated. "We keep hitting dead ends. Why can't we get the break we need to get Claire back?"

"Guess we just need to be patient. It'll come; besides, if there's nothing at the municipal campsite, and nothing here, then we've eliminated two more locations." The only sounds around the men were all natural; a slight breeze rustling the trees, squirrels scampering around, and an owl hooting off in the distance.

Greg conceded, "There's nothing here. We may as well head back to the station." Once back at their vehicle, and when their goggles were placed on the back seat, they started back to the precinct. Greg picked up the radio and checked in.

"Daniel here."

Greg let out a sigh. "Dead end here. Did the other team have any luck?"

"None whatsoever."

"Okay we're on or way back."

CHAPTER TWENTY-ONE

4:00 — 4:20

Charles was again sitting in his chair relaxing. He had found a footstool across the room and had put it in front of his chair to place his feet on. He was relaxed knowing that his latest antic would cost Bill a whole hour. Time was running out for the sergeant. The way Charles saw it, he couldn't lose. If Bill didn't get Tom released, the baby would be dead and the smart cop's entire family would never forgive him. If he did manage to find the cabin, Charles would kill him. It was a win-win situation for Charles. At this point, he didn't really care if Tom got out of prison; his real goal was to eliminate Bill. He watched Jenny holding Claire while the baby slept, but her eyes were locked onto his. Charles was irritated. "Why do you have to constantly hold that baby?"

"She sleeps better when I'm holding her, and this whole kidnapping will run smoother for both of us if she isn't screaming. I don't want to listen to you complain if she's crying." She glanced down at her watch then asked Charles. "It's four o'clock. Aren't you calling Bill?"

"Thought I might let him sweat for a few minutes, besides, it might make him realize he has no option but to make sure Tom is set free."

Jenny inquired, "Does Tom know that you're doing this?"

"He knows that I'm doing something, but I spared him the details."

"Have you ever thought that he may not approve of your method of getting him out?"

Charles was instantly on his feet yelling, "You whine and snivel constantly that he's behind bars, and now you dare to judge my methods of getting him out?" Claire was startled awake and began crying. Jenny got up from her chair, and continued cuddling the frightened baby. Charles continued, "I suggest you just shut up and keep that baby quiet. Right now, it would be easier for me to kill both of you and just leave."

Jenny couldn't believe her ears. Charles had just threatened to kill both her and Claire. Hugging the child even closer, she moved to the far side of the room, well away from him. Her eyes darted around the room looking for a secret way out of the cabin, and this whole mess, but there was only one way in and one way out. The two of them were like caged animals and in less than four hours she and this tiny helpless child could very easily be dead. Tears overflowed from her eyes and she buried her face in the baby's blanket.

***

Bill was sitting at Daniel's desk waiting for his next call. He watched his officer's working frantically trying to solve this case. He observed Eric getting up from his desk and approaching Don with a file in his hands. Eric passed it to Don, they spoke a few words, and then Eric returned to his desk. Bill watched Don open the file and glance at the first page before flipping it over and looking at the second page. Don slapped the file closed and turning to Bill he rose from his desk and walked over to the sergeant, placing the file in front of him. "I thought you should see this before your next call."

Bill responded, "What is it?"

"It's the file on Charles' parents and his sister."

Bill glanced at his watch knowing he would only have time to skim it briefly as his next call was only minutes away. He opened the file and took a quick look at both pages. He then turned to Don. "Why didn't we know about this before? Who was the officer that went to the Lockman house years ago?"

Don looked apologetically at Bill. "It was Officer Debbie Mozer. We didn't recognize the name because it was her case and she went to the residence on her own to deliver the bad news. She's on maternity leave, so Eric decided to look into her cases, and this is what he found."

Bill ran his fingers through his hair in frustration. "This could change everything."

He sat studying the file and waited patiently for his next call. His body was starting to shut down once again from lack of sleep, but he knew he had to push on for Claire's sake. He crossed the room and filled his cup with coffee. Looking around the room, his officers were busy at work; looking for any angle to locate Claire. Bill already knew that when this was over, he owed the entire crew a case of beer; maybe even two cases. It was four o'clock and Charles hadn't phoned yet. He was worried that maybe something had gone wrong and he had done something stupid, and Charles was already on the run. He kept pacing nervously between Daniel's desk and the whiteboard. Everyone in the room was on edge. He returned to his chair and nervously tapped the desk, waiting. He never did drink his coffee. His mind was working overtime while he fought to stay on track.

Daniel looked worried and finally asked, "What's going on? Why isn't he calling? Do you think something horrible has happened?"

"I'm not sure, Daniel, but let's hope not." Bill then added, "He's running the whole show, so unfortunately, we have to play by his rules."

Bill was worried about Claire's condition. Had her tiny body already started to shut down? Once it started, how long would it be before it shut down entirely without her insulin? He should've asked Richard, but he also didn't want to know the answer. Bill was already on a tight timeline, and shortening that time would only add more stress to himself and everyone else in the station who was working so hard to find her. His thoughts went to Richard's house. He wanted to be there for support, but right now, Charles was in complete control of him. He didn't like bending over for a lowlife scumbag like Charles, but right now, the bad guy was overpowering him. Bill hated the insecurity that weakness gave him. He felt like a puppet controlled by a crazy person. If only he could cut the strings that Charles held, he could once again have the upper hand. The whole scenario became disconcerting. When the phone rang, Bill jumped out of his chair. Daniel was already pushing the record button as Bill answered, "Hello."

"Well, Bill thought I'd call late this time. By the way, how are you and your team holding up?"

"I'm doing fine and my men are preparing the tracking dogs for when we locate you." He then added, "Have you ever wondered how scent dogs are trained? On a normal case, a piece of clothing that a person has worn is waved in front of the dog's nose. The animal is able to pick up the scent of sweat from the clothing and they follow it to where the criminal is hiding."

Charles laughed, "Too bad you don't have anything of mine to put in front of the dog's nose."

"Don't need it. Some animals can smell the shit that comes out of a criminal's ass. That would be you, so you should start to worry."

"I'm not worried in the least. The hours have slowly managed to creep up on you, and that must be stressful for you and your family. They're probably beside themselves as the hours fly by and you are slowly failing. Guess the superhero sergeant may be demoted to cleaning bathrooms at work and will no longer be welcome at home."

Bill was irritated. "That's assuming I lose. What about if I win?"

Charles' laugh caught Bill off guard. "You started this adventure at midnight. It's now four o'clock. You haven't exactly made much progress in those four hours."

"How do you know what progress I have or haven't made?"

"It's just an educated guess."

It was Bill's turn to laugh. "You didn't strike me as an educated man."

"Forget the chit chat. How are the plans going for Tom's release?"

Bill saw this as his chance to address the file in front of him. "First we need to have a discussion."

"Sure. If you want to kill off a few more precious minutes from your granddaughter's life, I'm okay with that."

"My men have dug up some interesting information about your parents and sister."

Charles became very upset and aggressive. "You high and mighty officers wearing your spiffy uniforms and working in your fancy offices think it is okay to pry into people's personal lives. You think you're Sherlock Holmes with your funny hat, magnifying glass, and pipe jutting out of your mouth and your team thinks they're all Dr. Watsons." Charles needed to take a breath. "Who the hell do you think you are?"

Bill had to defend his fellow officers. "My men see dead bodies, have guns pointed at them, have been shot, and attacked with knives from crazy people like you. Do you think we do it for fun?" Bill was now shouting, "We do it to keep our community safe for the people who live here. We do it for people like Joan Wilks. Unfortunately, your brother snuck through the cracks. I'm sure it won't be the last time we have to clean up the streets from assholes like you. Dirt bags like yourself and your brother are a waste of oxygen." Bill picked up the first piece of paper from the file. "Nikki Lockman died from crib death. Do you know what that means?"

"It means Tom and I killed her and that's why our parents abandoned us."

Bill added, "Her death is commonly known as sudden infant death syndrome. It can happen in perfectly healthy babies. They just forget to breath. It had nothing to do with you or your brother. It just happened. Instead of blaming you, they should've taken the time to explain why she died and that it was no one's fault."

"Why are you telling me this?"

"I think it's important for you to realize her death had nothing to do with you or your brother." Bill paused and turned to the second page. "I think I also have an accurate explanation for Tom's drug use and why he shot Joan Wilks."

"I don't want to hear it."

"Well, you're going to hear it anyways. My team dug up the obituary of your parents and it appears they both died from an overdose. It was a case of double suicide. Years after your sister Nikki died, your parents were still unable to handle her death, so chose to die in each others arms. We didn't have that information available to us until now, as it happened out of province. After Officer Debbie Mozer visited Tom and Jenny to tell them the news of their death, Tom went out and bought a gun several days later. He was probably considering suicide himself and knew that he couldn't do it without being high on drugs, just like his parents were. He ingested the drugs plus a shot of alcohol, so they would kick in much faster. We aren't sure where he planned to take his life, but obviously he never made it to that location. The combination of the two substances hit him too quick, and unfortunately poor Joan Wilks got in his way. Tell me, Charles, why didn't he seek professional help? There are groups out there that could have helped him."

Charles paused slightly. When he spoke, Bill was taken aback by his answer and unusually soft reply. "I don't know why." He immediately switched back to the impending business and his more common snarl. "You have no idea what it feels like to lose someone you love!"

Bill answered, "I know exactly what it feels like."

"Tell me, Mr. Big Shot. Who did you ever lose?"

Bill hesitated. "I don't reveal my personal life to criminals, so you'll just have to take my word for it."

Charles laughed, "Just another one of your bullshit stories."

"Take it for what it is."

Charles snapped back. "Where is my brother?"

"We can play this game all night, but he still can't be released before nine o'clock." Bill had to regroup his thoughts. "How can you be so sure that I'm not zeroing in on your location right now?"

Charles started laughing. "How do you know that I'm not moving around to throw you off?"

Bill hadn't even thought that Charles might be outsmarting him. "Just a guess, but I don't think you're smart enough to figure that out. Besides, packing up three people in the middle of the night and moving would require you to know that your next location would be empty. Not many people are out at this hour of the morning, but are you willing to risk that someone might see you and report it to us?"

"Maybe, but I still have more aces up my sleeve than you do."

Bill replied, "Maybe I'm holding a few jokers." He then added, "Funny, I don't see you as a card shark."

Charles responded, "I've done my share of gambling with some success."

"Can't have won that many times or you wouldn't have taken up kidnapping in your spare time." Bill added, "That's enough bullshit, let's get down to business. Have you considered my latest offer?"

Charles was irritated. "What latest offer?"

"You give me Claire's location and I give you that one hour head start. It's a good offer, but keep in mind that I will hunt you down and put you behind bars, maybe even next to your brother."

Charles let out a blood thirsty laugh. "Not going to happen."

"Okay then let's get down to business. I need to talk to Jenny to get an update on Claire."

There were some shuffling noises as the phone was passed to Jenny. Charles glared at her. "Don't say anything stupid. Just say that the baby's fine." Charles hated it when Bill would only talk to her. He was starting to realize that Jenny was showing signs of being soft and might secretly reveal their location. His eyes bore into hers. He ran his finger across his throat as a warning. "Don't screw up!"

Jenny finally spoke, "Claire's still fine. She's sleeping."

Bill quickly asked, "Are you changing locations?"

Bill knew that could be a risky question for her to answer, but she answered anyway. "No."

Charles took the phone back and yelled at Bill, "What did you ask her?"

"Simple question. I just needed to know that you weren't hurting Claire."

"From now on, Jenny is out of bounds. You talk to me, and only me."

"Not how it works, Charles. You do remember that I don't trust you, just like you don't trust me?"

"Okay. Now you know the baby's fine, at least for now."

"You know, Charles, you can't win at this game as the odds are against you."

"How do you figure that?"

"I've watched enough good guy bad guy movies to know that good always wins over evil."

Charles let out a laugh that sent shivers down Bill's spine. "You know, Bill, you were unable to protect your granddaughter, so what makes you think you can protect the rest of your family?"

Bill froze. "What do you mean?"

"I see that I've got your attention. While you've been busy doing nothing towards getting Tom out of prison, I've been taking extra measures to ensure his release."

Bill's face turned white and he started to sweat as he looked across the table at Daniel. Both men felt like they had been slapped in the face. They weren't sure what Charles had done. Maybe Bill had misread Charles. He already knew he was crazy, but maybe Bill underestimated how crazy he really was. "What're you talking about?"

"Oh come on, Bill. I'm sure you want to know what I've done, but there's no rush. Let me enjoy the moment."

Bill shouted into the phone. "There's no moment to enjoy, you wacko!"

"I don't see it that way. Victory is only a few hours away."

Bill had to calm down as he repeated, "My team have their guns loaded, and in a moment's notice will be hunting you down." Bill felt like he was suffocating. He got up, walked to the whiteboard, and wrote, 'not moving around.' He returned to his chair and took several deep breaths to calm down his nerves.

"Okay, Bill. I guess I've kept you in suspense long enough." He half laughed and spoke at the same time. "Have you talked to your wife or the doctor and his wife lately?"

Bill panicked and turned off his phone, hearing Charles laughing in the background. Daniel had already shut off the recording device when Bill inquired, "Anything?"

"Sorry, nothing at this point, but I'll review it to be sure."

Bill left the common area and went into his office, slamming the door behind him, and slowly dialled Richard's number, afraid to find out what Charles had done.

CHAPTER TWENTY-TWO

4:20 — 4:45

Charles' last taunting statement on Bill's four o'clock call had sent fear trembling through his entire body, so when Richard answered the phone at his house, the sergeant felt instant relief.

"Are you three okay?"

"What's going on Bill? I tried to call you, but your phone was steady busy. We heard what we thought were gunshots outside, so I sent the ladies into the bathroom and told them to lock the door behind them. When I peeked outside the window, it looks like someone set off a package of firecrackers on our front porch. Why would anyone do that?"

"Don and I are on our way! Don't open the door for anyone!" He then hung up. "Don, we need to leave right now!"

Don could tell from the urgency in Bill's voice that something was terribly wrong. Both men picked up their weapons and ran from the station towards a cruiser. They were in the vehicle and speeding to Richard and Kimberley's house before Don inquired, "What's up, boss?"

Bill chose his words carefully. "Looks like Charles is starting to play dirty."

"What do you mean dirty? What did he do? Where are we going?"

"Over to Richard and Kimberley's place." Bill felt like he couldn't breathe. He was worried sick about Claire; and now he had to add Richard, Kimberley, and Beatrice to the list. Bill explained, "Someone just let off fireworks on Kimberley's front porch and scared the hell out of them. They thought it was gunshots."

Don was shocked and said, "I don't understand. Why is this happening to them? He already has your granddaughter, so why terrorize the family any further? How the hell is he doing this if he's not in town?"

Bill answered, "I guess the guy will do anything to beat me. I'll take great pleasure in eliminating him from this planet and the entire gene pool. He must have had an accomplice set off the firecrackers."

Their vehicle stopped in front of Richard and Kimberley's house. Both men got out and ran towards the front of the house. Don and Bill scanned their surroundings before Bill suggested, "I'll go around the left side of the house while you check the right. I doubt that whoever did this is still here, but we need to be sure that the coast is clear." Don nodded his approval then both men drew their weapons and went in opposite directions around the house.

The druggie across the street was horrified when he saw the police cruiser pull up in front of the house he had just left. He suddenly felt as if the man that hired him had shafted him. What he thought was an innocent prank had suddenly become a police issue. He was confused and wondered what he had got himself into. Was it really worth the fifty dollars, especially if he got caught? He would just have to lay low until they left and he could then return to the safety of his overpass.

The two officers met at the back of the house.

Bill asked, "You find anyone?"

"No, the coast is clear, but I didn't really expect anyone to still be here. Let's get inside and check on everyone." Both officers secured their weapons and returned to the front yard and rushed up the stairs. Right in front of the door was a scattered pile of red paper that was definitely the remnants of a package of firecrackers.

Bill said, "I'll collect this as evidence. You go inside and check on Richard and the ladies."

Don replied, "I can bag the evidence. Why don't you go in and check on them?"

"Thanks, but I need a few minutes to compose myself, to kind of regroup, so I'll take care of it, thanks anyways." Bill had a key to Kimberley's house in case of emergencies so he unlocked it and let Don in.

When Don opened the front door, he called, "Bill and I are here. Are you all okay?"

Richard and the two ladies came out of the safety of the bathroom. "We are, and thank God you're here."

Beatrice looked behind Don and inquired, "Where's Bill?"

"Right behind me, he's just finishing off some business on the front porch." Beatrice tried to walk around Don, but he stopped her dead in her tracks. "Don't be too hasty." He then added, "I was told to keep everyone indoors until he's finished investigating outside."

Bill slipped on a pair of surgical gloves and then bent over and carefully placed the scraps of red paper into a zip lock bag before sealing it. He carefully tucked it into his jacket pocket, not knowing if he would need it as part of the investigation that would follow this nightmare. His feelings right now were in overdrive. How dare Charles try and attack his family a second time. It would be hard for Bill to not kill him on sight. He started to wonder why this whole event even happened. Was it meant as a distraction, causing Bill to lose an entire hour? He rubbed the tight muscle in the back of his neck and pretended to be in control. Bill entered the house, hoping he looked like everything was alright, knowing perfectly well it wasn't. Beatrice flew into his arms and refused to let him go. He had never seen her that scared before, even when the tsunami wave had hit the Panorama Room and Richard and Kimberley were helplessly trapped inside. That horrific event was over in a matter of hours, but this disaster just kept on going with no end in sight.

Bill held Beatrice even tighter, refusing to let her go. She was frightened at first as he had never held her so tight before. She wiggled her arms free and threw them around his shoulders and instantly felt the tension in his upper back. He buried his head in her hair and the warmth from his breathing helped her relax. Beatrice could slowly feel the tension releasing from his body as well. He slowly moved her away and kissed her passionately. Don looked away as he felt he was intruding on a very private moment.

Bill slowly moved away from Beatrice and inquired, "Are you all okay?"

Beatrice hung onto Bill's arm and asked, "Why is this happening to us?"

Bill admitted, "It's all my fault and I promise I'll fix it." He turned to Richard. "Can you get me a phone book?"

"Sure." He went into the kitchen to retrieve it, then handed it to Bill. "What do you plan to do?"

"Don and I can't be here, but the three of you need protection. I have a friend who owes me a favour. He's a retired officer that I trust completely. I need every officer on site and this friend will protect the three of you with his life. It's time for me to collect on that favour." He looked up the number and dialled it, waiting for an answer at the other end.

The answering machine kicked in. "Hi there. You have reached the residence of Glen Forner. I can't come to the phone at this time, but if you leave a message after the beep, I'll get back to you as soon as possible."

Bill waited for the beep then said, "If you're there Glen, please pick up. It's an emergency!"

Glen grabbed the phone and answered, "It must be an emergency or you wouldn't have called me at this ungodly hour. What's up?"

"I need a favour."

"Anything. How can I help?"

"I need you to protect my family. I'll fill you in once you're here." He then added, "Come armed."

"I'm on my way. What's the address?"

"30 Maple Crescent."

Bill hung up the phone then gestured for Don to go out to the front porch with him. As they waited for Glen to arrive, Don whispered, "Don't turn around, but I think I spotted someone across the street hiding behind a tree. He appears to be watching us."

Bill thought for a few seconds, then said, "I'll create a distraction. See if you can get behind him and catch him off guard."

Don looked like he was leaving the scene as he announced, loud enough for the stranger to hear. "I'll call it in, boss." He mimicked getting into the cruiser and picking up the radio, when in fact, he had crouched low and walked part way down the street before crossing over to the other side. He drew his pistol and, being light on his feet, surprised the mysterious onlooker. The kid had actually lost interest in the officer talking on the radio and had turned his attention to the other officer on the front porch. Don appeared behind the young man and confronted him. "Kind of late to be out walking, don't you think?" He then grabbed the man.

"Let me go. You ain't got nothing on me."

"What're you doing snooping around this neighbourhood at this time of night?"

"There ain't no law against taking a stroll in the middle of the night."

"No there isn't, but hiding behind a tree across the street from a crime scene makes you look pretty suspicious."

The kid was suddenly scared. "This ain't a crime scene. Is it?"

"Why do you think we're here in the middle of the night? Do you think we've come for coffee and donuts? The people inside are scared to death. They heard what they thought were gun shots outside their house."

The kid started to stutter, "What do you mean gunshots? All I did was set off a package of firecrackers." Don was about to throttle the kid, but had to find out why he trespassed and frightened the three people in the house.

"Why did you do that?"

"Some guy paid me fifty bucks to do it. It seemed innocent enough at the time."

Don put handcuffs on the kid and pushed him across the street. Bill looked at the young man and asked Don, "What do you know about this guy?"

"Apparently he was paid handsomely to set off firecrackers on this porch."

Bill studied the young man. "Someone paid you to do this?"

"That's right."

"What did he look like?"

"Kind of creepy."

Bill inquired, "What kind of creepy?"

"Didn't see his face tonight because he was wearing a dark hoodie, but several months ago when we first met, it was daylight so I got a good look at him then."

Bill continued to investigate. "Okay kid, what did he look like?"

"He was about your height, kind of skinny, no hair, and an ugly scar across his face."

Don turned to Bill. "You stay here and I'll take him in. He might appreciate a dry cell for the night."

"You can't do that! I have rights!"

"Don't push me kid. I can do it and I will." Don loaded the suspect into the cruiser and called to Bill. "I'll be back when this character is behind bars."

Eight Hours

A few minutes, later Glen arrived and met Bill on Richard's front porch. "Hey Glen. It's been a long time. Thanks for coming man."

"No problem, but what the hell's going on here?"

"Let's get inside." Bill introduced Glen to Beatrice, Kimberley, and Richard. He shook their hands. The two officers sat across from each other as Bill explained the situation. Glen watched the three innocent people in front of him as Bill filled him in on the case. The details that Bill told him slowly turned his sensitive stomach sour. He knew that Bill had to deal with terrorists over the years, but this case was a little too close to home. He shook away the negative thoughts that were forming in his mind and concentrated on what was being said. He listened intently and was already planning his strategy to keep Bill's family safe.

Glen inquired, "Is the outside of the house secured?"

"Don and I did a walk around when we first got here. Don discovered a kid hiding across the street and has arrested him. When we're back at the office, he'll be interrogated, but when Don returns, he and I both have to get back to the office. If I miss my five o'clock call, it'll be all over."

Don soon returned from the precinct and the two men said their goodbyes to Bill's family. Kimberley made it a point to cross the room and give Bill a big hug. "You be careful out there, you hear me?"

"Loud and clear."

The two officers left Glen in charge of protecting Bill's family. Neither officer spoke the entire way back to the precinct. Bill was upset that he hadn't foreseen Charles' every move and Don couldn't get the image of Beatrice's tearful face out of his memory. Would this evening ever end, and if it did, how would it end? Either way, there would be tears of joy or tears of despair.

Glen could see that the three people in front of him were like a wrecked bus, maybe not upside down, but definitely on its' side. He knew it was essential to try to calm them down and make them feel secure.

"If you don't mind, can I take a walk through your house? I want to make sure that the inside is secure." Kimberley nodded her approval.

As Glen walked to each room, he glanced around, checked closets and even under beds. He really wanted to be thorough. Before leaving each room he checked that the window was secure and the curtains were completely closed. When he got to the nursery, he paused, trying to imagine what had happened there only hours earlier. Noticing the window nailed shut gave him some comfort; the room was secured. He covered the damaged window frame with the curtains and left the room. Once all the rooms were inspected, curtains were closed, and he was sure that both the front and back doors were locked, he returned to the living room. Glen glanced between the two ladies and Richard and he knew he had to break the ice.

"Sorry, guess we have never met before tonight, but Bill and I go back many years, far too many. We both took courses in Vancouver and shared a few graduations together. I stayed in Vancouver and Bill came here. We kept in touch over the years. Bill knew I was drowning in the big city and encouraged me to move here. Best thing I ever did."

Beatrice looked at Glen. "You look tired. Can I make you a coffee?"

"It's not too often that I get called in the middle of the night for an emergency. A full pot would be great, that is, if it's not too much trouble." He then added, "Sorry, but I was in such a rush that I forgot to comb my hair." He tried smoothing it out with his fingers.

Beatrice spoke before leaving the room. "Your hair looks fine." She soon returned with the coffee pot full to the brim and a single mug.

While Beatrice poured his coffee, Glen looked between both women and Richard. "Well I'm really sorry that this is happening to you. I'm now on the scene so house rules fall into place. First, the doors are locked, and they are not to be opened unless I do it. Secondly, I have closed all curtains and they need to remain closed. No exceptions. Thirdly, I am the only one who answers the phone. Any of you have a problem with those rules?"

Beatrice smiled. "Not at all. Thank you for helping two distressed women and a frightened doctor. What shall we call you officer?"

"Glen is fine." He picked up his mug and slowly drank it.

CHAPTER TWENTY-THREE

4:40 — 5:20

Charles had already relived his brother's trial over and over in his mind, and he knew Tom's conviction could have gone either way. Here he was, reliving it again.

The judge remained in his seat and was mulling over the evidence set in front of him. He glanced up. "Would Tom Lockman and his defence please rise for my verdict." Both men stood and faced the judge. "Tom Lockman, I know that drugs are prevalent in your community, actually in most communities, but one has to be responsible enough to not touch them, and if they do use them, they have to be accountable. I've been told that this is your first offence, and drugs were not an everyday use for you. However, an innocent woman was murdered while you were on your drug trip. Shooting an unarmed woman in broad daylight wasn't the smartest thing you've ever done. Suppose Mrs. Wilks had her children with her, would you have killed them too?" The judge paused. "I can only guess that on the day in question, you felt like you needed a high. But during that high you committed a most horrific crime. Not only are you responsible for the cold-blooded murder of Joan Wilks, but you have also left her children motherless and her husband without a wife. Not only have you ruined a family, but your defence is trying to find a loophole that doesn't exist. Pleading temporary insanity. What does that mean? There's no such thing as temporary insanity, it actually doesn't exist. You're either crazy or you aren't. A person can't say that they'll shoot a person one day and claim insanity, but the next day they go to work perfectly normal. It's about time that loophole was closed; it should no longer rule the justice system. Therefore, I am sentencing you to twenty-five years in prison with no chance of parole for ten years. This court is adjourned." The judge rose from the bench and went into the inner chamber.

Tom was mesmerized as he looked at his lawyer in disbelief and then turned to Jenny with tears in his eyes. He was in shock as his lawyer was the one who suggested pleading temporary insanity, as it could get him a lesser sentence. Twenty-five years was a long time to spend behind bars. Even the possibility of the sentence dropping to ten years for good behaviour still felt like a lifetime. How could his lawyer have screwed up so bad? Tom had to entertain the thought that perhaps he had the same medical problem as his brother. Charles was the over-protective brother that always seemed to be controlled by demons. Many a night would pass when Tom had heard him going from one nightmare to another, never really sleeping soundly. Now it was Tom's turn to start his own nightmare behind bars but his would be real.

Jenny was reaching for him, but he was quickly swept away from the courtroom. She and Charles were in utter shock. Hearing the judge's verdict and watching Tom being led away by two officers sent Charles' mind into a whirlwind. His hate for Sergeant Bill Smithe and this Doctor Jackson was something to be reckoned with. His revenge would come slowly as he had to plan his next move with expertise. Jenny was beside herself so Charles had to grab her and drag her out of the courtroom.

Coming back to the present, Charles topped up the wood fire and then returned to his chair. Jenny was pacing the inside of the cabin while cradling Claire on her shoulder. "I told you not to get too attached to her."

"Charles, there's something wrong with her. I think she's sick."

"What do you want me to do about it?"

"We need to take her to a hospital."

Charles' vacant black eyes glared at her. "I hope you're kidding. That's not going to happen; besides she'll be dead by eight o'clock regardless."

Jenny's face turned a sickly white. "Why do we have to kill her?"

"Because, you idiot, Bill can't have Tom out of jail by the deadline, and I always follow through on my threats."

"You're going to kill a baby?"

"Sounds like I won't have to. If she's sick, we just leave the cabin with the baby inside. Some lucky fisherman will find her body, or should I say her skeleton, in the spring on their first fishing trip. Doesn't really matter because we'll be long gone by then."

"Do you think Tom would want you to kill an innocent baby just for his freedom?"

"If Tom wasn't so spineless, he wouldn't have been in jail in the first place. You two actually belong together." He paused. "You're both weaklings. Now shut up!"

Charles closed his eyes and concentrated on what his approach would be for the next call. His mind drifted back to when he and Tom were children, playing in the living room with Nikki, their newborn sister, who was fussing. Their mother yelled at them to quit making so much noise because it was scaring their sister. It didn't matter what Tom or Charles did, both their parents yelled at them, or worse, hit them. Charles couldn't remember how many times they were sent outside to play so the baby could sleep in peace and quiet, but once they returned inside, they were punished for being gone so long. Either way, it was a bad situation for the two young boys. Tom and Charles tried several times to play with their little sister, but their mother would scold them and send them out of the room. It wasn't long before both boys detested Nikki, however, neither one of them had ever wished her any ill will. The day she died, both parents put the full blame on the boys and started leaving them alone for days on end, and then one day they never returned. Since the death of their little sister, Charles had never again liked baby girls; his sister's death had further broken the love connection that both boys should have had with their parents.

Charles sighed and looked at Jenny. "I need to make my next call!" Jenny started to tremble as she watched Charles enter the one-digit number that connected him to Bill.

"Hey, Charles, time's running out for you, so thought I'd give you a second chance at my last offer."

"What offer was that?"

"The one-hour head start of course. It could still work to your advantage. Smart guy like yourself, I may never find you, but if I were you, I wouldn't hold my breath on that. I'm actually a very persistent officer, and I don't give up easily."

"Save your breath. I'm still not interested."

"So I guess we're still playing the game then. Guess you know I'll find you, if not in the next hour, then eventually. Do you want to spend the rest of your life looking over your shoulder? Just so you know, if anything happens to Claire, I'll make it my life long mission to find you and put you behind bars." Bill hesitated then added, "No, maybe I'll just shoot you; that works for me. Scumbags like you don't deserve a prison cell with three square meals a day. You deserve to be six feet below ground in an unmarked grave." Bill paused. "Yes, I could comfortably kill you with no regrets. Do you know, Charles, that if I discharge even one shot from my weapon; I have to fill out pages of paperwork? It's time consuming, but it will be well worth the effort."

Charles was out of his chair and once again pacing around the cabin. What was it about Bill that drove him so crazy? "I could just leave her here and walk away. A baby her size might last a few days, but would eventually starve to death. Sounds like a painful way for an infant to die."

"Not as painful as the death you'll have when I find you."

"That seems to be the problem, Bill, isn't it?"

"What is?"

Charles let out a terrifying laugh. "You haven't found me yet."

"You have no idea how close we are to your location."

"I venture to say that you're not even close to finding me."

"Believe what you want, but be prepared because we're closer than you think. The highway roadblocks are set up so there's no easy escape for you. Let's cut to the chase and let me talk to Jenny."

"Not going to happen. I don't trust you."

"Feeling's mutual. I don't trust you as far as I can spit."

"The baby's fine."

"I already told you, her name's Claire. She has parents and grandparents who love her."

Charles cut him off, "How do you know that she isn't dead already?"

"I know she's still alive."

"How can you be so sure?"

"I've dealt with enough criminals like you to know that the only way for you to truly hurt me and get the satisfaction you crave is for you to kill her in front of me."

Charles hadn't thought about that. He slowly spoke, "That's a great idea. I'll have to consider it."

Bill responded, "Enough bullshit, let me talk to Jenny."

Charles covered the receiver and handed the phone to her. "Put the kid down on the bed and talk to Bill. I don't have to remind you what to say."

Jenny carefully put Claire on the bed between the pillows then took the phone and softly spoke, "Claire's not well. I'm not sure what's wrong with her."

The phone was ripped out of Jenny's hand. Charles was so mad that he slapped her hard across the face. Jenny screamed and fell to the floor. Blood was running down her chin from the cut on her lower lip and her face had already started to swell up. She slowly crawled over to the bed and lifted herself up to face Charles. Outraged, she pulled the rusty knife from her pocket and started running towards him. She stopped dead in her tracks when she saw the gun pointed at her head. The eyes that stared at her from beyond the gun terrified Jenny, and she dropped the knife. She started to back away, but Charles didn't lower the gun. She saw him cock the trigger.

She pleaded, "No, Charles! Don't shoot! Please don't do this!" In despair, she raised her hands to protect her face from the inevitable bullet. The scream she let out sent chills down Bill's spine, but the gun shots sent him into despair. He glanced at Daniel and then back at the phone. He hated not knowing what was happening at the other end of the line, but he also knew it wasn't good for Jenny or Claire.

Bill yelled, "What's going on, Charles?"

His reply was full of anger and vengeance. "Guess who's in control now?" The call abruptly ended.

Charles stormed out of the cabin, screaming like a maniac, randomly firing bullets into the air until his gun was empty. He cursed under his breath, hoping there was no one close enough to hear the shots. If anyone did, hopefully they would think that a hunter had just shot an animal and could now provide enough meat to feed his family for the winter. Charles reloaded his gun and continued wandering into the bushes, kicking at anything that got in his way. His foot was still tender from the last time he went on a kicking rampage, so he was more careful this time. Somehow he avoided the two remaining traps.

Bill wasn't going to beat him. He needed to kill the cop and that doctor who had testified against Tom. He was okay with killing Jenny and Claire, then just disappearing. Tom could rot in jail as far as he was concerned. Just means the first people arriving at the cabin would find two dead bodies instead of one.

Out of the corner of his eye, he spotted movement. Not wanting to fire anymore shots, he slowly pulled his knife from his back pocket and turned to find the same deer from his earlier encounter had returned to the cabin. With a loud shout, he lunged at it and drove the blade into its' throat.

"This is my cabin and you're trespassing!" He was amazed at the thrill he got watching the animal die. Charles whispered, "Maybe Bill's right, and I really am crazy."

He wiped the bloody knife blade on his shirt before putting it away. Dragging the carcass deep into the woods, he left it there to rot. Under different circumstances, he probably would have dressed it and given it to Tom and Jenny to help them get through the winter, but that wasn't going to happen as he had murder on his mind, not preservation. Charles walked around, checking on the last two bear traps, which were still intact. Satisfied, he returned to the cabin, but first went to the trunk of his car. He pulled out the bottle of whiskey again.

Charles conceded, "Damn, may as well drink this myself." Alternating between swigs of alcohol and puffs on his cigarette, he slowly took control of his temper. A few more hours and this nightmare would be over. He was now pleasantly drunk, but felt that he would be sober enough before eight o'clock. Staggering his way back into the cabin, he flopped into his chair and glanced across the room at Jenny. She was slumped in a heap on top of the bed, her back facing Charles. Claire was curled under Jenny's arm. Even though her face was away from him, Charles thought he could see that blood was still flowing from her split lip. She got what she deserved, he shrugged.

Charles was very pissed off. Bill had no right prying into his family. It was obvious he had done his homework or had got his officers to pry into his history. His record was somewhat clean up to this point, only a few violations, but this latest venture would scar his life forever. He would be the one to take the fall if this went sideways, as Jenny was unaware of his intentions when they kidnapped the baby. His only consolation was that he wouldn't get caught. If Claire was eliminated and there was no body, Charles could imagine Bill's despair. Years later, her case would still remain unsolved. He could imagine the baby's photo on the side of milk cartons with a phone number to call if you knew any details about the child. Charles knew there were places he could hide where Bill wouldn't be able to find him. He had friends that would take him in, no questions asked.

CHAPTER TWENTY-FOUR

5:10 — 5:50

Bill's body was trembling as he looked across the table at Daniel before placing his phone on the desk. Hearing gunshots at the other end of the line threw Bill into a state of disbelief and panic. He recalled himself screaming after he heard the shots. 'What's going on Charles?' He also remembered Charles' reply, 'Guess who's in control now?' What had Bill done wrong? He had played by the rule book and look where it got him. He started to question his qualifications as a good negotiator. Bill was slowly suffocating, so not saying a word he rose from his chair and walked towards his office. The entire force was in shock and was speechless as they watched their sergeant leaving the room. Closing the door behind him, he leaned against it, feeling like a defeated man. Being upset with himself, Bill just wanted to hit something. His imagination was working overtime. Had Charles really shot Jenny and Claire? Had they both died instantly or was the wacko now watching them die a slow and painful death? Bill hadn't used his negotiating skill for several years, but he was warned against bringing in additional help, so he felt responsible for everything that had gone wrong. Knowing Charles would only deal with him meant that Bill was at the top of the maniac's agenda, and maybe setting his brother free was not his main objective. He tried to clear his head and remain positive while mumbling, "What did Charles have to gain by eliminating Jenny and Claire when there were still over two hours left?"

Glancing around his office, his eyes zeroed in on his three certificates hanging on the wall. Bill stood in front of them and roughly pulled them off the wall, shoving them into the bottom drawer of his filing cabinet. He had already decided that if this case turned bad, he was going to burn all of them. He had to clear his head and try to think. Sitting at his desk, in frustration, he slammed his fists hard onto its' surface. What was his next move? If Don came to him asking for advice, what could he tell him?

There was a soft tap at his door, and Don inquired, "You okay, boss? Can I come in?"

Bill tried to compose himself. "Sure, why not."

Don entered the room and closed the door behind him. First thing he noticed, other than Bill sitting at his desk looking distressed, was the lack of certificates hanging on his wall. He didn't mention the missing degrees, but instead approached Bill carrying a file and placed it in the center of his desk. Bill inquired, "What's this?"

Don took the seat across from him. "Sam just gave me this file. It's the medical report on Charles."

Bill was shocked. "How did he get it so quick?"

"You don't want to know boss. He had to call in a lot of favours."

When Bill opened the file he was silent and then shocked, but not totally surprised. Charles showed signs of schizophrenia. The report also noted that he refused medication for the condition. Earlier Bill had suspected Charles' condition, but he never mentioned it to Don, as he wasn't one hundred percent sure. Now seeing it in black and white confirmed it. He should have followed his gut feeling. It had always worked in the past.

Don looked across the desk at Bill. "You don't look surprised."

"I was hoping that this time my gut feeling was wrong."

Don changed the subject. "I've already told the men that your last call doesn't leave the building. We're still not one hundred percent sure that Jenny and Claire were shot. If he'd killed them, then he wouldn't have any reason to continue the game. He's going to want to beat you into the ground, so killing them at this time makes no sense."

"I agree," Bill mumbled, but knew he didn't sound convincing. He started to break down. "Don, she's just a baby. How could he possibly be so callous as to shoot a baby, let alone his brother's wife?" He rose from his chair and went to the window. "We're running out of time, and I don't know about you, but I'm not sure what our next move even is." He turned to Don. "What am I going to tell Beatrice, Richard, and Kimberley? I really screwed up this case. I'm afraid my marriage is over, and the trust I had with Kimberley and Richard has been shattered."

Don responded, "You were right to send Tom to prison, so don't second guess your decision. He's a murderer and jail is where he belongs, plus who knew that his conviction would come back to bite you years later."

Bill looked at the ceiling and spoke with defeat in his voice. "What do I do? I became an officer because I believed in the justice system and look where it's got me. If I beat Charles and get Claire back, will there always be someone else following in his footsteps? Do you have any idea how many crooks I've put behind bars?"

"No, I don't Bill, but I'm sure they all deserve to be there. You're second guessing yourself. You're a good officer, well respected by every man that works under your leadership."

Bill looked worried. "I'm just afraid that I'll start getting calls at midnight on a regular basis. How can I protect my family from further threats?"

"You can't do it on your own Bill, but the force will always be there to help you protect your loved ones."

"I don't think I could survive another episode of this nightmare. I'm tired, and I guess you've already figured out that I don't want to do it anymore."

Bill heard the sharp knock on his door before it opened. Daniel entered the office with a wide grin on his face. "I think we just got the break we need. You're going to want to hear this."

Bill shot out of his chair as if he'd been hit by a bolt of lightening. His chair smashed against the outside wall of his office. He immediately turned his despair into hope as he and Don rushed out to Daniel's desk. The three men sat in front of the recording device and slipped on their headsets. Bill was ready to listen, knowing that this might be his last chance to save Claire. Daniel pushed the play button and the entire call that he had just finished played out for him. Sparing Bill the pain of the last few seconds, Daniel stopped the tape before the gun shots. At the end of the recording, Bill looked puzzled and then questioned Daniel. "I thought you said there was a break in the case?" Bill thought he must be over thinking. If Daniel said there was a break in the case, it had to be there.

"You didn't hear it?"

"No, what was I supposed to hear?"

Daniel stood up and spoke to the officers in the room. "Hey guys, we need complete silence, just for a few minutes please." This time the headsets were put aside and all officers listened intently. Daniel rewound the tape and hit the play button a second time. "Okay, listen again."

Partway through the recording, Bill asked, "What's that in the background?"

Daniel was pleased. "So you heard it too. I wasn't sure if I was imagining it."

Don spoke with excitement. "Play it again, but this time pause briefly just before the sound."

Daniel hit the pause button when he heard the sound and slightly rewound the tape to just before the unknown noise then played it through. He repeated this several times as all officers listened intently before Daniel spoke, "I've tried to play around with the settings, but maybe I can enhance the background more and soften the conversation." He played around with the buttons until he had accomplished what he hoped would help. "Let's try this again." Although the sound was faint, the entire force was listening carefully.

Bob and Jim used their skills from when they searched the Panorama Room. With their eyes closed, they both concentrated on the tape being played. Both of their eyes shot open at the same time and they spoke in unison. "Clickety clack, clickety clack, it's a train!"

Don was excited. "Oh my God, you're both right."

Bill shot out of his chair and ran to the whiteboard, adding train to the bottom of the list. He then turned to his men. "Okay guys, this is the break we needed. This could be our last chance, so let's work it to our advantage. Bob, you call the local train depot and find out the schedule from here to Sidville. If Charles is hiding between these towns, we should be able to narrow down the search site."

For the first time in several hours, Bill felt he was making headway. He only hoped that Charles had not eliminated Claire and Jenny, but he was struggling to put those feelings aside. He felt a glimmer of hope.

Bob was already looking up the number. "On it, boss."

Bill then turned to Jack, but he was already ten steps ahead of his sergeant. "I'll call my fishermen and hunter buddies to find out if there are any cabins they could be hiding in."

In a very short time, Bill felt like he was finally making headway on the case, knowing that now he and Don could do their jobs. Bill felt a load lift from his shoulders, but still hoped they could find Claire in time and alive. By now, her sugar levels would be way off, so every minute counted. The place was bustling with officers on their phones, connecting with friends or family who could help narrow down the search site.

Bob called across his desk to Bill. "I just got off the phone with Jim Baxter who is the night shift supervisor at the train depot. According to him, the train would be about the halfway point to Sidville, which means the location is somewhere on the flats."

Bill's mind was once again overwhelmed with an old memory. His glimmer of hope was turned back to despair. Several years ago, a small child was out hiking with his parents in this same location and became separated from them. It took Bill and his team eighteen hours to find that child. Claire didn't have that much time. He was well aware of the massive thirty square miles that had to be searched. He started to despair again. His men couldn't possibly cover that great an area in the two hours left of Charles' game. Bill had been in charge of the rescue operation back then, and once again it had been a fight against the clock as fall had been closing in on his men.

Although Bill was frustrated he now had to somehow manage to cut sixteen hours off the search time. If he couldn't do it, then the game was over. His men would still have to deal with bears going into hibernation, cold temperatures, plus the wet terrain that was left after the big storm. The search several years ago had been stressful, but the boy's parents had assured Bill that their son had warm clothing. He tried not to compare the cases, but the child must have been so scared, whereas Claire was too small to know what was going on. The boy's parents were beside themselves, but were also very active in the search.

Not only were the flats extensive in area, but they were also heavily treed, with trails meandering off in all directions and few regular roads. Their main advantage now was that they were sure Charles must be in one of the cabins, so suddenly, the thirty square miles became a manageable area. Bill managed to calm himself somewhat, being partially confident that Charles was most likely hiding out in a cabin somewhere in those thirty square miles.

Years earlier, all his officers had been called in for the land search, while Bill had called in helicopters to search from the air. The area was massive, but Bill never gave up. He had officers doing eight-hour shifts, using flashlights at night and constantly calling out the child's name. After a long eighteen hours, the child was found huddled under a tree, very cold, hungry, scared, and crying. He was carried out to a waiting ambulance where his parents were overjoyed at their son's safe return. A doctor had checked the boy's vitals while he lay under a warm blanket with a cup of hot soup in his hands. Bill was relieved once he was found and hoped Claire's outcome would also be positive.

Several rivers and streams had eroded the earth tonight, making road access difficult, especially after that earlier downpour. The precipitation that had fallen previously could very easily hamper their search. It may be almost impossible to cross some of those rivers.

Bill went to the whiteboard and drew a horizontal line on the board. At one end he put Blue Ridge and the other end he put Sidville. He made an ellipse at the halfway point. "That's a big area guys, so we need to narrow it down even more."

Bill noticed Jack who raised his finger while he was on the phone. "Thanks buddy. I owe you a case of beer." Jack got up from his desk and went to the board. He marked four Xs inside Bill's ellipse. "These, gentlemen, are the locations of four cabins that Charles could be hiding in."

Don, Jack and Bill moved to the topographical map that was still on Don's desk, and Bill drew an ellipse around the new area incorporating the four cabins.

Jack added, "My friend is sending us the GPS coordinates, at least as close as he can estimate them."

Bill responded, "Gentlemen, put them on your phones; it'll help us to locate the cabins quicker."

Don turned to Bill. "Things are going to start to move quickly, so now would be a good time to call Richard and tell him to be prepared. We leave here just after your six o'clock call."

Without thinking, Bill responded, "On it, boss."

Don laughed, "I think now is a good time to turn the last of this case over to you. Don't fret, I'll still fill out the paperwork and sign it."

Bill went to his office and closed the door behind him before calling Richard's house.

Kimberley, Richard, and Glen were whispering across the room while Beatrice was once again napping on the couch.

Glen asked, "How can she sleep with so much going on around her?"

Kimberley grinned. "Guess it has to do with her spiked tea."

Glen was slightly taken back. "You spiked your own aunt's tea?"

Richard interjected, "No, I did it." He then added, "It's just two crushed Tylenol tablets mixed in with her tea."

Kimberley added, "We were both concerned with her health so he gave her a sedative to help her relax."

Richard laughed, "Do you think she'll ever forgive me for spiking her tea? Or for that matter, ever trust me to make her tea again?"

"I won't tell her if you don't."

The phone next to Glen rang. He checked the caller ID before answering, "It's the station."

Beatrice immediately woke up. "What did I miss?"

Glen whispered, "It's Bill." He then answered, "Hello."

"I need to talk to Richard."

Glen passed the phone over to him, and Richard answered, "Hello."

"I've got some good news. Our team has narrowed down the site where Claire is being held. My call from Charles is in fifteen minutes. After that, we'll swing by and pick you up. Don't forget your medical bag."

Richard was ecstatic. "Not a chance. I'll be ready." He hung up the phone and smiled as he announced, "They know where she's being held. I leave here just after six o'clock."

Bill hung up, then returned to the common area and glanced at his watch.

"Okay guys. Our next call is in fifteen minutes. After that, we hit the road. Jack and Bob, you're my snipers. I want you in full gear. That means bulletproof vests, headsets, sniper rifles, and night vision goggles. We can probably use them for at least an hour or so until daylight breaks."

Daniel motioned for Bill to come to his desk. "Just heard from Eli and Muhammad. No action over at Jenny's place."

Bill responded, "Maybe Charles isn't as stupid as we thought. I think we finally got the break we were waiting for, so tell them to come back to the office." Bill was about to leave when Daniel stopped him once again. Bill queried, "You need something else?"

"Once this call is over, I need your cell phone."

"Why do you need it?"

"Bill, there's no cell service on the flats."

He instantly froze. "I need my phone working for my seven o'clock call in case we haven't found him before then."

"You'll have it. I just need to program your satellite phone to work on your cell number."

"You can do that?"

"I can do almost anything involving electronics, so yes, I can do that. However, I won't be able to record the call."

"Hopefully you won't need to."

Daniel winked. "It'll work out, Bill. We'll find her."

"I sure hope so." Bill nodded his appreciation then went into his office to take another two Tylenol and pick up his weapon and ammunition. When he returned, his men were bustling around, getting their gear on and all the equipment they would need to take Charles out if necessary. He sat across from Daniel and waited for his call.

CHAPTER TWENTY - FIVE

5:55 — 6:30

Charles was counting down the minutes before his next call. He was still feeling the effects of the whiskey that he seemed to need more regularly to calm his nerves. Luckily the bottle was empty and he had discarded it somewhere in the bushes beside the cabin. The bottle shattered as it disappeared from Charles' sight, obviously hitting a rock. Right now, it was important for him to sober up. The cool fresh air around him slowly cleared his mind. He figured a short walk would work to his advantage, but when he stepped in a mud puddle his temper flared up to the boiling point again.

This game he had dreamt up was taking far too long to finish. Bill was supposed to find him by now. What would he do if eight o'clock came and went without him knowing anything about his brother's release? In frustration, he shook off his wet foot and went back into the cabin. Maybe his brother deserved to be there. Oh well, one thing he was sure of, when he passed through Sidville on his escape, with or without his brother, he would purchase another bottle of whiskey and another package of cigarettes. At that point, he may have lost the game, but he would be back a second time. Bill needed to be eliminated and he was prepared to modify his second round, making it foolproof. Obviously, he wouldn't be able to kidnap his granddaughter a second time, but maybe someone else close to him, possibly his wife or niece. That would require mastering a perfect plan. It was easy stealing a child in the middle of the night, but an adult would have to be unconscious and couldn't be moved easily to another location. That kidnapping would have to happen in daylight, so would require a lot more planning. His mind was already working overtime as it processed a possible second kidnapping.

He picked up his flashlight and made another trip to the outhouse. He then checked on his two remaining bear traps again, carefully manoeuvring around them so as not to trip them himself. He had found out the hard way that they were impossible to reset. He still had a sore foot from kicking the bear as his proof. He had marked the trap locations by breaking several branches on the tree closest to the traps, but Bill and his team wouldn't know to look out for that. Happy that both traps were still intact and ready for a victim, Charles could visualize either Bill or one of his officers taking that fateful step. On his way back to the cabin, Charles got wet from the trees that were still dripping from the earlier rainstorm. Once he was clear of the trees, he looked up at the sky and noticed a few stars peeking through the clouds that were slowly opening up. The ground beneath him, however, was still saturated and it forced him to walk around the puddles to keep his feet somewhat dry.

All was quiet around the cabin, except for the odd creature moving within the trees, hopefully not tripping his last two traps. He could hear an owl off in the distance, but it was nothing to be concerned with.

Once back in the cabin, he spoke to Jenny. "You awake?" There was no response so he shrugged her off. "Fine, be that way. I don't need you on the phone anyway. You don't know how to follow the rules." He plunked himself down in his chair and patiently waited for the hour to pass before his next call. Glancing around the cabin, he was somewhat pleased with his choice of locations. The building was cozy with the fire heating the entire building, but Charles knew that soon he would have to let the fire go out, and it wouldn't take long for the cool air to take over the once warm site. He planned on returning at some point and going hunting and fishing, that is, if it was safe for him to return at all. He glanced down at his watch, then punched the number, waiting for Bill to answer.

Bill answered, "Hello."

Charles didn't skip a beat. "Hey, Bill. Time flies by when you're having fun, at least it's fun at my end. You must be at whit's end, trying to locate me."

"Not at all, but how do you know that my team and I aren't already close to your location?"

"I'm not stupid, Bill." Charles continued, "I've already walked around my location and everything is quiet, like this baby next to me. She really is beautiful, guess she didn't get her looks from you."

"Why would she? I'm not her father."

Charles asked, "How awful of me for not asking about the baby's parents. How're they handling the little time they have left before their baby dies?"

"I've already talked to them and both are ready to testify at your trial. Isn't it coincidental how dysfunctional your family really is? Soon you'll be joining Tom in prison." Bill then added, "No, maybe you'll be in a different prison. I think a separate location would work better. Don't want the two of you getting too chummy."

Charles was very aggressive when he asked, "It's already six o'clock, so any news on my brother?"

Bill ran his fingers through his already messy hair. "Hey Charles, our last call ended with gunshots. Is everyone there okay?"

Charles laughed, "Wouldn't you like to know."

"Actually yes I would. Are Claire and Jenny safe?"

"Maybe yes, maybe no."

Bill was starting to sweat. Charles was now starting to play hardball. "Guess I'll find out soon enough. Let me talk to Jenny."

"She's not available right now."

"Okay. Where is she?"

"Asleep."

"Wake her up, I can wait."

Charles was losing his patience. "She's not available, so take it from me that the baby is fine, plus Jenny doesn't want to talk to you anymore." Charles then added, "New rule, you talk to me or no one."

"Here's my new rule, I talk to Jenny or this call is over. Don't think of me badly, but I still don't trust you."

"You either hear it from me or not at all."

"Tell you what. When she's available, you call me, then we'll talk." The line went dead.

Charles couldn't get his swear words out fast enough. He knew the only way to release all the stress building up inside him was to murder Bill and anyone else who got in his way. He stormed out of the cabin, totally enraged and mumbling, "You're dead Sergeant Bill Smithe." Snarling, he added, "Too bad for your wife, it'll crush her to have lost two husbands and a grandchild. It'll be another blow when I kill the doctor. So much tragedy for one person to have to live with. Her niece will never forgive you for not saving her child." He sneered. "Two widows in one family would be devastating."

Charles was somewhat pleased with how he was thinking. He was tired of playing this game, so he returned indoors and walked around the cabin looking for ways to vent his anger. He crossed the room and looked at Jenny who was still lying on her side, facing away from him. There was blood on her pillow, which he expected had come from her lip when he hit her. He wasn't sure why she was always challenging him. His plan was perfect and it was about time that she realized it.

Jenny had an arm over the baby as if she was protecting the child. The baby was pale, but sleeping soundly. Charles poked Jenny in the center of her back, but she didn't respond, so he became instantly confused. Had he really shot and killed her in one of his fits of rage? He wasn't going any closer to feel for a pulse or look at her face. At this point, he couldn't change what he had done, so was prepared to lie his way out of it. Tom only had to know that Jenny was dead and one of Bill's officers had pulled the trigger.

Charles moved towards the table and drew out his knife. Slowly but meticulously, he started carving two words into the rough wood surface, 'Bill's Dead.' As he slowly destroyed the tabletop, he repeated to himself. "Bill's dead." He felt his body slowly relaxing. Stepping back from the table, he admired his handy work. Every fisherman or hunter who came to the cabin would see the table and wonder about the story behind the artistic carving. Charles thought about signing his initials, but decided it was better to leave it as is. He returned the knife to his back pocket.

The alcohol was slowly being absorbed by his body, and Charles knew that he had to be spot on for his confrontational visit with Bill, if the smart cop indeed managed to locate him. Knowing that Bill was a professional, their meeting was inevitable, and he was prepared for the climax of his well laid out plan. Charles had been going to the target range for several years, so he felt prepared to take on the sergeant and the entire Blue Ridge Police Department if necessary. Charles knew for a fact that Bill wouldn't come alone, so hopefully the bear traps would improve his odds of killing Bill, thus ending this ridiculous game. Nine times out of ten, Charles hit the bulls-eye, as long as it was stationary. He had done some bird hunting in the past, but didn't do so well with a moving target, so hopefully Bill would be standing still. If Bill had a gun pointed at his chest, hopefully he wouldn't be stupid enough to move.

Charles felt safe within the walls that surrounded him. Planning this kidnapping and seeing it fall into place was rewarding. There were four cabins in the vicinity, but this one offered the best protection. Two of them were rotted out shacks that offered no warmth or security and were about to collapse in on themselves. Charles never looked at the last cabin once he had found this place. From the front window, anyone who approached could be seen. Yes, he had definitely made a wise choice. Glancing at his watch, Charles was pleased that he managed to not only vent his anger, but also kill half an hour before his next call. He was pleased that the next two calls would be to his advantage. Jenny wouldn't take the receiver from him again, not after she fouled up the last call.

It was time to let the fire go out inside the cabin. It would get cold fast, but it was important that when Bill found him, the place would appear to be empty. If Charles suspected that Bill was approaching the cabin, he would hide himself outside and attack before the cop even got close. He smiled as his plan was coming together.

He once more glanced at Jenny and decided that if she was going to ignore him, he would do the same. She served her purpose at the beginning, which was to take care of the baby, but she was no longer necessary. If she was dead, so be it. If she was still alive, she wouldn't give him anymore flack and he would simply abandon her at the cabin. There's no way that she could walk out to the main road and hitchhike. It was too far, and staying here meant she would starve to death. Charles returned to his chair and found a chunk of wood lying on the floor next to his seat. He picked it up, then pulling his knife from his pocket, he sat down and started to whittle. He found the process of hacking away at the wood relaxing. His next few hours could prove to be busy, so he needed to clear his mind and be prepared for the end of his game, meaning Bill's death.

CHAPTER TWENTY-SIX

6:05 — 7:00

Muhammad and Eli had just returned from their stake out at Jenny's to an office scrambling around getting ready to hit the road. Bill nodded when they entered the room. "Okay guys. These next few hours are going to be critical. Greg, Jim, and Eric, you stay here and hold down the fort." Bill nodded and turned to the rest of his men. "Get ready, guys, it's time to go hunting. Just so you all know, Charles is mine. I prefer to kill him, but we need to bring him in alive if possible. Death is too easy an out for him, prison is what he deserves."

Bill walked into his office, put on his bulletproof vest and grabbed his coat. He glanced at his empty wall and half considered re-hanging his certificates, but until Claire was safely in her parent's arms, they would stay tucked away in his filing cabinet. He didn't want to jinx the mission, so they would stay in the cabinet. He took a quick glance out of his window. All was still dark, but not for much longer. He was finally able to clear his mind and concentrate on the case. Bill looked across his desk to the picture of Beatrice, taken on their wedding day. He picked it up and studied her face. She was so beautiful and all smiles. He hoped in a matter of a few hours her face would once again look radiant. He quickly placed a kiss on the picture and returned it to his desk. "I love you, Beatrice, and I'll bring Claire home safe, I promise."

He returned to the common area where Daniel signalled for him to come to his desk. "I need your phone, Bill. It'll only take me a few minutes to set it up."

Bill waited and watched how easily Daniel accomplished the task. His officers all had different talents and this was just one example. Once he had the satellite phone in his jacket pocket, Bill said to Daniel, "I need you to stay here and man the phones. If this satellite phone should fail, I need you here to talk on my behalf."

"That isn't possible. Your number is now on the satellite phone and not on your cell phone. You can't have one number on two phones at the same time. Right now, your cell phone is numberless, useless."

"Fingers crossed then, just hope that doesn't become an issue."

Daniel looked at Bill and inquired, "What do I say if he calls the office on a regular line looking for you?"

"I don't know, use your imagination and tell him I'm sick in the bathroom throwing up, just anything to distract him. Tell him I've gone to comfort my wife and Claire's parents and I probably left my phone in my vehicle."

"Leave it to me. I'll deal with it."

Seeing his two teams were all geared up, Bill motioned them over to Don's desk. "We use two vehicles with a sniper in each car." The GPS co-ordinates for the four cabins had been marked on the topographical map. "Bob, your team will take the two closest cabins from here, snap a photo of the cabin co-ordinates and you're ready to go." He then added, "Wear your headsets men, we need to keep in close contact, and if one of these cabins pans out, you call for backup immediately. Richard has to be there for the takedown as Claire will need her medicine ASAP, but the doctor has to be kept safely away from the main action until it's safe for him to approach." He then turned to Jack. "Take a photo of our co-ordinates and then we're off to pick up Richard.

"Already done, boss."

Bill, Jack, and Muhammad left the building. As Bill was about to climb into the passenger seat of the cruiser, he noticed the damaged windshield. "What the hell happened here?"

Jack responded, "It's a long story, boss, but not mine to tell. You'll have to ask Bob or Jim, but the story circulating is that a grizzly decided to try and get into their vehicle with them inside." Jack ran back into the precinct to exchange the vehicle keys for a different car. He slipped into the driver's seat. Bill was already on his phone calling Richard's house.

Glen answered at the other end. "Hi Bill, Richard's ready."

"I'm on my way. Make sure he remembers his medical kit."

"It's already in his hands."

"Glen, I can't come in, our time is running out. Tell Beatrice and Kimberley that I love them."

"I will."

"Be there in five minutes."

Richard was standing on the sidewalk as the cruiser drove up. He jumped in the back seat carrying his medical bag. Bill looked at the front porch and saw Beatrice and Kimberley hugging each other and Glen waving at them. Bill yelled to Jack. "Stop!"

Jack obliged and Bill jumped out of the vehicle and ran to the house quickly to kiss both ladies before running back to the cruiser. He called behind him, "Love you both."

Tears were streaming down the ladies' cheeks as they watched Bill disappear inside the vehicle. Jack hit the gas peddle and they were soon swallowed up by the darkness.

Richard said to Bill. "I'm not sure if I'm out of line, but I ordered an ambulance to be close to the rescue site, just in case Claire needs something that I don't have in my bag. I just need to tell them where they're going." He added, "Hopefully nothing unforeseen will happen, but if it does, I'll cross that bridge if I have to."

Bill was impressed. "Good thinking, but just to be safe, let's bring a second ambulance just in case. Here are the four sets of co-ordinates you can send to them. Tell them no lights or sirens and tell the drivers to stay back until they hear from us." Bill watched Richard texting the co-ordinates to the first ambulance that was waiting for instructions and asked them to forward the information to the second ambulance. Bill was overwhelmed with guilt and still feeling sick to his stomach. He should have told Richard about the last call, but he didn't want to admit that he may have failed, which meant that his adversary had won. He was still muddling everything through his mind, and it just didn't make sense. If Charles really wanted his brother free, he would keep Claire alive, right up to the last minute, especially if he thought Bill wasn't even close to finding him.

Although it was dark inside the vehicle, Richard could sense the stress that Bill must have been going through. He felt like he could cut the emotions and tensions inside the vehicle with a surgical knife. Richard knew that something was obviously on the sergeant's mind. He inquired, "You okay, Bill?"

"As well as can be expected, considering the circumstances. I'm not sure how this is going to play out, but just so you know, I'm committed one hundred percent to getting Claire back. I just want you to know that."

"I know that Bill, but can I ask you a question?"

"Fire away." He backtracked. "Maybe that's a poor choice of words."

Richard sighed. "Good does win over evil, doesn't it?"

Bill didn't hesitate. "It sure does. Why else do you think I became an officer? I picked the winner's side. We're starting our search at the furthest point, in hopes that Charles would want to be closer to Sidville for a fast escape, while the other team is concentrating on the cabins closer to Blue Ridge." Bill turned his attention to Muhammad. "Thanks for helping with the search. You really weren't obligated to come in for another couple of days."

"Glad you called me. I've always believed that bonding immediately with my fellow officers is extremely important. I want them to know that they can count on me in a moment's notice." He paused before continuing, "Do cases like this one happen very often here?"

Bill responded, "First one to my knowledge."

Jack answered, "I hope to hell it's the last one. We're getting too old for all nighters."

Bill half laughed, "I'm the oldest one in this vehicle, and right now I feel like shit. I'm convinced the entire force would just as soon shoot Charles rather than let the system take over. If he walks, he better move to Timbuktu, well away from Blue Ridge or he'll be constantly stalked by every officer in the province."

Richard was beside himself. His imagination was working overtime. He had seen numerous patients come into the hospital with diabetes problems, some already in a coma. Treating an adult patient in that state was manageable. He only had to read their sugar levels, inject the insulin into them, and then leave the nurse in charge. Claire was an entirely different situation. Being a baby meant that she had little body weight so her insulin dose would be tricky, and if she had already slipped into a coma, she would require constant monitoring. He would have to try to get her to drink lots of liquids to keep her from dehydrating any further and if she was already unconscious could require intravenous.

Richard felt the vehicle jerk as it turned off the highway and started the bumpy drive on the gravel road. As much as Jack tried to avoid ruts and potholes, there were just too many, so he ploughed on. Richard turned to the newest officer, Muhammad. "I heard you were new to the area. Thanks for coming out and helping me get my daughter back."

"You're welcome. How're you holding up?"

"I've had better days."

"So you're a doctor?"

"Yes, I am."

"Glad to have you here just in case the takedown goes sideways."

Richard replied, "Not exactly a good start on your first day of work."

"Best to be thrown into the deep end, that way the team can see your true value." He laughed, "It's not like they can exactly fire me, but I do want to be accepted and productive."

"You married?"

Muhammad replied, "I am. We used to live in Alberta." He laughed again. "My wife thought that when we arrived in Edmonton we must have made a wrong turn and were actually at the North Pole. Neither one of us could stand the cold winters, so we were more than ready to move on. One day we went exploring and came upon the magnificent Rockies. The next summer we drove through them and came out to beautiful British Columbia. We were both smitten. When the posting came out for Blue Ridge, we both looked at each other and started packing as soon as I had been accepted. We'll never look back. Neither one of us misses the cold winters and flat terrain. We've been told that the scenery in this area is breath taking. Really looking forward to exploring this area, but night time doesn't exactly do it justice."

Richard spoke, "It really is a beautiful part of the province." He then turned his attention to Bill, who seemed deep in thought. "Bill, I know that you and your entire team are working hard to get Claire back, and if anyone can save her it's you." Richard was extremely nervous and added, "Just before I go into surgery, I'm always anxious. Even taking out an appendix, which I can do in my sleep, still comes with risks, and those risks scare me the most."

He was about to speak again when the vehicle swerved dangerously to the right, tossing the men around inside the cruiser.

Jack shouted, "Shit! Almost hit the bastard!" He regained control of the vehicle then said, "Sorry guys. I forgot about the damn moose that would be grazing and crossing the road without any warning. An accident at this time is not even an option."

Richard nervously inquired, "How far away are we?"

Bill looked at Jack's GPS. "Close now."

Jack turned a few more corners then shut off the engine. Bill turned to Richard. "You stay in the vehicle for now. If we find her, I'll come and get you."

Richard nervously replied, "Okay."

Bill, Muhammad, and Jack loaded up their gear and placed their night vision goggles over their faces, then followed their GPS signal. The technology of night vision goggles had been around for some time, but it was only recently that the Blue Ridge Police Department had got their hands on this new technology. The darkness was instantly turned to a bright green and the officers were able to manoeuvre efficiently in the darkness surrounding them.

With weapons drawn, Bill whispered to Muhammad and Jack through their headsets. "I don't want him to know that we're on to him, the element of surprise is our best option at this time."

Richard grabbed his medical bag, put it on his lap, and watched the three men hunched over, weapons drawn and hugging close to the bushes as they moved along the side of the road. Once the men disappeared into the darkness, Richard felt alone and helpless. The void that surrounded him was also the same darkness that he felt within himself. Nervously, he locked the doors to the vehicle, closed his eyes and said a silent prayer for his baby daughter.

As Richard sat quietly in the dark vehicle, he suddenly he felt a slight nudge against the side of the cruiser. Thinking he was imagining it, he brushed it off as a nervous reaction. The second nudge turned into a terrifying fear for his life. He quickly placed his medical bag on the seat and then slumped down onto the floor, hoping the intruder wasn't this Charles character. He had no weapon or means of protecting himself. He didn't have a headset, so stayed paralyzed on the floor, hoping whoever was outside didn't know that he was there. His breathing seemed to overtake the silence inside the vehicle and surely whoever was outside could hear him. He thought about reaching up and hitting the horn to scare whoever was outside away, but he knew that the noise could also alert Charles that they were close, so he remained hunkered down and kept silent.

According to their GPS, the cabin was just around the next corner. The air was cool and the officers' breath misted in front of their faces. Shadows from moving trees and underbrush kept them on full alert. Night vision goggles meant the men were able to dodge puddles that had accumulated from the earlier downpour, but the uneven road meant their walk was slower than they had hoped for. Giving up, they plunged forward, hitting every puddle, leaving their feet soaking wet. Bill glanced down at his watch.

Jack inquired, "How's our time?"

Bill was frustrated. "Only fifteen more minutes before he calls again. I sure hope this is his location and I can take his call and then organize the take down."

Jack responded, "I hope so too."

As the cabin came into view, it was obvious that it was empty. No sign of a vehicle or fire burning within the building. Bill stood behind some bushes to keep out of sight as Jack and Muhammad indicated they were going in for a closer look, especially behind the building; looking for a vehicle. Bill quietly moved between trees and bushes, slowly getting closer to the building. The cabin was more of a rotted out lean-to, with only a few boards holding up the entire frame. Bill stayed in the shadows as he approached the shack and cautiously glanced into the window. Once he was convinced the place was empty, he opened the door and glanced in. The odour hit him like a brick wall. The smell was a mixture of rotting food and bear droppings. He backed out of the building and closed the door. Jack and Muhammad came around the corner to find Bill looking rather green.

Bill wrinkled up his nose. "Don't go in there."

Jack responded, "Why not?"

"Fine, go if you want, but the smell is almost toxic."

"Gotcha. Thanks for the heads up."

All three officers were frustrated and quickly ran back to the vehicle. Bill stopped dead in his tracks, warning his men not to approach the cruiser. Bill began to panic. "Where the hell is Richard?"

Jack responded, "In the vehicle where we left him."

Bill was shaking now. "Why can't we see his shadow through the front window? He's not here! Damn! Charles must be close by and when he saw Richard on his own, he grabbed him." Bill was upset that he screwed up once again. "Why didn't I leave one of you with him?" Bill felt sick to his stomach. Mentally, it was like he was riding a rollercoaster. Half an hour earlier he had felt a real high with the latest tip, but that was once again taken from him as he felt the car going over the crest of the ride, only to plunge down into a deep depression once again. Bill wasn't sure how much more his body could take. He was drowning in frustration and exhaustion. Claire was dead without Richard. If Richard was with Claire right now, would Charles allow him to treat her? How could he possibly explain to Beatrice and Kimberley that he had also lost Richard? Bill felt like he was in a bad dream, getting one step closer to Claire, and then being pushed two steps backwards. Was there no end to this nightmare?

Muhammad slowly moved to the side of the vehicle and pointed at the front passenger door. He whispered into his headset. "There's damage to the door. Ouch. This door is going to need some repairs." He also observed a massive amount of slime running down the outside of the window. "Not sure what the hell that is on the window, but I'm not touching it." He was able to look beyond the yucky window and see inside the car.

Bill was frustrated. "First a windshield and now a door." He slammed his fist onto the front hood, mentally kicking himself for another mistake he had made.

Muhammad flashed a light inside. He whispered a second time. "Richard's bag is still on the back seat."

Bill commented, "Won't do Claire any good if Richard doesn't have it on him."

Jack carefully worked his way to the other side of the vehicle and pointed his flashlight into the back seat. He shouted to Bill who was not only depressed, but had also moved away from the front of the car, wanting to wallow in his feelings of despair. Jack shouted, "He's here Bill! Not sure why he's on the floor, but he's here."

Bill felt a weight lifted from his shoulders. "Are you sure?"

"Definitely." Jack unlocked the door and all three officers saw a very scared Richard crouched down behind the front seat. "No time to ask questions right now. Let's hit the road and we can talk to him on our way to the next cabin."

Once they were all loaded up and on the road, Bill turned to Richard, who by now had calmed down. "What the hell happened, Richard?"

"I was scared to death, that's what happened." He was still somewhat shaken up and added, "I was trying to stay alive."

Bill inquired, "What do you mean trying to stay alive. What happened?"

"I was attacked by a moose smacking against the side of the vehicle. Once I saw it, I hit the floor hoping I wasn't spotted. After the third nudge, I glanced up and saw it hitting the side of the vehicle with his big head. I slid back down onto the floor, hoping the animal hadn't spotted me inside. It eventually moved away, leaving me shaken but relieved."

Halfway to the next cabin, Bill quickly looked at his watch. It was already seven o'clock. Where had the last hour gone? When his phone rang, Bill shouted to Jack, "Stop! Shut off the vehicle and everyone stay silent. It's him and I don't want him to know how close we are to his location."

CHAPTER TWENTY-SEVEN

6:15 — 7:00

Kimberley, Beatrice, and Glen were standing on the front porch when Bill and Jack arrived at the house to pick up Richard. He had already hugged both ladies and was waiting for the cruiser to arrive. Glen had already told the ladies that Bill was not stopping, but sends his love to the two of them. His timeline was too short for even a quick visit, but once Bill saw the two ladies hugging each other; his instincts told him that he had to at least hug and kiss the two of them before leaving. Both women were so relieved when Bill jumped out of the vehicle and ran to them.

Bill hugged Kimberley, and she whispered into his ear, "Be safe, Bill. I love you."

"I'll bring her back, I promise."

He then turned to Beatrice and softly kissed her. His eyes were filled with a mixture of exhaustion, concern, and compassion. That special moment between the two of them was short and no words except 'I love you' were spoken between them. Glen watched in sorrow as he couldn't imagine what was going through Bill's mind. He wished there was something more he could do, but protecting Bill's family was just as important as saving Claire. That didn't mean he wasn't concerned for his friend and fellow officers. He would protect Bill's family with his life, as they were family to him too.

As Bill hurried back to the vehicle, he heard Glen shout after him. "You're family's safe with me!"

"Thanks, Glen, and see you soon."

Bill was in the car and gone within a matter of seconds. The three of them returned inside the house and Glen relocked the front door. He glanced at the two ladies. "I'm going to take another look around the inside of the house." He really didn't need to be concerned with the search, but felt that Beatrice and Kimberley could use some space to sort out their feelings. Glen didn't search outside the residence but was continuously peeking out windows to assess the outdoors and make sure nothing was out of the ordinary. That incident with the firecrackers was just meant to frazzle Bill, and it had served its' purpose. He figured Bill was most likely at wit's end, but he also knew his friend wasn't a quitter.

Both ladies went into the living room and once again sat in silence. Time was moving too fast for the two of them, plus they were physically and mentally exhausted. Kimberley observed Beatrice for a short time, then got up and walked over to her. "Can you do me a favour?"

"Of course I can sweetheart. What do you need?"

"I want you to lie on the couch and get some rest."

Beatrice was somewhat puzzled. "But I just woke up not that long ago." She then added, "I need to be awake. Besides, if I'm sleeping, we aren't supporting each other."

"Do you know why I want you to get more rest?"

Beatrice smiled. "Sounds like you're trying to get rid of me."

"Is that what you think?" She immediately added, "When we get Claire back, we're all going to be so tired from a lack of sleep and stressed from the night's events that not one of us will be able to take care of her. She is going to be getting up and ready to go for the day, while we'll all want to go to bed. You could take care of her while we catch up on a few hours of sleep. You would be doing Richard and me both a big favour. Besides, Glen is here to keep me company."

Beatrice seemed to think the idea over before she conceded, "You might be right, but promise me you'll wake me up if you get an update."

"Of course I will."

Kimberley helped her aunt lie down on the couch, and then placed a blanket over her before kissing her cheek. She then turned off the living room light and went into the kitchen.

Glen had returned to the living room but followed her back into the kitchen to refill his coffee cup. "You certainly have a way with her."

"Don't you mean a way to trick her into thinking she needs another nap. I'm really worried about her and especially Bill. It isn't his fault this is happening, but I know he blames himself. I still can't imagine the stress he's under."

Glen took a seat at the table and watched Kimberley cleaning a kitchen that was already clean. "How're you holding up?" He noticed a tear slide down her cheek, but let her have that private moment.

Kimberley paused. "How does any mother feel when someone has kidnapped her baby? First words that come to mind are afraid, anxious, fearful, and the list could go on and on. I just want this whole mess to go away." She was now leaning against the sink, somewhat defeated. "I need to know if Bill is going to bring her back to me unhurt."

Glen tried to reassure her. "If anyone can bring Claire home safely, it would be Bill."

Kimberley turned and looked at the empty coffee pot. "Oh, I'm such a terrible host; I'll put on a fresh pot of coffee for you."

"Thanks, but there's no rush. I really needed those first several cups to wake me up, but now I'm not too bad." He got up from the table and moved to the back door window to peer outside. His thoughts went back to his wife, who was taken from him far too early. When she was sad and upset he would pull her into his arms and comfort her. He wasn't sure if it was appropriate to comfort another man's wife, so he chose to leave the room and settle in a soft chair in the living room, enjoying the darkness surrounding him.

Sitting in the kitchen, it didn't take Kimberley long before she felt like she was being smothered. She wanted to keep busy, but also didn't want to wake up Beatrice who was now sound asleep, looking so peaceful and snuggled up in her soft blanket. Glen sat quietly in the shadows, but he was aware that she had come back and was checking on Beatrice. He whispered, "Are you okay?"

"I'm fine, just checking on her." She then added, "I'm going to get dressed and clean my bedroom. I'm not good under stress so I need to keep busy. Do you want me to fill your coffee cup before I leave?"

"No, you go ahead. I can get it myself, thanks."

Kimberley knew keeping busy would help to pass the time, but what she really wanted was to slow down time, giving Bill and his men enough time to find Claire. Refusing to look at the clock on the living room wall, Kimberley headed to her bedroom to clean the room. After the bed was made, she pulled on her clothes and threw open the curtains. Seeing that it was still dark outside, she quickly closed them again. Kimberley started to shake uncontrollably and tears freely ran down her cheeks. Walking across the hall, she entered Claire's room. It felt so empty, almost like when the nursery was first completed and she and Richard were waiting for the arrival of their first child. Standing beside the empty crib, she immediately pulled off the sheets and comforter and replaced them with fresh ones. Kimberley thought she could smell the odour of the intruder, who had been in the room only hours earlier. She wanted clean sheets for when her baby was back in the crib. Sneaking into the kitchen, she got the disinfectant, a bucket of warm water, and a soft cloth, then went back into the nursery. Glen watched her fill the bucket with water and head back down the hallway. He followed her.

Upon seeing her in such distress, he whispered, "Looks like you could use an extra set of hands to help clean the room. What can I do?"

"That's not necessary. I'm just trying to get everything perfect for when she's home."

"My wife used to work, so it was expected that I help out with the chores. I'm really quite good at scrubbing."

"Thanks, but I'm almost finished. How about in a few minutes we meet in the kitchen for a cup of coffee together."

"Deal."

Kimberley continued scrubbing the entire room and when she was finally convinced that all traces of Claire's abductor were erased from the room, she sat in the rocking chair holding Claire's favourite elephant stuffy. Rocking helped to calm her down. She softly whispered nursery rhymes to herself and slowly fell asleep.

Glen went into the nursery to check on her and found she was napping on the chair and holding one of Claire's special toys. He quietly left the room and returned to the living room. A short time later, she woke up, and for a few seconds, forgot where she was. Rising from the rocker, Kimberley put the stuffy in the corner of the crib before picking up the bucket of dirty water and going into the kitchen. Beatrice was still sleeping on the couch.

Kimberley quietly emptied the water and rinsed the bucket before putting it away.

Glen came into the kitchen. "I checked on you and you were out like a light. Thought you may have needed a short nap so I didn't want to disturb you. I could sure use that coffee you promised me earlier."

"Of course."

"Are you going to join me?"

"Sure. I really need one." She poured two coffees, setting one in front of him and taking hers to the counter. She suddenly set her mug down and quickly moved around the kitchen, remembering Richard had said to bake cookies for when he comes back with Claire. Taking out the recipe file, she flipped through the cards until she found the chocolate chip cookies that everyone seemed to like.

Glen watched her with concern. "What're you doing?"

"I forgot that Richard told me to bake cookies for Claire's coming home party."

Glen was amazed at the energy of the young woman standing in front of him. Although Kimberley tried to be quiet as she moved around the kitchen, Beatrice awoke and came into the room, rubbing her eyes. She crossed the room and proceeded to make a pot of tea. Beatrice turned to her niece in amazement. "Kimberley, what in heaven's name are you doing?"

"I'm baking cookies."

"Okay, but why?"

"I'm trying to keep busy. Besides, Richard told me to have some fresh cookies for the officers when they return with Claire. We'll deliver them to the office as a thank you."

Beatrice smiled sadly. "I do remember Richard saying that. It's a wonderful idea. Let me help you."

The two got busy, both happy not to be waiting around worrying and doing nothing. Glen watched as the two ladies mixed the ingredients in a bowl, then placed the dough onto cookie sheets. His mouth was already starting to water in anticipation of the hot, gooey cookies he could dip into his coffee.

Kimberley was about to put the cookie trays into the oven when she turned to Glen and said, "Bill happened to mention that you owed him a favour." She hesitated then added, "Sorry, you don't have to explain that. Guess I'm nervous and trying to make conversation." She placed the tray of raw cookies into the oven, set the timer, and then sat across from him. Beatrice had her cup of tea so joined the two of them.

Glen studied both ladies before saying, "Bill and I go back many years, and actually we went to the same academy and became partners and close friends. We shared many a beer together at the end of a shift, responsibly I might add. We went to hockey games, football games, you name it and we went together. We were inseparable, and neither one of us had a girlfriend. We were just two guys who worked together and enjoyed each other's company, no need for any women, at least that's what we thought. Some of our fellow officers always tried to set us up on blind dates. When one of us refused to go, they told us how disappointed the young lady would be if we were a no show. Eventually feeling somewhat guilty, whoever was set up for the night would meet the young lady for dinner. It never really worked out."

Glen started to chuckle and continued, "Believe it or not, Bill set me up on a blind date once with a young lady. I told him I wasn't interested and if she was such a nice young lady, he should meet her for the date instead. He told me that she was a better match for me than himself. I got the same story that the lady would feel bad if she was stood up, so I met with her. Bill said her name was Jeannine. He gave me her address and told me where he had made the dinner reservation. He also told me she liked carnations, so I picked up a bouquet, went to the lady's apartment, and softly tapped on the door, hoping she wouldn't hear it and I could leave. When she opened the door, her beauty took me off guard. The dinner was wonderful and the company was exceptional. Bill was right when he said we had so much in common. We both loved sports, Italian food, movies, and even junk food. I dated that beautiful lady for a year then decided to marry her. Bill was ecstatic, and he was our best man."

He paused before continuing. "I really loved that lady, and we had a short blissful marriage before one morning she woke up not feeling well, so I took her to the doctor. After lots of testing and medical procedures, the outcome wasn't good. She had breast cancer. Bill and I both struggled with her ups and downs from the chemotherapy treatment. Bill was as devastated as I was when she passed away. We both needed each other for support, knowing neither one of us could do it without the other. We both decided that maybe leaving Vancouver would give both of us a fresh start, so Bill moved to Blue Ridge, and I followed not long after. I chose to retire while Bill kept on working. Bill was there to help me through the worst time of my life, and I feel I owe him big time. Bill always told her he would protect her, and once we were married, she had two officers watching over her. How could he possibly keep that promise when he was competing with such a nasty disease? I'm still not sure he's fully accepted her death. We finally started seeing less and less of each other, although we still kept in contact. When his fiancée died in a car accident, it was another blow to him. He kind of went into a protective bubble where he felt safer from the outside world. Then he met you, Beatrice, and he was once again able to move outside of his small world."

Both ladies looked at each other and Beatrice spoke, "Jeannine must have meant a great deal to both of you."

The puzzled look on both women's faces told Glen that they were unaware of her. "Has Bill never mentioned her?"

Beatrice was rather embarrassed. "No. What does your wife have to do with Bill?"

Glen looked sadly between Kimberley and Beatrice. "She was Bill's sister."

Beatrice was stunned. "He's never mentioned her. Why wouldn't he tell me about her?"

Glen looked at her with compassion. "He never talks about her, bad memories I guess."

Kimberley looked at Glen. "I'm sure that I can speak for both of us when I say we are so sorry for your loss." Kimberley then changed the subject. "Bill's fiancée who was killed in that car accident was my mother."

"I'm so sorry, I didn't make the connection."

"That's okay. Bill helped Beatrice and me through a very difficult time and he was there for us. He's a very giving man."

Glen responded, "Don't I know it."

Kimberley's mind traveled into the past, back to when her mother was alive. "I was eight years old when my mother died. She and Bill had been dating for some time. He was so good to her, and he was fun to have around. Bill brought my mother flowers and always had a single carnation for me too." She paused. "I never knew my father then. He and mom dated for a short time and fell madly in love with each other. He was a truck driver so was constantly on the road. When he found out that my mother was pregnant, he got cold feet and left. My mother was devastated. Beatrice was there for my mother's entire pregnancy, even in the delivery room. When mom went back to work, Beatrice babysat me every day and once I started school, she watched me before and after classes. I first met my father when I was seventeen. Guess he was feeling somewhat guilty after abandoning her and I suppose he was curious to know if he was a father or not. He swore that he was still in love with my mom and was upset that she had moved on without him." Kimberley shrugged. "Would you care to guess how I finally met my father?"

Glen was intrigued. "I'm hoping you'll tell me."

"My first introduction was when some friends and I were at a soda shop and a friend told me that some weirdo was watching me. I thought he was just a loser. When we left the shop and I noticed him following me home I panicked. Beatrice called Bill and he came and scouted out our house. Bill was livid and several days later arrested my father for being drunk and disorderly. I asked permission to see him and when we met, a set of steel bars separated the two of us. He told me he still loved my mother and was devastated to find out she was engaged to Bill." Kimberley threw up her hands in frustration. "Did he really expect her to hang on to the idea that one day he would return?"

Glen just shook his head. "That would have been a long time for your mom to wait."

Kimberley sighed. "Exactly. We eventually did accept each other and now he comes to see us whenever he's in town, but he especially comes to see Claire. She's his one and only grandchild and he spoils her rotten." Kimberley's body trembled as she mentioned Claire's name. "Bill supported both Beatrice and I through the most tragic event that anyone should ever have to go through, plus he was also going through the same feelings himself. We shared my mother's death together. He came around daily to check on us and somewhere along the line he fell in love with Beatrice."

The timer on the stove rang. Kimberley got up and took the two trays of cookies out of the oven. Glen's mouth was watering as he spoke, "Those cookies smell amazing. May I try one?"

Kimberley replied, "I would be offended if you didn't."

Glen went to the coffee pot and refilled his mug, then grabbed a few cookies on his way back to his seat. They were still warm and smelled delicious, so he woofed both of them down in no time. It had been a long time since he'd had fresh, homemade cookies, and they were heavenly.

Kimberley smiled at him and asked, "Can I interest you in a few more?"

Glen chuckled. "I think I'm good, thanks. I'm going to take another look around the rooms again."

Once he was out of the room, Beatrice turned to Kimberley. "Why do you think Bill never told me about Jeannine?"

"I'm not sure. That's a question you'll have to ask him."

"I'm such an awful wife. I was so worried about myself and you, I never once asked him about his family."

Kimberley looked sadly at Beatrice. "I suppose he was going to tell you when the time was right, but that time isn't now. Glen said it still isn't easy for him to talk about her, still too fresh in his memory. Just give him some time."

"I guess you're right, but we've never kept secrets from each other, at least I didn't think so until now."

Kimberley hugged Beatrice and whispered, "Just because Bill didn't share the loss of his sister with you, doesn't mean he loves you any less."

"You're right again." The two ladies tidied up the kitchen and left the remaining cookies to cool on a rack before they returned to the living room.

CHAPTER TWENTY-EIGHT

6:20 — 7:00

Don drove the twenty or so miles to the turn-off that lead to the two cabins his team were in charge of searching. Their two cabins were on the west side of the plateau and further back into the forest. It would take them longer to get to the first one, but once there, the second one was close by. All four officers were silent, which they often were before a big takedown. Each officer knew that clearing their minds and mentally concentrating on the job they were facing often ended in better results.

Don figured Bob was deep in thought and inquired, "What's going on in that head of yours?"

Bob responded, "Lots of things, some good, some not so good." He turned towards Don. Even in the darkness he could see the outline of his face. "What if we don't find her in time?"

"Not an option, so just put that idea to rest. Our objective right now is to get Claire back safely and into the arms of her parents. We've rescued people before; the only difference here is our timeline. If we give up, we fail. If we push on, we have a chance of success. That's all that's important right now."

Bob sighed. "You're right. I don't know about you, but I'm exhausted. We need to get through this case and then sleep for a week. I expect the rest of the team is feeling the same."

Don turned to the newbie. "So, Eli, how long have you been an officer?"

His answer surprised the three other officers in the car. "Pretend or real?" When he got no response, he started laughing. "When I was a child, my life long dream was to be superman. I really liked his cape and thought it would be cool to be able to fly. My parents shot down that idea. Told me it wasn't realistic, whatever that meant."

Sam replied, "I think that was every little boy's ideal dream job."

Eli continued, "Once my parents shut down my first career opportunity, I thought the next coolest job would be a policeman. I figured if you wore a gun, no one would mess around with you. That worked for many years. Halloween after Halloween, I was a policeman, costumes just got bigger and bigger. Once I had made that final decision to become a policeman, I realized that having a gun didn't mean that you were any safer than anyone else. There're a lot of wacko's out there and finding them and putting them behind bars became my mission. I expect we're all trying to make this world a better place for the good people."

Don snickered and directed his next comment to Eli. "We play a game with all newbie's. You in?"

Eli was nervous. "Is this an initiation into your private club?"

Don half shrugged. "At the end of each case there's tons of paperwork to fill out, enough to keep all of us busy for hours." He then added, "We usually do rock, paper, scissors."

Sam started laughing. "Hey man, we're just messing with you. Four officers can do it four times faster if we work as a team. Besides, maybe Bill will give us a day's grace before it has to cross his desk."

Don responded, "Now that would be nice." He then added, "If this is indeed the cabin, what's our strategy?"

Sam answered, "We don't have one up to this point. If you remember, Bill said we call him if this is the location, and then wait for backup. Richard has to be here to treat Claire."

Don sounded frustrated. "I remember, but it just seems pointless for us to sit and do nothing when Claire's life is at stake. What if we kill him, and then when the other team arrives, Richard can treat her. That's the end of the case."

Sam responded, "True but have you thought that maybe Charles is in this cabin, but Claire and Jenny are being held somewhere else?"

Don was frustrated. "Never even thought of that. Certainly Charles isn't smart enough to leave Jenny at another location where she might be able to escape and get help."

Eight Hours

Bob responded, "Look around you, where could she possibly go in the dark, carrying a baby, miles away from anywhere? She wouldn't take the chance of getting lost and perishing in the woods. Also, there's a chance of coming across bears heading into hibernation. Let's hope she realizes that it's just too risky to leave her present location."

Don glanced at Bob. "Why do you always have to be right? I'm the gung-ho person and everyone else in this damn car are the practical ones. Guess that's why we make such a good team."

Bob laughed, "Guess that's why Bill put us together and trusted us to break in Eli."

Eli responded, "Trust me, guys. I was already broken in while Muhammad and I staked out Jenny's house. It was as boring as hell."

All four men were silent for several moments, driving on the bumpy gravel road, their headlights barely guiding their way. Don couldn't go any slower, if he did, reaching the cabin before Bill's next call was out of the question. Even with their seat belts on, the four officers were being bounced around the inside the vehicle. Avoiding potholes was almost impossible. Poor Don couldn't see the holes quick enough to miss them, especially not with mud being splashed all over the front windshield, leaving the glass a dirty mess. He was constantly spraying the window with cleaning fluid and squinting to see the road in front of him.

Bob glanced at his phone to read the GPS, checking how far they were from their destination. He exclaimed, "Oh my God, this is taking forever. Can't you go any faster?"

Don's response was quick. "Not if we want to get there in one piece." He asked rather frustrated. "Are you blind? The road is not only twisty, but it's also dark outside and I'm fighting to see ahead of me. I'm not going to be the one to call Bill if we're in an accident. If you think you can do better, you're more than welcome to take over the driving."

Bob felt bad. "Sorry, I think the whole team is under stress right now, including me. Never was good with timelines, too much pressure."

Don asked, "How close are we anyways?"

Bob glanced at his GPS again. "Still two to three miles ahead."

Don inquired, "How close do you think we should get to the cabin before we park?"

Bob thought before answering, "With the co-ordinates that we have, a quarter of a mile sounds good? We don't know how thick the bush is in that area and we need cover for the vehicle."

Don replied, "Works for me."

Finally arriving at a safe distance from the cabin, all four men got out and loaded up their gear. Placing their night vision goggles over their heads, they locked their vehicle and started the short run to the cabin. Each man tested their earphones to make sure there were no problems.

Bob turned to the others. "We all ready for this?"

Eli responded, "Let's get the son of a bitch."

Even with the night vision goggles on, headsets in place, and weapons drawn, navigating was difficult with potholes full of mud hampering their progress.

Don spoke into his headset. "Should have worn my boots, but who knew that our call at midnight would turn into this fiasco?"

Bob answered, "Certainly isn't our typical call out."

Don stepped into another puddle. "No shit. If Bill doesn't kill Charles, I'll do it myself."

Bob's response was quick. "Stand in line buddy."

With all of their feet soaked, the foursome carefully worked their way towards the cabin. Open to all the sounds that surrounded them, there were several encounters with bears, but only one that slowed them down.

Don paused. "Hold up team."

All three men answered in unison. "We hear it."

The team froze, moved off the center of the road, and then slipped into the bushes. The night vision goggles showed a single bear, which was not yet aware of their presence; and it was not in any hurry to move along. They lost more precious time waiting for the bear to cross in front of them before they could continue.

When they moved out of the bushes and again started towards the cabin, out of nowhere, the team was suddenly swarmed by bats. Quickly removing their night goggles, all four officers flailed their hands above themselves and tried to protect their faces.

Don shouted, "Where the hell did they come from?"

Bob immediately yelled, "You're aware that bats come out at night?"

"I know that, but we don't have time for this."

Bob responded, "Let's get back into the bushes until they pass."

"You don't have to tell me twice," Don exclaimed.

Once the bats had passed over the team, Bob looked at his GPS. "It's not far now."

All four men replaced their night vision goggles and continued on. Glancing cautiously around them, they were still unable to dodge many of the mud puddles in front of them. It was like an obstacle course they were unable to navigate. Their feet were soaking wet and cold, but they pushed on. As they approached the cabin, they were all discouraged. The building was so old and rotten that it had collapsed in on itself.

Bob shook his head. "What a waste of time this has been."

Sam answered, "Well there's one good thing; we can eliminate this location and move to the next one."

Bob was again frustrated. "Hope we have better luck there. Once we're back at the vehicle, I'll radio Bill and let him know." Bob felt sick knowing that he had to deliver the bad news to Bill; hopefully his team had had better luck. By the time they reached their vehicle, they were not only soaked, but mud was also caked onto the bottom of their shoes and halfway up their pants. The team threw their gear onto the back seat, kicked the mud off of their boots, and then set off to the next location.

Bob contacted Bill over the radio. "Sorry boss, this first cabin was a bust. It's just a pile of rotten wood. How did your team make out?"

"Not good here either."

Bob continued, "We're off and moving to our next location, we'll keep you updated."

He turned off the radio and the foursome was on their way to the next cabin. In their cruiser, heading towards their next search site, Bob and Don now remained silent. Each was wrapped up in their own thoughts. Trees flew by them and bushes scratched the side of their car. They came to a junction where they turned off and headed east. This road was even worse, as several times Don found himself dodging small trees that had fallen across their path, most likely from the recent storm. He managed to navigate around one of them and drive over another.

While bouncing about on the back seat of the cruiser, Sam said to Eli. "It's definitely an interesting first day of work for you?"

Eli answered, "Every day on this job is interesting. No two days are ever alike."

Sam inquired, "What was the hardest case you ever worked on and how long did it take you and your team to solve it?"

Eli thought for several moments before replying, "A young boy was kidnapped 15 years ago. He disappeared from a local campsite. The family's summer vacation turned into a nightmare. It's a little like the one we're dealing with tonight. As far as how long it took to solve, it remains an active file. Theory is he was sold on the black market and is no longer in Canada."

Bob turned towards the officers in the back seat. "Gentlemen, this case will be solved tonight. We have to find this crazy lunatic before it's too late. I can't imagine what Bill and his family are going through. It must be hell on earth for them."

Don kept his eyes on the rough gravel road ahead of them. He tried to make good time, but the ruts and potholes jolted the car, leaving the men thinking that they were on a circus ride. Although they were jolted around the inside of the vehicle their seatbelts held them secure. Don said, "I agree, sure hope this car can handle this torture test."

"It has too." Bob looked at his GPS. "Not too much further." He then suggested, "Do you think we might be able to get a little closer to the cabin this time? It'll cut down our walk time, or should I say run time to the location?"

Don responded, "I agree. How close are we now?"

Bob looked at his phone. "We're within a couple hundred yards."

Don moved the vehicle off the road and parked. "Let's stop here."

They all climbed out of the car and grabbed their gear from the back seat, and once again locked the doors.

Bob suggested, "Let's get moving, but once we are closer, we'll duck into the bushes and observe before approaching the building."

Seeing the cabin appear in front of them, they noticed there was no vehicle in front of it. Don motioned to the right and whispered, "I'll check for a vehicle out back."

Eli whispered into his headset. "I'll take the left."

Bob nodded and watched the two men move slowly and quietly through the bushes, trying not to make a sound. They both disappeared behind the building, out of sight for a few minutes, before reappearing and shaking their heads. They both removed their night vision goggles and then moved to the only window in the building. Eli carefully peered inside. When he was convinced the building was empty, he turned on his flashlight and shone it through the window. All four men regrouped.

Don spoke first. "Another bust! Now I'm really pissed off with this Charles character."

Bob shook his head. "Me too, but there's no time to waste, we need to get going." The four men put on their night vision goggles and set off running back to their vehicle, now knowing which cabin Charles, Jenny, and Claire must be in. They knew it wasn't either of theirs, plus Bill had eliminated his first cabin, so that only left one remaining possibility.

The mud clinging to the bottom of their shoes slowed them all down, but there was no time to scrape it off and it would only build up again on the next few steps. Once back at their vehicle, Bob looked at his watch. It read 6:45. All four officers once again kicked the mud off their footwear. All the gear was put into the vehicle again and Don started the car, turned around quickly, and was soon heading back down the dirty, bumpy road. Bob picked up the radio. "I need to call Bill and tell him this location is another bust." He quickly called their sergeant.

"Bill here, any luck?"

"Sorry, another dead end here."

Bill sounded defeated. "Looks like we were wrong assuming it was the one closer to Sidville. I'll send you the co-ordinates for the last cabin. Don't want you going to the wrong location. He has to be there."

"Sounds good. We're on our way."

Bill sounded tired. "How far away is your team?"

"Probably fifteen to twenty minutes, if we don't run into any bears or other wildlife. How close are you?"

"We could be there in fifteen minutes."

"See you there." Half way into their rush to the last cabin, Bob wrinkled his forehead as he realized that he knew this section of the road. His eyes looked off into the distance, as if he had a plan in place. He shouted to Don. "Stop the car! Back up!"

Don hit the brakes hard. "What the hell! You scared the shit out of me!"

Bob shouted again. "Back up and turn left!"

"Why would I do that?"

Bob replied, "I know where I am."

Don was unsure. "It's dark outside. How do you know where we are?"

Bob repeated, "Back up! You have to trust me."

Don conceded and threw the car into reverse.

Bob shouted again. "Stop here!" He rolled down his window and shone his flashlight outside the window. He pointed to a sign hanging on a tree about three feet from the ground. "My hockey team put that sign up in the summer. It was kind of like a beacon for the team so we knew where our base cabin was."

Don sharply turned the wheel and headed into the unknown. "I trust you buddy, so I hope you're right."

"I know I am. Trust me. This is a short cut to the last cabin."

Don looked puzzled. "Why didn't you mention that sooner?"

"I knew what it looked like, but wasn't a hundred percent sure which cabin it was. Don't forget, I was looking at a topographical map with four cabins close together. I had no way of knowing which one was correct."

Don tried to make up more time. He had no sooner hit the gas, when he immediately slammed on the brakes. All the officers were jolted to an immediate stop as their vehicle came face to face with a huge fallen tree. They could neither manoeuvre around it nor drive over it. Frustrated, they knew that turning back would cost them valuable time. Bob grabbed the radio and called Bill.

"Bill here, what's up?"

Bob responded, "We've run into a glitch or should I say a tree. It's blocking the road. We're going to have to hoof it the rest of the way. We'll get there as fast as possible."

Bill replied, "Copy that. Hope to see you here soon."

The four men picked up their gear, leaving their night vision goggles in the vehicle, as the sun slowly approached the horizon. Locking the vehicle, they set off on a dead run. Bob was very concerned as he was one of the snipers, which meant not only did he have to get there fast, but he also had to hope his heart rate would slow down enough before he had to make an accurate shot.

Don was breathing deeply as he asked, "How much farther?"

Bob looked at his GPS. "At least another half a mile." All four men continued running down the old road, hoping they would arrive around the same time as Bill and his team.

All four men stopped dead in their tracks as they faced what should have been a creek, had now turned into a narrow river blocking their progress. Sam looked ahead of them. "This river must be a result of the earlier rainfall."

Eli was already crossing the muddy water. "I think we're going to get a little wet guys." The water level was up to his knees and the slight pull of the water made his crossing slower than it should have. "Look at the positive side, the river will clean the mud off our shoes. We should be able to make better time with the lead weights off our feet."

Don watched Eli's progress and was the next officer to take the plunge. "This night really sucks."

Sam followed behind him but lost his balance. Before he knew what had happened, he was up to his waist in dirty water. "Why can't we catch a break? Our search of the two cabins was a bust, then a tree blocks our progress, and now I'm soaking wet up to my waist. Can anything else possibly go wrong?"

Bob laughed, "Don't jinx yourself, Sam. This isn't over yet."

Once all four officers had crossed the swollen, muddy creek, they continued running towards Bill and his team at the last cabin.

CHAPTER TWENTY-NINE

7:00 — 7:30

After Bill's team had eliminated the first cabin and were on their way to the second one, his phone rang for the seven o'clock call. With everyone in the cruiser silent, Bill turned to Richard. "If you as much as breathe too loud, it's all over. No matter what I say, you absolutely must not react. This is my last phone call and also my last chance to save Claire. Can you do that?" Bill studied Richard. "If not, I suggest you leave the vehicle before I answer it."

Richard was scared but whispered, "I can be quiet."

Bill turned his attention to answering his phone. "Hello."

Charles shouted, "Where the hell are you, Bill? You should've been here by now?"

"We're surrounding your cabin as we speak."

Charles jumped up from his chair and ran to the window. I don't see you. Show yourself."

"I will in due time. I'm just getting my troops ready to take you down."

Charles simply laughed, "You're too late. Times run out."

"I thought I had until eight o'clock. You change the rules again?"

"Not exactly. I need to be on the road by eight, and it's only obvious that you haven't got Tom out of prison yet."

Bill was very irritated. "I think we both knew that wasn't ever going to happen." He paused. "The justice system doesn't make deals with terrorists, and you're a terrorist, but you must already know that."

Charles laughed, "I need to see Tom within the next forty-five minutes or I win the game. Are you willing to sacrifice your granddaughter's life over Tom's release?"

Bill looked directly at Richard and put his finger up to indicate he was to remain silent. "How do I even know she's still alive? You won't let me talk to Jenny. Maybe she's dead too."

Richard closed his eyes and leaned his head against the back of his seat. His body was instantly tense, but he didn't say a word. Visions of Claire's small body being rocked to sleep by Kimberley seemed a dim reality. He had to trust Bill, knowing the pressure he was under.

Charles laughed again. "You don't know do you? You're just going to have to trust me."

It was Bill's turn to laugh. "I think we've had this trust talk before. Let's not flog it to death. Neither one of us trusts the other." Bill looked at his watch, knowing time was running out, and knew that it was a good time to hang up. "See you in a few minutes, Charles." He then hung up his phone. Bob immediately started the vehicle and off they sped towards the hostage site.

Richard was sweating and he asked to borrow Bill's satellite phone. "If you don't mind, I'm going to update the ladies. By now they're probably worried sick." He glanced at the phone before entering the numbers. "What do I tell them?"

Bill thought for a moment before answering, "Tell them we've located the cabin where Charles is holding Jenny and Claire and we'll be at the site in ten minutes."

Richard looked skeptical and hesitated, so Bill reached across and took the phone back from him and entered the numbers. Beatrice and Kimberley were sitting at the kitchen table when the phone rang. Glen rushed into the living room with the ladies right behind him. Recognizing the number, he answered, "Hello, Bill."

"Hi, Glen."

"Tell us good news, man."

"We've almost found her."

"That's very good news." Both ladies appeared relieved knowing that Bill and his team were one step closer to rescuing Claire. Luckily, they didn't hear Bill's next comment.

Bill tried to sound positive. "I just hope we aren't too late. Is Beatrice there?"

"Sure is, hold on. Beatrice, it's Bill. He wants to talk to you."

She grabbed the phone. "Bill, please tell us good news?"

"I don't have long to talk so listen carefully. We're closing in on where Jenny and Claire are being held. We're about ten minutes from the cabin. Once the team is in place, we'll try to talk Charles outside and take him down. I'm hoping that he'll leave Jenny and Claire inside until he knows what's going on with Tom."

Beatrice cut him off. "I love you Bill, but promise me you'll be careful. I really need you to come home safely to me." Through her tears, she added, "And carrying Claire."

"I love you too, and I'll do my best."

"That's all I expect from you."

"I'm going to pass the phone to Richard. I'm sure he wants to talk to Kimberley." Bill handed the phone back to Richard.

Beatrice passed her phone to Kimberley. "Richard wants to talk to you."

She took the phone and spoke softly. "Richard, where are you? Have you found her yet?"

Richard knew exactly what Kimberley was going through, as his feelings were equally as strong. "We're close. Bill says the cabin is only ten minutes away and his team is pumped up and ready to go."

Kimberley started crying at the other end of the phone. "Save our baby, Richard, that's all I ask of you."

Richard's voice choked as he responded, "When we find her, you know that I can treat her, and will bring her home safely to you."

Just as Kimberley thought she had no more tears to shed, they started all over again. She had never cried so much in her life. "But will you find her in time?"

"We have to. Now no more tears. Within the hour she will be in my arms and safe from that bastard who stole her. After that, I don't give a flying crap what Bill does to Charles; he can rot in hell as far as I'm concerned."

Kimberley somewhat settled down. This was the first time she had ever heard Richard actually express his feelings, and hers were mutual. Charles was a lowlife piece of shit; that they both agreed on. Should he go to jail for his crime? Yes. Should the team take him out? Yes, if they had to. Both scenarios worked for Richard and Kimberley, although the second choice would prove to be cheaper on the justice system. Either way, Bill or his team would be the ones to make the ultimate decision. "Tell Bill I love him."

"I'm sure he knows that, but I'll definitely pass it on to him."

Kimberley remembered. "Beatrice and I made those cookies you ordered." She glanced at Glen who was standing next to her. "Glen seems to enjoy them."

"Don't let him eat them all, they're for Bill's officers."

"I'll tell him that. I love you Richard, but be careful."

"I love you too, and I know that I'm safe with the entire force watching over me, since I'm the only one who can ultimately save Claire. Sorry, I really have to go. Love you both and will be calling back soon." He then hung up, and spoke to Bill. "Kimberley told me to tell you that she loves you. I think she's really worried about you."

"Hell, I'm worried about myself too. I haven't pulled a twenty-four-hour shift in a long time. Just have to hope the adrenaline stays kicked in."

Once Kimberley hung up the phone, she left the room. Beatrice and Glen listened as she went into the bathroom and threw up. Her poor body was shutting down from lack of sleep, but sleep was not going to happen as long as Claire was in danger. She stayed in the bathroom for several minutes, leaning against the wall and crying until there were no more tears left to shed. Her body was a wreck and there was nothing she could do to help herself. She longed to cradle Claire in her arms once more, read her a story, and then sing her a lullaby before she put her into the crib. With the nursery scrubbed clean, Kimberley just wanted her baby snuggled under her favourite blanket and her stuffy lying next to her. Kimberley tried to stay in focus, but she felt exhausted and deflated. With difficulty, she lifted herself up from the floor, splashed water on her face, and looked into the mirror. Her hair was a mess and her face was far too pale. This nightmare seemed to have no end in sight, especially with Claire's life uncertain. Kimberley knew that losing Claire would not only devastate her and Richard, but also Bill and Beatrice. Bill was working so hard to get her back and she wasn't totally sure how Bill was dealing with the case. He had to beat Charles or he would be a defeated man, reliving his failure over and over, day after day. Her aunt had been right about the four possible outcomes.

Beatrice gave Kimberley some space as she watched her niece head towards the bathroom. "Are you okay, dear?"

"I'm fine. I'll be out in a few minutes." As Kimberley made her way back to the living room, Glen noticed she was staggering and her eyes weren't in focus. He rushed to her side as she fainted into his arms. Glen was glad he was able to break her fall. He easily swept her up and crossed the room with her so he could lay her on the couch. Beatrice placed a blanket over her trembling body and went into the kitchen to get a cold cloth to place on her forehead. Glen stayed next to her until Beatrice returned with the cool cloth and a glass of water. Glen gently raised Kimberley up slightly so Beatrice could help her take a drink. She was then lowered down and the cool cloth was placed on her forehead. Glen slid a chair next to the couch for Beatrice to sit on, close to Kimberley.

"Are you feeling any better, dear?"

"I think so. It came on so quick. I didn't have a chance to make it to the couch. This is the second time I've fainted tonight." She turned to Glen. "Thanks for catching me. Maybe we're just two damsels in distress."

Glen responded, "I don't consider you damsels in distress, more like two ladies who are in need of protection from a wacko." He added, "When Bill and I took the negotiator course years ago we learned one important fact. The deranged person is crazy enough to confuse his objective. In Charles' case, he wanted to set his brother Tom free, but once that became unachievable, his objective changed to retaliation. His mind becomes confused about what he hopes to accomplish, so his brain automatically alters to a different outcome, one that he is able to achieve. According to Bill, Charles is unstable, but having said that, Bill knows how to bring him down. Rest assured that Claire is safe, because if she's no longer in the picture, Charles has failed his mission to get Tom out, and failure is not on his agenda. He will now be after Bill." Glen added, "Bill is a professional and has never let anyone down before, so I venture to guess that he won't today either." Glen turned to Beatrice. "Apart from Kimberley fainting, how're you holding up, Beatrice?"

Beatrice replied, "I think I'm safe to answer for both of us. We both feel like we've been run over by a bus, but we have to forge on, for Claire's sake." Kimberley nodded in agreement. The color was already slowly starting to return to her face, but Beatrice made her stay lying down.

Glen tried to put the ladies at ease. "Do you mind if I have another one of those amazing cookies?"

Beatrice knew what he was trying to do, so smiled and replied, "As soon as the tea is made. You do drink tea, I hope? They just don't taste the same with coffee."

"Tea it is then."

Beatrice left the room to put on the kettle, then set several cookies on a plate and brought them into the living room. Kimberley turned to Glen and chuckled.

"Richard told me not to let you eat all the cookies, they're for the officers, but what the hell, eat as many as you want. Beatrice and I can always make another batch. You've certainly earned them. I guess when you went to bed last night; you didn't expect to be babysitting two distressed women." Beatrice poured three cups of tea and passed around the cookies. Kimberley slowly sat up, but kept the blanket covering her.

Kimberley slowly sipped her tea and felt her body regenerating. "Thanks, Beatrice. The tea is just what I needed."

"Do you feel better?"

"I do, thanks."

Glen finished his cup of tea and ate two more cookies. "I'll take another look around the house." When he got to the nursery, he drew back the curtain and noticed signs of daylight starting. He nervously returned to the living room and looked at both ladies, then took a seat. He knew they were stressed as each minute turned into an hour. With the curtains drawn, neither one was aware that daylight was fast approaching. He needed to create a distraction, so he asked Kimberley. "How did you and Richard meet?"

Kimberley immediately relaxed. "Funny you should ask."

Beatrice interceded, "It's kind of my fault."

Kimberley agreed. "It sure is. After my mother passed away, and I moved in with Beatrice, she decided to get a job to help make ends meet. I guess I became a financial burden."

"That's not true, dear, and you know it."

Kimberley responded, "This is my story so let me tell it. As I was saying, she needed work, so had applied at the Jackson residence, Richard's parents' place, as a housekeeper, and she got the job. She loved cooking their meals and cleaning their house, which allowed Richard's mother to apply herself to her charities. The Jacksons had gone overseas on an extended vacation to Paris over the summer, but their son Richard had just graduated from medical school so was back home and in the process of setting up his own practice. He still needed his house cleaned and meals prepared. All was going well until one day when Beatrice fell and broke her ankle. She was worried she would lose her job, so we did the big 'switch.' Beatrice rested at home while her ankle healed, and I took care of the Jackson residence. Richard was unaware of her injuries. Luckily, Beatrice had taught me how to cook, but Richard's menu was so boring. I challenged him daily with food that was out of his comfort zone. I was constantly on alert while in his house and almost got caught several times. It worked for a short time, but unfortunately Richard discovered me one day and the rest is history."

Glen was intrigued. "That's a nice story."

Beatrice added, "She's always been a rather adventurous person, so seeing the long banister inside their house got the better of her, and one day she slid down it and landed in his arms."

Kimberley laughed, "It was rather frightening, but also romantic." She smiled. "He asked me on several dates, but his job always seemed to get in the way. I was starting to think he didn't really want to take me out. When his father was attacked on the streets of Paris, Richard went there immediately to bring him back to Blue Ridge. Being a doctor, there was no problem with getting him released from the Paris hospital." She added, "Our first date was at the Panorama Room, the night of the tsunami, where we were trapped with several other patrons when the wave hit. I actually drowned that night, but Richard saved my life." There were tears in her eyes when she looked at Glen and Beatrice.

Glen was amazed. "And I thought the night I met Jeannine was amazing, but yours has mine beat hands down." All three of them were startled when the phone beside Glen rang. He glanced at the caller ID.

Beatrice inquired, "Is it Bill?"

"I'm not sure who it is yet." He answered, "Hello." The phone went dead so Glen hung up and was suddenly on full alert.

Beatrice asked, "Who was it?"

"No one was at the other end." He got up from his chair. "I need to have another look around the house."

This time, he opened every set of curtains and had a good look around outside. Convinced that all was okay, he reclosed them and then returned to the living room and sat down again.

Moments later, the phone rang again, and this time Glen was prepared. "Hello." The recording at the other end of the line started talking about a compromised credit card and said to press one to speak to a representative. Glen was frustrated and hung up the phone.

Kimberley inquired, "Who was it?"

"It's just a scam call about your credit card being compromised. Why don't those people get a real job?" Glen looked at both ladies and made a suggestion. "Why don't the two of you lie down and try to get some rest. You may not be able to sleep, but just closing your eyes for a short time will regenerate both of you. I'm here to keep you safe." Neither of the two wanted to lie down, but they were so exhausted they agreed.

Glen watched the two of them as they both appeared to have fallen into a deep sleep. He got up and turned off the overhead light and sat in the dark watching them and listening for any sound that was out of the ordinary. Glen glanced down at his watch, which read 7:20. He had already been protecting Bill's family for three hours. He knew that Bill was close to rescuing Claire, but knew if it didn't happen soon, the game would have a bad ending. His ears perked up when he heard a dog barking outside. He crossed the room and glanced out the front window. He may have heard a dog, but there wasn't a soul in sight. The barking soon turned into howling and whining and both ladies woke up with a start.

Kimberley was frightened and asked, "Is everything okay?"

"I'm not sure yet." He walked around the inside of the house until he figured the barking dog was right outside the nursery and the sound wasn't moving. He returned to the living room and told Kimberley. "I need to go outside and figure out what's going on. You lock the door behind me and only open it for me. Do you understand?"

Kimberley was trembling, but she replied, "Yes."

Glen drew his weapon from his holster and opened the front door, slipped outside, and then closed the door behind him. Once he heard it was locked, he stood just long enough for his eyes to adjust to the partial darkness surrounding him. He then slowly descended the stairs and, staying close to the house, he worked his way around the side of the building. The animal was still barking and whimpering endlessly. Coming to the back of the house, he saw a man kneeling down next to the frightened dog.

Glen pointed his gun directly at the man and said, "Don't move, asshole."

The man jumped up and turned around quickly. When he saw the gun pointed at his head he froze and started pleading, "Don't shoot! Oh God, please don't shoot! I don't want to die!"

"What're you doing here?"

"I was out walking my dog and he got away from me. I ran around looking for him with no luck, and when I heard the whimpers, I found him here. His leash is stuck in the picket fence. I just want to free him and I'll be on my way."

Glen lowered his weapon, which put the man at ease. The owner turned back to his dog and wiggled the leash free, this time holding onto it tightly. The man turned back to Glen and inquired, "You have a permit for that weapon?"

Glen was rather taken back. "I'm a police officer and yes I have a permit for it."

The man inquired, "You don't live in this house so why are you here?"

"How do you know I don't live here?"

"Because Doctor Jackson and his wife and infant daughter live here."

"Let's just say I'm visiting them." With the dog freed from the fence, Glen suggested, "You best be on your way." The man left in silence, but Glen was still very cautious. He drew his weapon again and before heading up the stairs to the front door, chose to continue around the entire house as an extra precaution. When he returned to the entrance, he softly tapped on the door, not wanting to scare the ladies, and said, "It's me, Glen. Open up."

Kimberley unlocked the door and opened it. "What did you find?"

Glen slipped inside and closed the door, relocking it. "Just a dog with its' leash stuck in your picket fence and the owner trying to free it."

The three returned to the living room and sat quietly. Beatrice finally asked Glen. "Do you think Bill is okay?"

"One thing I know about Bill is that he's always super careful and can take care of himself. He also has the entire force behind him, so you can put those feelings to bed. This will all be over soon."

"I wish I could think as positively as you."

"I guess I've known him longer than you, so I know what he's capable of doing."

"Thanks, Glen." Beatrice was afraid to look at the clock, but she had to know what the time was. She drew in a deep breath as seven o'clock had come and gone long before now. She tried to remain calm, but her mind was working overtime. Glen saw the anxious look on her face.

"Beatrice, you took a job at the Jackson's residence to help make ends meet."

"That's correct."

He then addressed Kimberley. "You just told me that Richard saved your life and that you also survived your mother's passing with the help of Beatrice."

Kimberley responded, "That's also correct."

"It sounds to me like your family is capable of survival. I bet little Claire has got those same genes bred into her. She's lucky to have such strong family members behind her."

CHAPTER THIRTY

7:20 — 7:40

The cabin was starting to close in on Charles once again, so in boredom, he started counting the logs it took to build one wall. In his mind, the builder was a genius. Each log fit tightly together preventing the outside weather from coming in. Feeling the cool air that was settling into the cabin made him wish he had kept the stove going slightly longer. He pulled his hoodie over his bald head to keep it warm. Jenny was still lying in the same position, not moving a muscle. He became very agitated when he realized that he may have lost the game against Bill. Why couldn't Bill find him? Charles had to assume that Bill was not as good an officer as he had thought he was. Even though Bill had eight hours to find him, so far he had failed. He had to hope that Bill would be closing in on him, if not, then all would be lost. The sergeant absolutely had to find him or all his planning was for naught. The smart cop may be wearing a shiny silver badge, but there was no way Charles would be outwitted. Criminals did what needed to be done, to outsmart the police. The police academy couldn't possibly know all of the ins and outs of a criminal's mind. If they did, they would be criminals themselves.

He whispered, "You're getting careless in your old age, Bill. You're not as good a cop as you thought you were." He added with frustration. "I'm tired of playing this game of cat and mouse; it all ends here and now."

He crossed the room and approached the table, slamming his fists onto it. His carved words, 'Bill's Dead,' glared back at him. Jenny should be talking to him, her voice always seemed to calm him down, but she wasn't responding to his mood swings. Her silent treatment was driving him crazy, if only she would turn over and face him. Charles knew he'd hit her hard and her face must be swollen and sore, but that was no reason to ignore him. He realized that by now, he should've had Tom beside him, and the three of them should be safely leaving this hell hole, that is, if indeed Jenny were still alive. She hadn't moved since he fired those bullets.

He often had moments during the day when he was alert, aware of everything going on around him. Then there were times that were completely blank, sometimes a blur, and other times he remembered absolutely nothing. He tried to remember when he fired those shots at her. His intention was to shoot into the cabin ceiling, but maybe he had actually shot her in the head. He suddenly started to tremble, realizing that maybe he had actually killed her, but was afraid to look at her face. The blood was still on the pillow, but now it had changed from a bright red patch to a dirty, dried-up blotch of red. For the second time, he walked up to Jenny and poked her in the back, and once again got no response.

"You can turn the cold shoulder on me if you want, but eventually you'll have to talk to me. Get up and help me pack the vehicle." With no response, he shouted, "Fine, stay and wait for the police to arrest you, but I'll be long gone by then." He then added, "You'll be put in jail as an accomplice, so feel free to do prison time for both of us. Tom and I'll both be sipping on a bottle of whiskey while you rot in jail." He laughed, "He'll think you're dead so won't even be looking for you, but he'll probably go after Bill or his team for killing you." Glancing at Claire, he noticed she was paler than an hour earlier, and her puffy cheeks were void of all color. Charles knew there was something wrong with her, but there was also nothing he could do for her, so he walked away. In his mind, the child was collateral damage, a small price to pay for his brother's freedom.

With his seven o'clock call already made, Charles now had to start organizing his escape plans. He grinned to himself. How dare Bill think he could outsmart him? All those years of planning the perfect crime and it was nice to finally see it falling into place. It was time for Charles to finish off his game. Looking around the cabin, he had to decide what needed to be put into his friend's vehicle for his victorious escape. The car needed to be back in the friend's driveway before he went to work three hours from now. Charles realized that apart from himself and Jenny, nothing else needed to be removed from the cabin. His backpack was already in the trunk of the vehicle with his few possessions inside. Jenny came with nothing as she only had the clothes on her back. He was more than ready to hightail it out of there in a moment's notice. With just under one hour left, Charles half considered climbing into the vehicle and making a clean escape. The only problem with that choice was Bill would still be alive. Tom would be especially pleased to know that the sergeant who testified against him was dead, so Charles had to stay until the job was finished.

Charles returned to his chair and plunked himself down, recalling his seven o'clock phone call with Bill. When he had asked Bill where he was, Charles was shocked to hear that the cop could already be outside waiting for him. That didn't scare him as his gun was resting next to his chair and was already loaded. He did pick it up when he got up to look out the window to see if Bill was indeed there. He was relieved to see the coast was clear. Asking Bill to show himself confirmed that he was no where in sight. When Bill said, 'in due time,' Charles could only speculate how close the sergeant might be and he found that disconcerting, but also exhilarating. Charles thought that by saying, 'your time's run out,' he may have drawn Bill out from his hiding place, but that hadn't happened so Charles didn't need to panic. Also, saying he wanted to be gone by eight o'clock would force Bill to show himself. Charles knew there was no way Bill was that close. It irritated him to know that Tom wouldn't be released. He knew it, of course, but since that wasn't his primary goal anymore, it made no difference.

How dare Bill preach to him about the Justice System and tell him he was a terrorist. He already knew that, but didn't want to hear Bill actually say it. Charles wasn't about to admit defeat, so giving Bill another forty-five minutes was his last chance at defeating him. Bill simply wouldn't swap his granddaughter's life for Tom's. His statement that Jenny was probably already dead turned Charles' stomach sour. He actually wasn't sure if she was dead or alive and the fact that he wouldn't let Bill talk to her confirmed that it could be true. When Bill heard Charles say, 'you're just going to have to trust me,' he had laughed, 'There's no trust between us remember. See you soon.' That had pissed Charles off even more. It didn't really matter at this point because once eight o'clock arrived and Bill was officially dead, the game would be over and Charles would have completed the first chapter of his revenge. Chapter two would be the elimination of Doctor Jackson, which would prove to be easier as the doctor could be taken out with a single shot to the back while walking down the street. It would be a simple elimination compared to the planning Charles had done to lure Bill to his demise.

His positive outlook of the game was soon turned to dismay. His mind once again became confused and he needed some fresh air. Charles left the building, wandering around aimlessly. One minute, he felt victorious and the next, he felt defeated.

"Damn, maybe I should've got those lousy pills the doctor told me I needed. I can't keep my head on straight." He wandered around the property, taking a final look at his two remaining bear traps and was pleased to find them still ready. Daylight was fast approaching and still, all was quiet around him. A plane flew high above him, leaving a white stream of vapour behind it, like a thin thread of string that slowly dissipated into the atmosphere. Charles already knew that Bill would come with a team to back him up, but they wouldn't know about the bear traps. If any of Bill's officers stepped into either of the remaining traps, Charles could be at a real advantage. The unfortunate officer who made the mistake of stepping into the trap would be in such excruciating pain that Bill would run to help him. That would be when Charles would shoot Bill in the back, giving him instant gratification, while the poor officer died a most painful death. He would then sneak into the bushes, avoiding his last trap, and carefully work his way to the hidden vehicle to make his dynamic escape. He went inside the cabin one last time and took another look at Jenny.

"So I see you're still playing dead. Well, I don't need you anyways." Glancing down at his watch, his last hour was slowly counting down. He crossed the room and glanced out the window, noticing the sunrise just below the horizon. Tapping on the glass, he was surprised to find it wasn't glass at all, but plastic. He grinned and repeated over and over. "Bill's dead. Bill's dead." If Bill was indeed close, he needed to be set up for his attack point, so he made one last trip to the outhouse before sneaking into the bushes.

CHAPTER THIRTY-ONE

7:40 — 8:10

Jack got as close to the cabin as he could without Charles discovering their arrival and turned off the engine. He and Bill climbed out from the front of the car while Muhammad and Richard climbed out of the back. Richard grabbed his medical bag and then all four men quietly closed their doors, hoping Charles wouldn't hear them. The ambulances with two paramedics in each had been told which cabin to come to and they parked well behind the police. The attendants remained inside their vehicles. Richard stood against the police vehicle and watched the three officers gearing up for the takedown. Glancing up, the sun was starting to light up the sky, indicating that Claire's time was almost up. He stared patiently but nervously, pacing back and forth, waiting for Bill and his men to get into place for the takedown.

Bill had received a call from Bob saying they were delayed by a fallen tree across the road, and he realized that when they overtook the cabin, he would be four officers short. He had to hope they showed up soon for backup. "Okay, Jack. Looks like you're our only sniper. Make it count."

"I won't let you down, boss." Jack added, "I'll see if I can get a hold of Bob on the radio and find out how soon they'll be here." He returned to the cruiser and radioed the second team. "Pick up! Where the hell are you guys?" With no answer, he went back to the group. "No answer, boss. Something must have gone wrong. They're not answering the radio. Also tried their earpieces, but no reply means they're out of range."

Bill tried to imagine the cabin and its' surrounding area. "Jack, stay far enough back so you aren't discovered, but keep in mind your trajectory point.

Position yourself slightly off to one side of the cabin, it doesn't matter which side at this point. Stay low and out of sight. You may only get one chance at a shot."

Jack shook his shoulders several times, loosening up his muscles. He wasn't sure what position would give him the best shot, so surveyed the area before turning to Bill and saying, "I'll be off to the right side of the cabin."

"Okay then, get into position." Bill took several deep breaths before announcing, "I'm going in alone with my weapon in my holster. No one shoots until I give them the signal."

Muhammad protested, "You can't be serious. He's already said his goal is to kill you, so why give him the opportunity?"

"I'm going to try to talk him down. He may be here, but we're not totally sure that Jenny and Claire are still with him. What if he has them at a different location? I'm just thinking of Claire's safety; and for Jenny's also, if the truth be known. I'm sure she's innocent and she may be the only reason that Claire is still alive."

Muhammad had to reluctantly agree with Bill. "So what's the signal?"

"I'll run my fingers through my hair."

The officers all snickered when Muhammad said, "I don't think your hair has seen a comb in days."

Bill agreed. "Good one. But also true."

Muhammad then added, "Where do you want me Bill?"

"I need you to slightly backtrack and protect our two ambulances, just in case Charles slips by us."

"On my way." Muhammad worked his way back to the two ambulances.

"What about me, Bill?" Richard finally asked. "Where do you want me to be?" "Well out of harms way. You only approach the cabin when this is all over. No exceptions."

Richard replied, "Okay, but be careful."

Behind the team, there was a rustle of bushes that put them all on full alert. All officers' weapons were drawn only to see Bob, Don, Sam, and Eli sneak around the last corner of the road. All four men were not only soaked, but also winded and bent over to catch their breath.

Don gasped and managed to get a sentence out. "Sorry, boss. You knew about the fallen tree over the road, but then we had to forge through a river that I'm sure wasn't there before the rainstorm hit."

Sam added between gasps. "We had to trek the last mile."

Bill responded, "Just glad you all made it here in time. Bob, are you still going to be able to make the shot?"

"Yes, as soon as I can get my breathing under control."

Bill looked at Bob. "Okay. Jack is positioned on the right side of the cabin. You take the left side." He then added, "Shoot signal is me running my hand through my hair. Nothing happens before you see my signal."

Don turned to Bill. "I'm going to have a quick look around, to get a feel for the cabin surroundings."

Bill stopped him. "Don't forget that Jenny said there were traps set up." He then turned to Sam. "I need you backing up Jack. He is on the right side of the cabin." Sam left and quickly slipped several yards behind Jack. Glancing over to his right he spotted something other than the forest. He slowly moved towards the object and discovered Charles' vehicle. He spoke into his head piece. "Bill. I just found Charles' escape vehicle."

Bill replied, "Stay there just in case Charles tries to leave the site."

"Copy that."

Bill then glanced at Eli. "I need you right here protecting Richard. Absolutely nothing can happen to him."

Eli nodded. "You got it boss."

Bill took a deep breath. "Be careful out there. No officer dies on my shift."

Don moved into the trees and worked his way closer to the cabin, assessing how to best overtake Charles. Edging closer, he spotted the dead bear with its' paw removed which was still stuck in the nearby trap.

He spoke into his head piece. "Heads up guys, it looks like Charles indeed has set up bear traps, which are highly illegal. I just came upon one with a bear paw attached to it."

Bill responded, "Jenny said there were three of them, so now we're down to only two. Walk with care and trip them if you see any. At this point, we're not sure where he has them positioned. He must know we're coming and hopes that at least one of us will step into a trap, so tread lightly men."

Don slowly and cautiously worked his way around the side of the cabin, and into the forest. He stopped when he found signs of a second trap that was well hidden in the leafy underbrush of a tree. He picked up a stick and touched the sensitive center of the trap, causing it to instantly spring closed. The lethal device snapped shut with such force that not only would it crush a person's foot, but also shatter every bone it came in contact with. Bill's team was now strategically positioned, within sight of the cabin, but still well hidden in the surrounding foliage.

Don spoke into his headset a second time, but much softer. "Found a second one. It's tripped. Only one left."

With both snipers in place, Bill nervously started walking towards the cabin.

Bob and Jack were in position, close enough to hear what was being said, but far enough away to not be discovered. They could both make a clean shot and take Charles out of the picture, but were patiently waiting for Bill's signal.

Charles came out of the outhouse. He slowly turned around with not only a grin on his face, but also his gun pointed directly at Bill. "I heard one of my traps snap. Guess no one stepped into it." He had an evil grin on his face. "You must be really rusty, Bill."

"Why do you say that?"

"You should've been here hours ago. You come alone?" He then added, "You'd be stupid if you did. Who's here with you?" None of the officers revealed their locations. Eli took his eyes off of Richard for only a split second. That was enough time for Richard to walk towards the cabin and stand next to Bill.

Shaking his head, Bill looked at him before speaking, "I thought I told you to stay away from the cabin?"

"I just wanted to meet face to face with the man who kidnapped my daughter."

Charles couldn't believe his good luck. His laugh sent shivers down both men's spines. "Looks like the gods are on my side today. Doctor, you were also on my hit list. It'll give me great pleasure to kill both of you at the same time."

Richard screamed, "Where's my daughter?" He then realized there was dried blood on Charles shirt. "If you hurt her, I'll kill you!"

"Those are big words for an unarmed man."

Bill shouted, "Where are Claire and Jenny?"

"They could both be dead by now. You were supposed to be here hours ago," Charles exclaimed.

Bill asked, "Are they inside the cabin?"

"Maybe yes, maybe no."

Richard was getting desperate. "My daughter needs her medicine." He then pleaded, "Please let me treat her."

Charles ignored Richard's plea and turned his attention to Bill. "Take off your jacket."

"Why would I do that?"

He then screamed, "Do it!"

Bill slowly unbuttoned his jacket and let it fall to the ground.

Charles looked at him. "Carefully remove your weapon and put it on the ground."

Bill slowly removed his gun and placed it on the ground.

Charles then added, "Kick it away from you."

Bill gave it a slight nudge, just out of his reach.

Charles yelled, "Is that the best you can do?"

"Afraid so, arthritis restricts my movement. Do you want me to pick it up and move it physically?"

Charles snarled, "That won't be necessary." Charles then looked Bill directly in his eyes. "Remove your bulletproof vest."

Bill replied a second time. "Why would I do that?"

"Because I told you to."

Bill nervously removed his vest and tossed it onto the ground next to his gun. "Happy now?"

Charles chuckled. "Just wanted to even out the playing field. You can put your jacket back on. I don't want you to die from pneumonia. I plan on shooting you."

Bill slowly picked up his jacket and put it back on, carefully buttoning it up. He wasn't sure if it was safe to take Charles out, but he had to make a quick decision. He raised his hand and ran it through his hair. When nothing happened, he did it a second time, wondering why neither of his snipers was taking Charles out. Bill heard Jack speak to Bob through his headset, "I don't have a clear shot. Do you?"

Bob replied, "Negative, Richard's blocking my shot."

Jack responded, "Shit, Bill's blocking mine! One of them has to move."

Hearing that he and Richard were blocking the trajectory for an accurate shot, Bill slowly started moving towards Richard in hopes of opening a window for at least one of his shooters.

Charles saw the movement from the corner of his eye and stopped Bill dead in his tracks. "Don't do anything foolish."

Richard started to move towards Charles and then froze. "One more step and the sergeant's dead." He growled, "Of course you realize he's going to die today anyways. So make your choice, it's either now or later."

Richard stopped and toned down his voice, while still pleading, "I just want my daughter back. Please let me treat her. Without her medicine, she'll die."

Jenny could hear voices outside the cabin and carefully got out of the bed. She had lain in the same position for so long that her body ached. She was petrified. Each time Charles had been in the room, she had slowed down her breathing so he wouldn't notice she was still alive. Twice when he had poked her in the back, it had hurt, but she still didn't move a muscle. She now stretched out her aching body then carefully picked up Claire and went to the door.

Behind Charles, the cabin door opened and Jenny came outside holding Claire. Charles heard her and yelled, "So you're not dead after all!"

Jenny ignored Charles, slowly descended the stairs, and walked up to Richard. Their eyes met and Richard could see the split lower lip and dried blood that had formed there. Her face was also red from where he assumed Charles had hit her. She whispered, "I'm so sorry. She's not well." Tears were streaming down her cheeks as she gently passed Claire to her father.

Bill felt instant relief knowing that Claire and Jenny were still alive. All his doubts and fears about whether he had made the right choices over the past few hours now evaporated in front of his eyes. Now it was time to take Charles out. The two snipers were cursing as they still didn't have a clear shot. Moving positions at this point would give away their locations and put Bill and Richard in deeper jeopardy, so they waited patiently.

Jack and Bob relayed to Bill, "Neither one of us have a clear shot yet."

Charles was enraged that Jenny was again defying him and had given Claire back, so he quickly ducked behind her, expecting no officer would shoot him while he had a human shield. He slowly started backing up and pulled her along with him.

Bill grabbed his weapon from the ground and shouted, "Let her go Charles! Your games over, you just lost! You can't escape! I have men surrounding the cabin!" He softened his voice. "It's over." He then whispered to Richard. "Go. Take care of Claire. I can finish up here." Richard quickly ran towards the closest ambulance. Both ambulances had been radioed to move in closer to the cabin and came around the last corner. Richard jumped into the back of one and started treating Claire.

Charles kept backing away from Bill, slowly moving towards the front corner of the cabin. Once he was there, he snarled at Bill, but whispered into Jenny's ear. "You playing dead makes me think that you should be." He moved her slightly ahead of him and then pulled the trigger. Jenny's face went blank as she slipped to the ground like a rag doll.

Bill watched in shock as Jenny fell to the ground and Charles ducked behind the cabin. He shouted at Charles. "You just shot an unarmed, innocent woman. You're no better than your scumbag brother!"

Charles was already around the corner and headed into the thick bush. Don called into his head piece. "I need a medic here pronto, Jenny's down."

Richard heard the shot, and the message that Jenny was down, but had to concentrate on Claire for the moment. Hopefully nothing else bad would happen before Richard could help out.

Three medics arrived with a stretcher and assessed the situation. Jenny was turned over and the back of her dress was cut open to get access to the wound. At first glance, they were positive no vital organs were damaged, but they still had to slow down the flow of blood. Two of the men quickly got her onto the stretcher, on her side, and headed towards the ambulance, while the third medic applied steady pressure to her back. Her breathing was steady, but shallow, so once they had her in the back of the ambulance, they placed an oxygen mask over her face as a precaution. Her vitals were acceptable, so the problem for the three medics overseeing her was keeping her blood loss to a minimum. One medic stayed in the ambulance with Jenny, applying pressure to her wound, while the second one climbed out and into the driver's seat. The third medic stayed behind and returned to the second ambulance. The driver called ahead to Blue Ridge to make sure a surgeon would be onsite when they arrived, and they sped off over the gravel road towards the highway. Although Sidville appeared to be closer on the map, by the time they hit the main highway, Blue Ridge was actually closer so they swung that direction.

Bill had his weapon and ran after Charles, listening to hear where he was heading. Charles kept glancing behind to see how close his opponent was getting. Feeling that Bill was closing in on him, he ran even faster, ducking under branches and jumping over fallen trees. Charles panicked as his world was now rapidly falling apart. He once again was caught between reality and fiction and became confused and disoriented. He planned on getting far enough into the forest, and then circling back to his vehicle and making his escape. The roadblocks that he knew would be waiting, he could simply plough through. Right now, Charles had to stay focused and escape Bill.

For a moment he was fine, but in his rush he forgot about the broken branches next to his last well-hidden bear trap. It was too late to avoid it. Before he knew what was happening, his leg buckled beneath him. The trap snapped so hard that it shattered his ankle. Charles screamed out in pain, dropped his gun, and vainly tried to open the trap. Tears streamed down his face and sweat poured off his forehead. Bill heard Charles' blood curdling scream and ran towards him. Instantly seeing the pain he was in, he holstered his weapon and said, "Let's get you out of that contraption."

Charles howled, "Stay away from me!"

Bill froze. "I only want to help you, Charles. Please let me help you."

Charles paused for only a slight second then picked up his weapon and pointed it at Bill's chest.

"Don't do this Charles!"

The pain running through Charles' body was overwhelming, but in spite of it, he started laughing, "The great Sergeant Bill Smithe is pleading for his life. Well, Bill, it won't work."

The sound of the gun firing was deafening and it reverberated through the woods. The bullet that slammed into Bill's chest knocked him to the ground. He was conscious for only a few seconds before he blacked out. He thought of his beautiful Beatrice and was sorry that he had broken his promise to her, to come home safely. At least he knew Claire was safe. He knew that if she was safe, he would willingly sacrifice himself. Then everything went black.

Charles continued laughing, "Gotcha, Bill. I won."

Jack had just arrived to see Bill hit the ground. He stated, "Sorry, asshole, you lose." He shot two bullets into Charles, one to the head and one to the heart. He blew the end of his pistol like they do in the movies. "The first shot was for Bill, the second was for Jenny and Claire. Nobody shoots my boss and gets away with it. At least you got what you deserved." He then holstered his gun and ran to Bill. He yelled into his head piece. "Officer down! I repeat, officer down!"

Richard heard the first shot fired and heard that Jenny was down. He struggled to keep in complete focus while treating Claire. He also heard the blood thirsty scream followed by agonizing cries and was sure it was Charles. When three more shots rang out, he instantly switched into overdrive. It was like he was working a night shift in the trauma ward. He had already tested Claire's blood sugar levels and had given her the insulin injection. To give her system an extra boost, he had also brought a bottle of water that she had to drink to keep hydrated. Don had just arrived at the ambulance to see how Claire was doing when he heard shots fired and the 'officer down' call announced.

He grabbed Claire and shouted to Richard, "You go and help the downed officer, and I can feed Claire the bottle."

Richard grabbed his medical bag and was on the run. "Thanks, man." He kept calling, "Where are you guys?" The two remaining paramedics picked up the stretcher and followed Richard to the fallen officer's side.

Finally, Jack responded, "We're over here. Bill's been shot."

Richard felt sick to his stomach and froze when he arrived to find Charles' body in a pool of his own blood and his leg a mass of blood and broken bones. Richard turned his attention to Bill. Judging from the bullet hole in his jacket; it didn't look good. His blood was already staining the jacket, and damn it, the bullet was spot on for his heart. "Damn, why did Charles have to be so accurate with this shot?"

Jack crouched down next to Richard. "You need some help, Doc?"

Richard answered, "Please, we need to get Bill's jacket off so I can assess the wound."

Jack switched into help mode. "You got it. Damn, why did he remove his bulletproof vest?"

Richard answered, "I think we all know why he did it."

Then Jack nervously asked, "Is he going to make it?"

"He has to or Beatrice and Kimberley will never forgive me."

The two paramedics arrived with the stretcher and stood back while Richard took care of Bill. Richard and Jack twisted and turned Bill cautiously, trying to rid him of his jacket. Once it was off and tossed aside, both men were astonished when they looked at Bill's chest. Charles' shot would have passed into Bill's heart if it hadn't been for his badge. The bullet had hit the centre of it and deflected off and into his shoulder. Relief was obvious on both men's faces.

Jack nervously said, "Bill just bought that coat so good thing Charles is dead because the boss would've killed him." Bill looked really pale. Both men first looked at Bill's chest then slowly turned him over onto his side.

Out of the blue, Bill moaned and complained, "If you don't quit hurting me, I'll fire both of you."

Richard grinned. "You may be able to fire your officers, but you can't do anything about getting rid of me. The medical board has to do that. You can report me if you want, but at least let me finish treating you first. You have no idea how lucky you were. The bullet is a through and through and it's only your shoulder." Richard couldn't resist asking him. "What were you thinking, running off on your own like that? You could've been killed."

"I didn't have time to think. I just didn't want the bastard getting away with murdering Jenny; it was a last-minute decision." Bill winced in pain as Richard worked on him. "Tell me something, Richard. Why am I still alive? Charles went for the heart shot and I thought it was all over. I've never been shot before and it hurts like hell."

Jack showed Bill exactly why he was still alive. He removed the badge from Bill's shirt. "Looks like the bullet ricocheted off your badge, barely missing your heart. You're one lucky guy."

Richard finished putting a bandage on Bill's front and back shoulder, then signalled to the paramedics that it was safe to transport him to the second ambulance. Once on the stretcher, Bill finally got a glance at Charles' body. He asked, "Who shot him?"

Jack responded, "I did. Sorry, but no one attacks my boss and lives to tell the story."

Bill looked away and inquired, "Is Claire okay?"

Richard pointed to Don who had just arrived at the scene and was holding her. "I'll let you be the judge of that."

Bill was relieved when he saw Claire grasping tightly onto one of Don's fingers. He again asked, "Are you sure she's going to be okay?"

Richard answered, "She got the best treatment a doctor could give her. I'll keep monitoring her over the next several hours, but I'm sure she's going to be fine, thanks to you and your team." He then added, "Sorry I treated her first."

"I'd expect nothing less." Bill was afraid to ask, but he had to know. "What about Jenny?"

"From what I could hear, no vital organs were hit and she's on her way to the hospital where a surgeon is waiting to operate, and remove the bullet." Richard then took Claire from Don and walked beside Bill towards the ambulance.

Bill looked down at the spot where Jenny had been shot and stated, "I knew I had an ally in Jenny. She kept Claire safe during this whole nightmare."

Richard answered, "We all owe her a big thank you."

The paramedics were almost to the ambulance when Bill shouted to his men. "What part of Charles is mine did Jack not understand?"

Jack laughed and responded, "If you wanted to shoot him, you should have when you had the chance."

Bill sighed, "I guess." He felt instant relief. "I can't believe it's all over."

Jack inquired, "How you feeling, boss?"

"I've had better days." The paramedics continued towards the ambulance, loaded Bill into it, and checked his vitals.

Eli, Sam, Muhammad, and Bob got the all clear message from Don that Charles was dead, but also heard that Bill was shot. The four officers ran back to the cabin to find out how he was doing. Relief was felt by all four officers when they saw Bill alert and sitting slightly upright while the paramedics checked his vitals. The four then all piled into one of the squad cars and headed back into town. Sam turned to Bob who was driving. "Do you think you could drop us off at our abandoned vehicle? It shouldn't be left out here over night."

"Sure thing."

Jack left Bill's side and climbed the few stairs to enter the cabin. Inside, it was still dim despite some light coming through the windows and he noticed a candle sitting in the center of the table so he drew out a match and lit it. Glancing around the interior, Jack was horrified at the conditions that Jenny and Claire had endured. He turned on his flashlight to help him investigate the areas that were still in shadows. Looking at a torn and weathered armchair, he imagined Charles would have sat in it, and then he saw a more comfortable smaller couch across the room that he knew would have been Jenny's. Next to the larger chair was a table, and on it was the infamous satellite phone, so he put on a set of plastic gloves that he always kept in his pocket, picked up the phone, and bagged it. Also on the table was Charles' pocketknife, the handle still covered in blood. It was also put into a separate bag and sealed. Next, he turned towards the bed, and beside it on the floor, he noticed an old rusty kitchen knife. It didn't appear to have any blood on it, but he still placed it inside a third plastic bag and sealed it shut. Glancing at the bed, he saw the bloody pillowcase so carefully removed it and also put it into a plastic bag. The bed was in very poor condition and he had a hard time visualizing Claire sleeping on it. He hoped that Jenny had cradled the baby on her chest and not laid the infant on the dirty sheets. He worked his way to the small kitchen area and opened each drawer, finding nothing of significance. Turning to the table, he froze when he saw what was carved into the wooden surface. He took out his phone and snapped a photo for evidence. Feeling that he had collected every piece of evidence within the cabin walls, he left the building. He came outside the cabin and went to check on Bill.

Bill was comfortably resting on the stretcher with both paramedics tending to him. Jack turned to Don. "I think you're going to want to see what I found inside."

Don replied, "What've you got."

"You're going to have to see it to believe it."

"Okay, lead the way." Once inside the cabin, Don glanced around the room, sickened at the state of the old building where Claire and Jenny had been held hostage. The room was cold and dim. He followed Jack to the table and his jaw dropped. In deep cut marks on the top of the table were the words, 'Bill's Dead.'

"This Charles was indeed a crazy man." Without missing a beat he added, "Take a photo of the table as evidence and then take it outside and burn it."

Jack replied, "Photo's already done, but we should hold off on destroying it."

Don crossed the room and grabbed a sheet from the bed then left the cabin. He next went into the bushes where Charles body lay and simply threw the cover over him so he didn't have to look at his disgusting face. Don glanced around and spotted a tree with a fresh cut on the bark. Going close, he saw a bullet half imbedded into it. He carefully carved the bullet free as further evidence, but also knew that when the case was over, Bill would want to keep it. Bill was resting in the ambulance, waiting to leave for the hospital, Don rushed up to him.

"Boss, I know you're going to want to keep your badge and this bullet as a souvenir, but for now they are both evidence in the case. Jack has been busy bagging all the other evidence, so I'll make sure he gets both of these."

"I sure will once this is all over," Bill replied.

"Jack and I will stay at the scene until the body has been removed. We'll hitch a ride back with the coroner. Rest assured that the cabin will be taped off until the investigation is complete."

"Thanks," Bill replied.

Richard carried Claire into the ambulance with Bill and the driver headed back towards town. Richard carefully laid Claire on Bill's chest while he made the call to the ladies. He dialled the number and Glen answered.

CHAPTER THIRTY-TWO

7:55 — 19:30

Beatrice and Kimberley were pacing the living room, both sick to their stomachs. It was almost eight o'clock and there was still no news from Bill or Richard.

Kimberley was beside herself. "They must not have found her in time."

She started trembling, and once again, bile started rising up into her throat for a second time. She was about to return to the bathroom, but instead decided to swallow it down. Now was not a good time to leave the room and miss the call. Glen watched them and knew their pain. When he had lost Jeannine, his whole world had turned upside down. It must be the same for these two distraught ladies in front of him. He wasn't sure how he could distract them once again.

Glen had been on similar jobs, where he had been stationed at a safe house, protecting witnesses before they testified in a court of law. There were also at least two more officers on site backing him up. Teams worked together to ensure the people who were under protection were kept safe. Those cases were far more intense, as criminals could quite easily locate safe houses by word of mouth and would do anything to eliminate the witness. The three officers watched each other's backs, and inevitably shots were fired, but so far, Glen had never lost a witness on his watch. This case was no different, except he was working alone and these ladies were family of a very close friend, so it became personal. He knew there wouldn't be shots fired outside the current house as this Charles appeared to be working alone, except for that skinny druggy that was arrested earlier.

He glanced between the two ladies, feeling their deep concern. He had felt a deep loss in his life, and he wanted to protect them from the same pain. That internal pain never really goes away. He was able to push it off to the side, but when he was in bed at the end of the day, his beautiful Jeannine entered into his dreams. He often woke up in a sweat and would have to get up to clear his head and splash water on his face. He was glad that she visited him most nights, but it was also overwhelming.

Both ladies looked defeated. Glen didn't need another coffee or more cookies, but he felt he had to say something. "Okay ladies, this is how it usually works in a take down." Both of them looked at him. "This is only a guess, but a good one. Once they find the cabin, they would've had to set up their team and strategy. Bill would have had sharp shooters ready if needed, but he would also have wanted to try to talk Charles out of the cabin. Charles wouldn't want Jenny or Claire beside him as he would lose his advantage, so they would be safe inside the four walls. Words would be exchanged and that's where Bill's negotiation skills would come in handy. He could very easily talk Charles into turning himself in, end of story." Glen sure hoped that his words helped the two ladies to think positively.

Kimberley seemed to relax somewhat. "When do you think they will call us?"

"I expect once it's all over."

"How long will that be?"

He looked at both ladies. "Not long I hope."

Kimberley refused to look at her watch again. Slumping into her chair, her body slowly started to shut down again. She didn't want to face the day without Claire in her arms. Beatrice went and sat next to her and held her hand. She collapsed further into her chair, defeated. Kimberley already felt it was all over. How would she and Richard survive the loss of their precious daughter? How would Bill feel knowing that the one case that was closest to his heart, he had failed to win?

Beatrice tried to comfort her. "Don't give up yet. It's not over until we get the call."

"But why aren't they calling? Maybe I should phone them."

Glen interceded, "Not a good idea. The phone ringing could be a distraction to the team, especially if they're in the middle of the takedown. We just need to be patient."

Kimberley's phone rang and all three of them jumped, their heart rates pumping wildly.

Glen answered, "Hello, Glen here."

Both ladies watched the expression on Glen's face, hoping to get a clue as to what was being said. Richard chose his words carefully, as he already knew that the ladies would be watching Glen closely. "First, Claire is fine. We got to her in time, and I've already treated her. She's a ball of energy right now. While her day is just starting, ours ended hours ago. The team is exhausted." Glen gave the ladies a smile and a thumbs up.

Both of them jumped to their feet and hugged each other in excitement. Tears of joy streamed down both of their cheeks and Kimberley went to take the phone. Before Glen could pass it over, Richard said, "I'll hold the line, while you pass that information to the anxious ladies, but please stay on, we need to talk."

The smile on Glen's face told the ladies that Claire was okay. Glen stopped Kimberley from taking the phone, saying, "You can have it in a minute, but first Richard needs to fill me in on something else."

Richard paused. "I'll give the phone to Don. He'll be better at telling you what went down here."

Kimberley looked confused and continued to watch Glen's face for possible bad news. Glen was anxiously waiting for more details, but chose to go into the kitchen for privacy. "What about Charles?"

Don sounded exhausted. "He didn't fair very well. Nasty man set up bear traps and managed to step into one himself. Guess he got what he deserved. Can you believe it; he shot Jenny in the back because he was pissed off with her. She's going to make it and most likely is almost to the hospital already where a doctor is waiting to operate on her."

Glen whispered, "You obviously have something that you don't want the ladies to hear right now, so spit it out."

Don's voice choked as he spoke, "Bill's been shot. Charles played dirty and made him take off his bulletproof vest. He took a bullet to his chest, but as luck would have it, the bullet hit his badge and deflected into his shoulder."

Glen inquired, "How bad is he?"

"He said it hurts like hell. Those were his exact words. It was a through and through, non-critical, so Richard has already treated him. Ambulance is on the way to the hospital as we speak. The ladies can meet them at emergency within the hour."

Glen replied, "I'll make sure the ladies are there."

Don added, "One more favour. Prepare Kimberley and Beatrice for Bill's injury. Assure them that he's fine. I think Richard wants to speak to Kimberley so I'm passing the phone on to him. Pass onto the ladies that the team did great work."

Glen went back into the living room and passed the phone to Kimberley. "Richard's on the phone for you."

Kimberley was shaking as she asked, "Hello, Richard. What's going on?"

"I have her, Kimberley, and she's fine. You can meet us at the hospital emergency room in about an hour. I want to have her checked out."

Kimberley burst into tears and Beatrice shared in that happy moment. "She's fine, Beatrice. They've found her. They're on their way to the hospital, and we're to meet them there in about an hour."

Glen felt instant relief for the two ladies he had been protecting over the past four and a half hours; he did, however, have to tell them of Bill's injuries.

"That's wonderful news about Claire's rescue." He paused slightly. "But it's my duty to let the two of you know that Bill was shot in the rescue operation." Glen watched the color drain from both ladies faces, and he quickly added, "It's just a flesh wound to his shoulder, so he's going to be fine."

Beatrice cried openly. "I told him to be careful."

"Richard has already treated him and Bill is sitting up playing with Claire." He smiled and added, "Guess that means my job here is finished. I'd love to drop the two of you off at the hospital on my way home if that's okay." Both ladies got up and hugged him in appreciation.

Beatrice looked puzzled. "Aren't you coming to the hospital to see Bill?"

Glen replied, "I didn't want to encroach on your family time. I can always see him later."

"Don't be ridiculous. You're family and I know for a fact that Bill will want to see you."

"Hospitals aren't exactly my favourite place, but I guess for Bill I could stop by to say a quick hi."

It was just after nine o'clock when Bill, Richard, Claire and the two paramedics arrived at the hospital. Kimberley immediately ran to Richard and hugged him before taking Claire. Their daughter was full of smiles and bubbly. Beatrice came over and kissed Claire's cheek. Richard led Kimberley behind an examination curtain where another doctor would be checking Claire over from head to toe. At the last moment, and before Kimberley went behind the curtain she turned to see Bill walking into the hospital. They made eye contact and Kimberley blew him a kiss. In return Bill waved to her, a wide grin on his face.

The doctor on call turned to Richard and Kimberley. "She's a spry one considering what she's just gone through."

"That she is." Richard replied, "Just like her mother."

With Richard, Kimberley and Claire safely behind a white curtain in the emergency room, Beatrice turned around looking for Bill. She watched him carefully step down from the ambulance and slowly walk towards her. His jacket was half thrown over his shoulders and was covering the bandages that Richard had applied only an hour earlier. She looked at him in horror. He had a big grin on his face.

Glen was standing next to Beatrice and shook his head. "Just had to get shot eh? How are you feeling?"

Bill grinned from ear to ear. With excitement in his voice he looked at the two of them. "We did it! We got her back!"

Glen smiled and announced, "Three's a crowd so I'm heading home to get some sleep. We'll talk later."

"Thanks man. Your debt is paid in full."

"Glad everything worked out in the end."

Beatrice snuggled up to Bill and softly kissed him. "I thought you said that you would be careful. What happened to you?"

"Oh, it's nothing. I just got in the way of a bullet."

She gently gave him a hug then asked, "What about the kidnapper?"

"It's over. While I was getting shot, my team took him out. It was Charles Lockman, the brother of Tom Lockman whom I put away for murder."

A nurse approached Bill and Beatrice. "Why don't the two of you come with me and I'll get a doctor to check you out."

Bill placed his arm on Beatrice's shoulder and they ducked behind another white curtain where a doctor was waiting to check Bill out. Bill spoke with confidence. "I knew we had an ally in Jenny."

Beatrice was not aware of any Jenny. "Who's Jenny?"

He smiled. "Claire's guardian angel; she's Tom's wife, so Charles' sister-in-law. Charles shot her and she's in surgery as we speak. We have to find out how she's doing before we leave here."

Beatrice looked at Bill. "We sure do."

Seeing that Richard was starting to leave, Kimberley turned to face him. "Where're you going?"

"I need to check on a patient, a very special patient. I'll be right back."

"Do you have to go now?"

Richard nodded. "I'm afraid so. This very special patient got shot saving Claire. I need to know she's going to be okay."

Kimberley was surprised. "Go then, but I also definitely want to meet her when she is allowed visitors. We could never repay her for saving our baby."

Richard left the room and talked to the nurses at the main desk. "Any word on Jenny Lockman's surgery?"

The nurse glanced up. "Hi Dr. Jackson, Jenny's out of surgery and everything went well. She's pretty groggy right now, but later today you could drop in and see her."

"I'll do that, thanks. I'm sure Kimberley is going to want to meet the woman who kept our daughter safe."

The nurse added, "We all heard about your terrible ordeal. We're all so sorry about what happened, but we're glad everything turned out fine." She then added, "That Jenny must have been a very brave lady to stand up to a killer, she's so petite and was obviously hit several times in the face by that monster."

"She's a hero in our eyes. Thanks for the update." He then returned to Kimberley and Claire and the three of them left for home. When they arrived, Richard called his parents and told them about the last ten hours. Both were flabbergasted and immediately came over to their house so their son and wife could get some much-needed sleep.

By ten o'clock, Bill and Beatrice were sitting in their living room having a cup of tea before they went for a nap. The two of them were beyond exhausted and snuggled up beside each other. Beatrice looked lovingly at her husband. "Are you sure you're okay?"

"I'm fine, but every time you ask me it starts to hurt again."

Beatrice moved away from him and asked, "So guess I shouldn't ask then. Maybe I should change the subject?"

"That works for me." Bill half grinned.

Beatrice looked deep into his eyes. "Why didn't you tell me about Jeannine?"

Bill looked shocked and embarrassed. "Who told you about her?" He then added, "It must have been Glen. How did you get onto that topic?"

"Glen just happened to mention his deceased wife and how much it had affected you. Why didn't you tell me about her?"

He looked sympathetically into her eyes. "It's still too painful for me to talk about her."

"Was she older or younger that you?"

"I was older." There were now tears in Bill's eyes and Beatrice hugged him softly.

"It's okay darling, maybe we can talk about it another time. I just wish I had known about her. So we've both lost a sister. This can be another bond between us."

He wiped the tears from his eyes and turned to her. "Guess now is as good a time as ever. I was born four minutes ahead of her."

"Oh my God Bill, she was your twin!"

"Yes, she was my baby sister. I taught her everything she knew. I even taught her ways to get around our parents. Drove my mom crazy as she knew I was always behind Jeannine's antics. I taught her how to ride a bicycle, helped her with homework. I protected her from real life, but I couldn't do anything when she got sick. Glen saved me from becoming an alcoholic, and I saved him from massive depression. The two of us were a wreck after her funeral." He added, "I'll never keep anything from you ever again. Let's get some rest. Later today, you and I and Richard, Kimberley, and Claire are returning to the hospital to see Jenny."

"I'd love that."

Right after dinner, the five of them met in the hospital waiting room and as a group, they all went into see Jenny. The hospital bed was slightly raised up so as they entered the room, Jenny spotted Claire and beamed from ear to ear. "Oh my little angel, you're safe."

Kimberley slowly crossed the room and gave her a gentle hug. "Thanks to you."

Jenny once again apologized to Richard. "I'm so sorry. I wasn't aware of what Charles had planned. I wouldn't have been part of it if I had known the details."

"She's safe and that's all that matters right now. How are you feeling?"

"I'm a little sore. Can I ask a favour?"

Richard replied, "Of course."

"May I hold her one last time?" Jenny beamed when Claire reached out towards her.

"It looks like she's glad to see you." Richard carefully placed Claire on Jenny's lap. "This won't be the last time you hold her. You're welcome to see her anytime you want."

Jenny had tears in her eyes. "She loved it when I sang softly to her and snuggled to keep her warm." Her tears started to flow freely. "Charles really scared me, that's why I played dead. I had to protect Claire and myself." She then repeated, "I'm so sorry and hope all of you can forgive me." She then had to ask, "What happened with Charles?"

Bill looked sadly at her. "I'm sorry, he's dead. My men had to take him out after he shot me."

Jenny looked horrified. "Charles shot you? Are you okay?"

"I'm standing in front of you, so that's a good sign. It was just a flesh wound. We really should let you get some rest. Sleep well knowing that you did the right thing by protecting Claire." Jenny got hugs from the four adults. Richard had to pry Claire's fingers off Jenny's thumb.

CHAPTER THIRTY-THREE

TWO DAYS LATER

Bill moved to the front door and picked up his jacket. Beatrice was right behind him.

"Let me help you, dear," she said.

"I can manage it, thanks." He turned to her. "How long are you going to pamper me?"

"For as long as it takes to get you back on your feet."

Bill laughed, "I'm standing, so I'm already back on my feet."

"Don't be difficult. We have to be at your office by nine o'clock for Claire's welcome home party. If we're late, Glen and the staff will have eaten all the cookies Kimberley and I made."

"You're right. Glen has always had a sweet tooth. Jeannine could never keep enough cookies in their house."

Beatrice was pleased. "It's nice to hear you speak so openly about your sister. I wish I could've met her."

"She would've liked you. She was also a wonderful cook and baker." Once his jacket was on, he announced, "I'm ready. Going to need a new jacket, though."

They arrived at the station to a bustling group of men all holding half eaten cookies and huddled around Claire. Bill approached Daniel and inquired, "Sorry, forgot to ask about our druggie who spent the night behind bars. Was he released?"

Daniel replied, "You bet. I told the Sidville officers who were here to cover for our dayshift about him. He was given a nice hot breakfast and sent on his way. He was told that we weren't going to press charges, but in the future he better keep his nose clean. He was happy to return to his home under the overpass."

Don approached Bill and pointed towards the sergeant's office. "I did some redecorating to your office before you came in."

Bill entered and found all his certificates once again hanging on the wall. "Thanks, Don. I wasn't sure if I would've ever hung them up again. I definitely had times where I was very unsure of my skills. What made it even worse was the personal nature of the case, and I had to try and separate myself from it and blend into the woodwork. Thanks for taking over for me and keeping the case on track."

"You're welcome. I couldn't have done it without your guidance." He half laughed, "Guess you don't want to help with the massive amount of paperwork that needs to be filled out?"

"No, thank you. If you recall, my name can't appear on any of it."

Don turned to Bill. "There's a table at the cabin that has inappropriate carvings on it. I've photographed it, but need your permission to return and cut that section out and enter it as evidence. Once that's done, I can officially remove the yellow tape so people can start using that building again. Also, with your permission, I'd like to take the rest of the table lumber to the old warehouse and donate it to the homeless who are using the location as their home for the winter."

"That's a good idea. Go for it."

Both men returned to the common area and Daniel made an announcement. "Bill, I think you should be the one to clean the whiteboard off so it can be returned to the back cupboard. Hopefully we never have to use it again."

Bill stood in front of it and, after reviewing all the tips that stared back at him, he slowly wiped it clean.

Parents: Ted Lockman – Mechanic   Betty Lockman - Waitress

Sister Nikki deceased

Charles Lockman – B & E's brawls no time in jail

Tom Lockman – Mechanic killed Joan Wilks   wife: Jenny – waitress   Ally
                                                   Address 16 Birch Crescent

~~Vacant buildings   Eric and Sam~~

~~Lighthouse   Jack and Greg~~

~~Panorama Room   Bob and Jim~~

Sound of crackling fire on tape

Charles didn't lose power

~~Search campsites Municipal   Bob and Jim~~   ~~No~~

~~Search campsite Rock Creek   Greg and Jack~~   ~~No~~

Three traps

Not in town

Eli and Muhammad stake-out Jenny's house

Not moving around

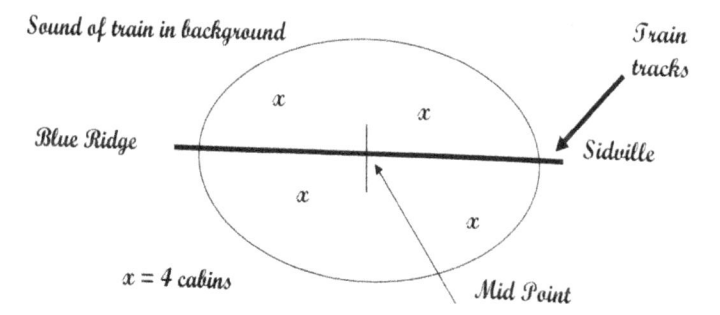

Sound of train in background   Train tracks

Blue Ridge ————————————————— Sidville

x = 4 cabins

Mid Point

He turned towards his men who were clapping and hooting as the whiteboard was cleaned and put away. Bill listened to his officers reminiscing about the case. Each officer had something to contribute to the conversation. All he heard was the odd word that caught his attention. Eric and Sam shared how they were attacked by bats at the vacant cannery, while Jack and Greg laughed about catching that young couple making out behind the lighthouse. Bill smiled as he moved from one set of officers to the next, catching all their adventures over those stressful eight hours. He moved to the next group of men where Bob and Jim were dramatizing their search at the Panorama Room and being attacked by a massive grizzly bear.

He approached both men. "Interesting story, but who do you think should pay for that windshield?"

Jim answered, "As long as it isn't either of us. Wasn't our fault the damn bear decided he might want to eat us for supper."

The group around them started laughing. Bill joined in on the fun. "Neither one of you necessarily look good enough to eat."

Jim answered, "Well said, boss."

Greg, Jack, Bob, and Jim all agreed that the search of the campsites was a waste of time, but also necessary. They couldn't leave any stone unturned.

Richard joined in on the conversation. "What about when I was attacked by a moose in the cruiser. You guys left me there defenseless."

Bill admitted, "That was my fault. I really felt like I had let the entire force down when we returned and thought you were gone. Thank heavens you were still inside." Bill paused. He raised his hand to get the team's attention. "Let's not forget about Jenny. She kept feeding us information with each hourly phone call. She must have been petrified when she took it upon herself to call and let us know about the three traps. Then she played dead for several hours, controlling her breathing and not moving a muscle. That must have been very difficult for her. She is the real hero of this story." There wasn't a single officer in the room who would dispute it. Bill approached Beatrice. "I'm sorry, darling. I have to leave, but I'll be back in time for dinner. One of the officers will see that you get home safely."

She looked at him. "What's so important that it has to be done right now?"

"Don and I need to officially close this case. We'll talk when I get home." He kissed her softly then left the office.

Don and Bill climbed on a jet bound for Edmonton to go to the Maximum Security Institution there, to confront Tom Lockman. Both were signed in at the gate and their weapons were taken for safe keeping, until they left the complex. They were then led through a series of locked doors. In the center of the building was a visitor's room, broken into smaller cubicles. Tom was already sitting in a chair with a wide grin on his face. He picked up the phone on his side of the protective glass and waited for Bill to sit down and take his. Don stood behind Bill, mostly for moral support. Tom looked very impressed. "Wow. Didn't expect you to personally come and escort me back to Blue Ridge. I'm honoured."

Bill didn't take his eyes off Tom. "Is that why you think I'm here?"

Tom's face turned white before asking, "If not, then why are you here?"

"To update you on your case." Bill paused before adding, "I'm here to inform you that your wife has been shot."

Tom sprung to his feet and yelled, "You shot Jenny! When I get out of here, I'll find you!"

"Don't waste your time. Your brother Charles shot her in the back. Then my officers shot Charles. He's dead, but your wife survived her surgery and is doing well."

Tom's eyes locked onto his. "You're lying."

Bill kept calm and added, "Your brother coerced your wife into helping him kidnap my granddaughter and the child almost died. You should be proud of Jenny. She almost died saving that innocent child. She's a real hero, plus she won't ever be lonely again. She's become an important part of our family." Bill stood up and looked at Tom for the last time. "Enjoy your stay here. Don't expect that you'll have too many visitors." Bill hung up the phone and then he and Don left the room.

Tom started smashing the phone on the table and screaming hysterically until the receiver was a pile of rubble. The officers dragged him from the room and put him back in his cell.

As the two men left the prison, they were given their weapons back and signed out. Don placed his hand on Bill's shoulder as they approached the waiting taxi. "You okay?"

Bill smiled. "I am. Sure glad that's behind us."

"I think you handled Tom really well."

Bill started laughing. "So now that you've been in my shoes, what do you think? There will be an opening one day, just in case you want to take the position."

"I definitely have lots to learn before that day comes."

When Bill and Don got back to Blue Ridge, Bill explained to Beatrice over dinner why he had to leave quickly that morning. Tom was the last link to the case and it needed to be officially closed. She understood completely.

Several months passed before Bill's damaged badge was returned to him in a sealed evidence bag, which also held the spent bullet. Beatrice was still amazed that the thin piece of metal protected him from that fatal shot. She was also upset that he had removed his bulletproof vest making himself a vulnerable target for Charles. He had told her time and time again that he did it to protect Claire. Although she knew it was true, she had a hard time grasping his objective.

Bill tore the bag open and took out his badge and the damaged bullet. The bullet had hit the center of his badge and left deep scratch marks as it deflected. Half of his number was no longer legible. The force had already replaced it with a new one. Bill looked at it in amazement. "It saved my life."

Beatrice's eyes filled with tears. "I almost lost both of you."

Bill hugged her and showed her the damaged bullet. This was the first time she had seen it. "Why are you keeping this?"

"It's a souvenir. All officers who are shot and live through it keep them. It's bad luck to throw them away."

Beatrice watched as he crossed the room and placed the badge and the spent bullet next to Claire's baby picture. "When Claire grows up, I want her to know that I saved her life with the help of my team."

THE END